George Alfred Townsend

Tales of the Chesapeake

George Alfred Townsend

Tales of the Chesapeake

ISBN/EAN: 9783337120207

Printed in Europe, USA, Canada, Australia, Japan

Cover: Foto ©Andreas Hilbeck / pixelio.de

More available books at **www.hansebooks.com**

TALES OF THE CHESAPEAKE

BY

GEO. ALFRED TOWNSEND

"GATH."

A fruity smell is in the school-house lane:
  The clover bees are sick with evening heats;
A few old houses from the window-pane
  Fling back the flame of sunset, and there beats
The throb of oars from basking oyster fleets,
  And clangorous music of the oyster tongs
Plunged down in deep bivalvulous retreats,
  And sound of seine drawn home with negro songs.

NEW YORK:

AMERICAN NEWS COMPANY,

39 AND 41 CHAMBERS STREET.

1880.

THE JOHN A. GRAY PRESS
AND STEAM TYPE-SETTING OFFICE,
Cor. Frankfort and Jacob Sts.,
NEW YORK.

TO MY FATHER,

REV. STEPHEN TOWNSEND, M.D., Ph.D.,

WHOSE ANCESTORS EXPLORED THE CHESAPEAKE BAY IN 1623,

AND WERE SETTLED ON THE POCOMOKE RIVER ALMOST

TWO HUNDRED YEARS, NEAR HIS BIRTHPLACE;

WITH

THE AFFECTION OF

HIS ONLY SURVIVING SON.

Of the following pieces, two, "Kidnapped," and "Dominion over the Fish," have been published in *Chambers's Journal*, London. The poem "Herman of Bohemia Manor" is new. All the compositions illustrate the same general locality.

INTRODUCTION.

MOTHERNOOK.

THE EASTERN SHORE OF MARYLAND.

ONE day, worn out with head and pen,
And the debate of public men,
  I said aloud, " Oh ! if there were
Some place to make me young awhile,
  I would go there, I would go there,
And if it were a many a mile !"
  Then something cried—perhaps my map,
That not in vain I oft invoke—
  " Go seek again your mother's lap,
  The dear old soil that gave you sap,
And see the land of Pocomoke !"

A sense of shame that never yet
My foot on that old shore was set,
  Though prodigal in wandering,
Arose ; and with a tingled cheek,
  Like some late wild duck on the wing,
I started down the Chesapeake.
  The morning sunlight, silvery calm,
From basking shores of woodland broke,
  And capes and inlets breathing balm,
  And lovely islands clothed in palm,
Closed round the sound of Pocomoke.

The pungy boats at anchor swing,
The long canoes were oystering,
   And moving barges played the seine
Along the beaches of Tangiers ;
   I heard the British drums again
As in their predatory years,
   When Kedge's Straits the Tories swept,
And Ross's camp-fires hid in smoke.
   They plundered all the coasts except
   The camp the Island Parson kept
For praying men of Pocomoke.

And when we thread in quaint intrigue
Onancock Creek and Pungoteague,
   The world and wars behind us stop.
On God's frontiers we seem to be
   As at Rehoboth wharf we drop,
And see the Kirk of Mackemie :
   The first he was to teach the creed
The rugged Scotch will ne'er revoke ;
   His slaves he made to work and read,
   Nor powers Episcopal to heed,
That held the glebes on Pocomoke.

But quiet nooks like these unman
The grim predestinarian,
   Whose soul expands to mountain views ;
And Wesley's tenets, like a tide,
   These level shores with love suffuse,
Where'er his patient preachers ride.
   The landscape quivered with the swells
And felt the steamer's paddle stroke,
   That tossed the hollow gum-tree shells,
   As if some puffing craft of hell's
The fisher chased in Pocomoke.

Anon the river spreads to coves,
And in the tides grow giant groves.
   The water shines like ebony,
And odors resinous ascend
   From many an old balsamic tree,
Whose roots the terrapin befriend ;

The great ball cypress, fringed with beard,
Presides above the water oak,
  As doth its shingles, well revered,
  O'er many a happy home endeared
To thousands far from Pocomoke.

And solemn hemlocks drink the dew,
Like that old Socrates they slew ;
  The piny forests moan and moan,
And in the marshy splutter docks,
  As if they grazed on sky alone,
Rove airily the herds of ox.
  Then, like a narrow strait of light,
The banks draw close, the long trees yoke,
  And strong old manses on the height
  Stand overhead, as to invite
To good old cheer on Pocomoke.

And cunning baskets midstream lie
To trap the perch that gambol by ;
  In coves of creek the saw-mills sing,
And trim the spar and hew the mast ;
  And the gaunt loons dart on the wing,
To see the steamer looming past.
  Now timber shores and massive piles
Repel our hull with friendly stroke,
  And guide us up the long defiles,
  Till after many fairy miles
We reach the head of Pocomoke.

Is it Snow Hill that greets me back
To this old loamy *cul-de-sac ?*
  Spread on the level river shore,
Beneath the bending willow-trees
  And speckled trunks of sycamore,
All moist with airs of rival seas ?
  Are these old men who gravely bow,
As if a stranger all awoke,
  The same who heard my parents vow,
  —Ah well ! in simpler days than now—
To love and serve by Pocomoke ?

Does Chincoteague as then produce
These rugged ponies, lean and spruce ?
  Are these the steers of Accomac
That do the negro's drone obey ?

KING OF CHINCOTEAGUE.

THE night before Christmas, frosty moonlight, the outcast preacher came down to the island shore and raised his hands to the stars.

"O God! whose word I so long preached in meekness and sincerity," he cried, "have mercy on my child and its mother, who are poor as were Thine own this morning, eighteen hundred and forty years ago!"

The moonlight scarcely fretted the soft expanse of Chincoteague Bay. There seemed a slender hand of silver reaching down from the sky to tremble on the long chords of the water, lying there in light and shade, like a harp. The drowsy dash of the low surf on the bar beyond the inlet was harsh to this still and shallow haven for wreckers and oystermen. It was very far from any busy city or hive of men, between the ocean and the sandy peninsula of Maryland.

But no land is so remote that it may not have its banished men. The outcast preacher had committed the one deadly sin acknowledged amongst those wild wreckers and watermen. It was not that he had knocked a drowning man in the head, nor shown a false signal along the shore to decoy a vessel into the breakers, nor darkened the lighthouse lamp. These things had been done, but not by him.

He had married out of his race. His wife was crossed with despised blood.

"What do you seek, preacher?" exclaimed a gruff, hard voice. "Has the Canaanite woman driven you out from your hut this sharp weather, in the night?"

"No," answered the outcast preacher. "My heart has sent me forth to beg the service of your oyster-

forms and images. Dip again, and help me to my hut with a few oysters, for I am very faint. Then all my knowledge and interest in this effigy I will surrender to you."

"Agreed!" exclaimed the Jew, plunging the tongs to the bottom again and again, in his satisfaction.

They walked inland across the difficult sands, the Jew carrying the crucifix jealously. Lights gleamed from a few huts along the level island. At the meanest hut of all they stopped, and heard within a baby's cry, to which there was no response. The preacher staggered back with apprehension. The Jew raised the latch and led the way.

The light of some burning drift-wood and dried sea-weed filled the low roof and was reflected back to a cot, on which a woman lay with a living child beside her. Something dread and ineffable was conveyed by that stiffened form. The Jew, familiar with misery and all its indications, caught the preacher in his arms.

"Levin Purnell," he said, "thy Christmas gift has come. Bear up! There is no more persecution for thee. She is dead!"

The outcast preacher looked once, wildly, on the woman's face, and with a cry pressed his hands to his heart. The Jew laid him down upon a miserable pallet, and for a few moments watched him steadily. Neither sound nor motion revealed the presence of the cold spark of life. The husband's heart was broken.

"Poor wretch!" exclaimed the Jew. "Mismated couple ; in death as obstinate as in life. Lie there together, befriended in the closing hour by the Jew of Chincoteague, a present—to-morrow's Christmas—for thy neighbors of this Christian island!"

He stirred the fire. Death had no terrors for him, who had seen it by land and sea, in brawls and ship-wrecks, by hunger and by scurvy. He laid the bodies side by side, and warmed the infant at the fire. Looking up from the living child's face, he caught the sparkle of the crucifix he had discovered, where it stood in the narrow window-sill. There were gems of various colors in it, and they reflected the firelight lustrously, like a slender chandelier, or, as the Jew remembered in the version of the Evangels, like the gifts those bearded wise men, of whom he might resemble one, brought to the manger of the infant Christ—gifts of gold, frankincense, and myrrh. Struck by the conceit, he looked again at the baby's face—the baby but a few days or weeks old—and he felt, in spite of himself, a softness and pity.

" It might be true," he muttered, " that a Jewish man, a tricked and unsuspecting husband of a menial, like her who has perished with this preacher, *did* behold a new-born baby in the manger of an inn, eighteen hundred and forty years ago."

He looked again at the cross. In the relief of the night against the window-pane its jewels shone like the only living things in the hovel. A figure was extended upon this cross, and every nail was a precious stone ; the crown of thorns was all diamonds.

" It might be true," he said again, " that on a cross-beam like that, the manger baby perished for some audacity—as I might be put to death if I mocked the usages of a whole nation, as this preacher has done."

The cross, an object as high as one of the window-panes, and suffused with the exuding dyes of its jewels, took now a dewy lustre, as if weeping precious gum and amber. The Jew felt an instant's sense of superstition, which he dashed away, and placing the child, already sleeping, before the fire, awakened rapacity led him to hunt the hovel over. He found nothing but a few religious books, and amongst them a leather-covered Testament, which he opened and read with insensibility—passing on, at length, to interest, then to fascination, at last to rage and defiance—the opening chapters and the close of the story of Jesus.

" Now, by the sufferings of my patient race ! I will do a thing unlike myself, to prove this testimony a libel. Here is a child more homeless than this carpenter, Joseph's, without the false pretence of coming of David's line. Its mother tainted with negro blood, like the slaves I have imported. Its father the obscurest preacher of his sect. I will rob the shark and the crab of a repast. It shall be my child and a Hebrew. · Yea, if I can make it so, a Rabbi of Israel!''

Issachar looked again at the cross. Day was breaking in the window behind it, and the rich light of its gems was obscurer, but its form and proportions seemed to have expanded—perhaps because he had worn his eyes reading by the firelight—and the outstretched figure looked large as humanity, and the cross lofty and real as that which it was made to commemorate. He hid it beneath his garment and walked forth into the gray dawn of Christmas. One star remained in mid-heaven, whiter than the day. It poised over the hovel of the dead like something new-born in the sky, and unacquainted with its fellow orbs.

"Christmas gift!" shouted a party of lads and women, rushing upon the Jew. "Christmas gift! You are caught, Issachar. Give us a present, old miser!"

It was the custom in that old settled country that whoever should be earliest up, and say "Christmas gift!" to others, should receive some little token in farthings or kind.

"Bah!" answered the Jew. "Look in yonder, where the best of your religion lie, perished by your inhumanity, and behold your Christmas gift to them!"

There, where no friendly feet but those of negroes and slaves had entered for months, the strengthening morning showed a young wife, almost white, and the most beautiful of her type, with comely features, and eyes and hair that the proudest white beauty might envy. The gauntness of death had scarcely diminished those charms which had brought the pride of the world's esteem and the prudence of religion to her feet, and lifted her to virtuous matrimony, only to banish her lover from the hearthstones of his race and make them both outcasts, the poorest of the creatures of God, even on Chincoteague. A slight sense of self-accusation touched the bystanders.

"He was a good preacher," said one, "and I was converted under him. He baptized my children. That he should have married a darkey!"

"She was a pious girl," added another, "and from her youth up was in temptation, which she resisted, like a white woman. That she should have ruined this preacher!"

"He was a poet," said a third. "'Peared like as if he believed every thing he preached. But, my sakes! we can't have sich things in *our* church."

"She loved him, too, the hussy!" exclaimed a fourth. "She would have been his slave if he had asked her. Oh! what misery she felt when she knew that his passion for her was starving him, body and soul!"

They slipped away, with a feeling that, somehow, two very guilty people had been punished in those two. The negroes made the funeral procession. The Jew walked amongst the negroes.

"O Father Abraham," he said, chuckling to himself, "forgive me that I stand here, no renegade to my faith, yet the only white Christian on Chincoteague!"

Issachar was oysterman, sailor, and sutler in one. He advanced money to build pungy boats, knit nets, and make huts. He kept a trading place, packed fish, and dealt with the Eastern port cities by a schooner whose crew he shipped himself and sometimes commanded her. He was a wrecker, too, prompt and enterprising; passed middle life, but full of vitality; bold and cunning in equal degree; and he had been, it was guessed, a slaver, and some said a pirate. He was called by the negroes the King of Chincoteague. His schooner was named The Eli.

Chincoteague is the principal inhabited island along the one hundred miles of coast between the capes of the Delaware and of the Chesapeake—a coast of low bars, divided into long and slender islands by a dozen inlets, which, almost filled with sand, permit only light-draught vessels to enter ; and it is destruction to any ship to go ashore on that coast, where five successive lighthouses warn the commerce of the Atlantic off, but are unable to intimidate the storms which sweep the low shores and almost threaten to leap over the peninsula and submerge it.   Chincoteague lies like a tongue between two inlets, and partly protrudes into the sea, but is also sheltered in part by the bar of Assateague, whose light has flamed for years.   Chincoteague is about ten miles long, and behind it an inland bay stretches continuously, under various names, for thirty miles, protected from the ocean, and scarcely flavored with its salt, except near the outlet at Chincoteague, where the oysters lie in the brackish sluices, and all sorts of fish, from shrimps to sharks, hover around the oyster beds.   In the green depths they can be seen, and there the crab darts sidewise, like a shooting star. In the sandy beach grows the mamano, or snail-clam, putting his head from his shell at high tide to suck nutrition from the mysterious food of the sea, and giving back such chowder to man as makes the eater feel his stomach to possess a nobility above the pleasures of the brain.   The bay of Chincoteague is five or six miles wide, and the nearest hamlet is in Virginia, as is Chincoteague island also.   The hamlet takes the name of Horntown, and not far from there is the old court-house seat of Snow Hill, in Maryland.   Every soul on Chincoteague was native there or thereabout, except Issachar the Jew.

He had appeared amongst them after a sudden storm, the solitary survivor of a wreck that had partly drifted ashore, and, as he said, gone down with all his fortune.   The mild air and easy livelihood of the spot pleased the Jew, after his first despair, and he set about making another fortune.   Capable, solitary and active, he soon outstripped all the people of the islands, and neither beloved nor unbeloved, lived grimly, as chance ordained, and until now, had never shown more than business benevolence. It was a surprising thing to the people of Chincoteague, when the news went round that he had been over to court at Drummond-town and given his recognizance to bring up the orphan boy—whom he named Abraham Purnell—so that the county should not be at the expense of him, and he also brought out from New York, on the Eli's next trip, a Hebrew woman to be the boy's matron. Suckled at a negro's breast, Abraham grew to a vigorous youth, resembling his guardian's race and his mother's as well, in the curling nature of his hair and the brightness of his eyes. The Old Testament Scriptures alone were taught him, and Issachar himself joined the family circle at daily prayer to encourage the faith of Israel in the stranger. The finest of the lean, tough ponies, bred only on Chincoteague, and renowned throughout the peninsula for their endurance, was bought for the boy, as he grew older. He was made Issachar's companion, and, in course of time, passed in fireside talk for a Jew, like his protector.

Only once the superior comfort and clothing of Issachar's *protégé* provoked the remark from one of a group of men that Abraham was "only a stuck-up nigger, anyway;" and then, like a maniac, Old Issachar dashed from his store with a boat-hook and struck down the offender like a dead man.

But the boy was of such docile and beautiful nature that he excited no general antagonism. He was four removals from pure African blood, and as his mother had been a freed girl, he was a citizen, or might be if he pleased. The certain heir of Issachar's possessions, the only thing except gold that Issachar loved, and of a parentage which linked misfortune with piety, his mysterious nativity gave him with the negroes a sacred character. They believed that he would become their king and priest and lead them out of bondage to a promised land ; and this involuntary homage so pleased old Issachar that his heart inclined toward the black race above the Christian whites around him. If an aged negro fell sick, the Jew sent, by his ward, medicine and food. If a very poor negro was buried, the Jew contributed to the expenses. He gave the first counsel of worldly wisdom to the negro freedmen, and gave them faithful interest on their savings. One slave that he possessed he set free, saying :

" By Jacob's staff ! 1 will not hold as cattle the blood people of my son !''

His enlarged benevolence made no difference in his business. It grew to the widest limits of that humble society, and by the accident of a younger life coming forward to bear his honor up, Issachar grew into sympathy with the social life of all the lower peninsula. If they wanted money for public enterprise on the mainland, the Jew of Chincoteague was first to be thought of. His credit, Masonic in its reach, extended to his compatriots in distant cities, and the politicians crossed the Sound to bring him into alliance with their parties. To personal flattery he was obtuse, except when it reached his ward, and then a melting mood came over him. At every Christmas he led himself the eloquent Oriental prayer, young Abraham responding with even a richer imagery, for his mind was alert, his schooling had been private and unintermittent, and his father's enthusiasm and his mother's docility made him a poet and a son together.

" My son," said the Jew, as Abraham's fifteenth Christmas approached, " the time is at hand when we must part for years. I am growing old, and the loss of thee, O my love ! is harder than thou canst know. The sands of life are running out with me, as from an hour-glass. With thee the heavens are rosy and the world is new. Thou beautiful Samuel, Jehovah's selected one ! wilt thou remember me when far away ?"

" Father," answered Abraham, " what besides thee can I love ? Every morning, and at noon, and again at night, I will face from the East to pray toward thee ;

for God will not listen unless I am grateful to my father.''

'' Thou art going to Amsterdam,'' said Issachar. '' There, amongst the noblest Jews of Europe, the descendants of the Jewish Portuguese, the Hebrew tongue in its purity, the law of Moses in its majesty, our lore in its plenitude, thou wilt learn. I look to thee, adopted child of Israel ! to give the promise of thy youth to the study of our grand old religion, and, like the infant Moses, discovered amongst these bulrushes of Chincoteague, to be the reviver of our faith, the statesman of our sect. Yea ! the rebuilder of our Zion. It has been ordained that these things will be done, and, by the stars of Abraham ! it shall be so !''

'' My father,'' said young Abraham, '' God will keep all His promises.''

The Jew took from a chest of massive cedar wood, empty of all besides, the precious crucifix.

'' Look on that,'' he exclaimed. '' Dost thou know what it represents ?''

'' No,'' answered Abraham.

'' It is the symbol of the faith in which thy father died. A Hebrew impostor, one Jesus, was nailed by the Roman conquerors of Jerusalem to a cross-piece of wood. He affected to be the son of David and the Saviour of men. My son, in the name of his punishment the children of Israel have been burned at the stake, dispersed abroad among the nations, and hated of mankind. Preaching his imposture thy father and thy mother were suffered to die for their consistency. See what I have done with the bauble ! The years I have expended on thy mind and comfort have cost me money. From that crucifix, one by one, I have plucked the precious stones for thy education. Here, from the side, where they say the soldier's spear was thrust, I have sold the costly ruby. The nail in the feet, a sapphire, paid thy Jewish matron. The emerald in this right hand purchased thy books. I send thee abroad with the price of the diamonds in the crown.''

" Father," said young Abraham, " the image is hallowed to me for thy piety. It' is Humanity, O my father ! that has made me devoutly a Jew, and thee, unsuspectingly, a Christian."

He sailed away upon the Eli. His parting words had affected old Issachar so much that his mind returned along the course of years to the Christmas night he had passed in the outcast preacher's hut, and the curious story of Jesus he had read there in the New Testament and in the presence of the dead.

" To-morrow is Christmas," said the Jew ; " a hallowed day to me, because it brought me a son whose obedience and piety have gratified the exile of my old age. Although these Christians have covered him with their despite, his excellent charity remembers it not. I will be no less magnanimous, and I will cross the bay and attend the Methodist worship at Snow Hill on Christmas morning, that I may communicate its frivolity to my son."

He kept his word ; and for fear thieves might discover and steal the valuable crucifix, he hid it beneath his vesture and carried it to the mainland. The little plank meeting-house at the edge of Snow Hill was filled with whites on the floor, but in the end gallery, amongst the negroes, Issachar haughtily took his seat, an object of wonder to both races, for his face and reputation were generally recognized. Perhaps it was for this reason that the young preacher, a gentle, graceful person, adapted his sermon to the sweetness of the Christian story rather than bear upon those descriptions which might antagonize his Jewish auditor.

He told the story of the world's selfishness when Christ appeared ; how the Jews, living in the straitest of sectarian aristocracies, inviting and receiving no accessions, had finally fallen under the dogmatism of the uncharitable Pharisees, who esteemed themselves the only righteous devotees and doctrinaires amongst the millions of people on the earth. Jesus, a youth of good Jewish extraction, and honorable family, had been bold enough to denounce Phariseeism and make its votaries ridiculous. He was scorned by them, if for no other crime, for the cheap offence, in a bigoted age, denominated blasphemy. Here the preacher, looking toward the Jew, paid a tribute to the antiquity and loyalty of the better class of Jews, and said that it was well known that one of his own forerunners in the Christian ministry, dying in penury from the consequences of a marital mistake, had been befriended in his death and in his posterity by a gallant follower of the House of Israel.

The congregation, facing about to look at the Jew in the gallery, amongst the negroes, were surprised to see tears on his gray eyelashes, and the colored elders, who loved Issachar exceedingly, exclaimed, in stentorian chorus :

" Praise God for dat Israelite, in whom dar is no guile ! Hallelujah !"

Then, as if the Christmas frost had melted, these grateful exclamations made warmth at once in both races, and encouraged the orator in his extemporization. Issachar began to appreciate the possibility of the founder of a more liberal sect of Jews, whose charitable hand should be extended to Gentiles also, and whose heaven should comprehend all the posterity of Adam. Perhaps his son's portrait was in his mind— that loving son who had but just departed in the interests of the law of Moses and the restoration of the Temple. At the end of the sermon alms were invited for the support of the minister and the propagation of such a gospel as he had preached. With a mixture of pride and humility old Issachar descended the gallery stairs and walked up the aisle, and, taking the crucifix from his breast, planted it upon the altar.

" There," he said, " if your sect asserts the sentiments of this sermon, you are entitled to this rich image. I am repaid for its possession by a son of Gentile parentage whose obedience has been the delight of my old years, and for the gift God has given me in him, I tender you this counterfeit of Jesus nailed on the Roman scaffold.''

The congregation gazed a minute at the golden cross. Ireful laughter broke forth, followed by rage.

'' The pagan ! The papist ! The Turk ! The idolater !'' they exclaimed. '' He mocks the memory of our Saviour on Christmas morning ! Out with him !''

The Jew recovered the crucifix and put it beneath his mantle. He vouchsafed no reply except a scornful '' Ha ! ha ! ha !'' and with this he strode out of the Methodist meeting, rejoined his boatmen, and returned to the island of Chincoteague.

Years passed, and the Jew grew very feeble. He had lasted his fourscore and ten years, and prosperity had attended him through all, and children loved him ; but, true to his first and only fondness, his heart was ever across the sea, where gentle Abraham, studiously intent amongst the Rabbis, communicated with his father by every mail and raised the old man's mind to a height of serious appreciation which greed and commerce had never given him. Although hungering for his boy, Issachar forebore to disturb young Abraham's studies until a bitter illness came to him, and in his gloom and solitude his great want burst from his lips, and he said aloud :

'' Almighty Father ! What will it avail to these old bones if the Temple be rebuilded, and I die without placing my hands on the eyelids of my boy and blessing him in Thy name ? I will pluck from this Christian image the last jewel and dispose of it, that he may return and place his hands in mine, and receive my benediction, and gladden me with his gratitude.''

The image was therefore wholly separated from the cross. Nothing remained but the figure in gold of that bloody Pillory on which He died on whom two hundred millions of human beings rely for intercession with their Creator and Destiny.

The days seemed months to the Jew of Chincoteague. The negroes gathered round his cabin to be of assistance if he should require it ; for they also looked for young Abraham as the Shiloh of their race, and would have died for old Issachar, unredeemed as they thought him, except by his goodness to their prince and favorite.

A high tide, following a series of dreadful storms, arose on the coast of the peninsula, as if the Gulf Stream, like a vast ploughshare, had thrown the Atlantic up from its furrow and tossed it over the beach of Assateague.

The sturdy ponies were all drowned. The sea was undivided from the bay. Pungy boats and canoes drifted helplessly along the coast, and the Eli alone was out of danger in the harbor of New York, waiting to receive young Abraham. At last the freshet crept over the house-tops, and nothing remained but the cottage of the Jew, planted on piles, which lifting it higher than the surrounding houses, yet threatened it the more if the water should float it from its pedestal and send it to sea. Every effort was made to induce the Jew to abandon it, but he was obdurate.

" By the tables of the law !" he said, " living or dead, here will I abide until my son returns."

The bravest negro left the island of Chincoteague at last, placing food beside old Issachar, and there he lay upon his pallet, with nothing to pierce the darkness of his lair except that sacred cross he had raised from the depths of the ocean. That object, like a sentient, overruling thing, still shed its lustre upon the wretched interior of the deserted hut, and, day by day, repeated its story to the neglected occupant.

The mighty storm increased in power as Christmas approached, in the year one thousand eight hundred and fifty——. Wrecks came ashore on the submerged shoal of Chincoteague, but there were now no wreckers to labor for salvage. The Eli, too, was overdue. One night a familiar gun was heard at sea, thrice, and twice thrice, and Issachar raised up and said, in anguish :

" It is my schooner. My son is at hand and in danger. Oh ! for a day's strength, as I had it in my

youth, to go to his relief through the surf.   But, miserable object that I am ! I cannot rise from my bed.
What help, what hope, in the earth or in heaven can I
implore ?''

The naked cross beamed brightly all at once in the
darkness of the cabin.   Issachar felt the legend it conveyed, and with piety, not apostacy, he uttered :

'' O Paschal Lamb ! O Waif of God ! Die Thou for
me this night, and give me to look upon the countenance of my son !''

The Jew, intently gazing at the cross, passed into
such a stupor or ecstasy that he had no knowledge of
the flight of time.   He only knew that, after a certain
dreamy interval, the door of his house yielded to a living man, and, nearly naked with breasting the surf and
fighting for life, young Abraham staggered into the hut
and recognized his father.

'' O son !''   cried Issachar, '' I feel the news thou
hast to tell.   The Eli is wrecked and thou only hast
survived.   The moments are precious.   Hark ! this
house is yielding to the buoyant current.   Stay not for
me, whose sands are nearly run.   I am too old to try
for life or fear to die, but thou art full of youth and
beauty, and Israel needs thee in the world behind me.
Let me bless thee, Abraham, and commit thee to God.''

The water entered the cracks of the cabin ; a pitching motion, as if it were afloat, made the son of the
negro cling closer to the Jew.

'' Father,'' he said, '' I have passed the bitterness
of death.   When the vessel struck and threw me into
the surf, I cried to God and fought for life.   The
waves rolled over me, and the agony of dying so young
and happy grew into such a terror that I could not
pray.   In my despair a something seemed to grasp me,
like tongs of iron, and my eyes were filled with light,
bright as the face of the I AM.   Behold ! I am here,
and that which saved me has made me content to die
by thee.''

The old man drew the dripping ringlets of the

younger one to his venerable beard. The house rocked like a sailing vessel, and the strong sea-fogs seemed to close them round.

"We are sailing to sea," whispered the Jew. "It is too late to escape. The next billow may fling us apart, and our bones shall descend amongst the oyster-shells to build houses for the nutritious beings of the water. Thence, some day, my son, from the heavens God may drop His tongs and draw us up to Him, as on this night thy father and I drew the casket, many years ago. Look there! Look there!"

The heads of both were turned toward the spot where the finger of the old man pointed, and they saw the denuded cross shining in the light of the agitated fire, so large and bright that it reduced all other objects to insignificance.

"It was a light like that," exclaimed Abraham, "which shone in my eyes through the darkness of the billows."

"It was on that," whispered Issachar, "that I called for help, my son, when thou wert dying. From the hour I dipped it from the water my heart has been warmer to the world and man. Is there, in all the hoary traditions of our church, a reason why we should not beseech its illumination again before it returns to the ocean with ourselves? Do thou decide, who art full of wisdom; for I am ignorant in thy eyes, and heavy with sins."

The cross, resplendent, seemed to wear a visible countenance. Wrapped in Issachar's arms, like a babe to its mother, young Abraham extended his hands to the effigy, and in its beams a wondrous consolation of love and rest returned to those poor companions, reconciling them to their helplessness in the presence of the Almighty awe.

"Child of God!" exclaimed the Jew, "thou beauty of the Gentiles, I gave thee life but for a span, and thou seemest to bring to me the life immortal."

The morning broke on the shore frosty and clear

after the subsided storm, and the earliest wreckers, seeking in the drift for Christmas gifts to give their children, found well-remembered parts of the Eli and portions of the tenement of its proprietor. A wave rolled higher than the rest and cast upon the shore two bodies—a young man of the comely face and symmetry of a woman, without a sign of pain in his features and dark, oriental eyes, and an old man, venerable as an inhabitant of the ocean and mysterious as a being of some race anterior to the deluge. In his rugged face the marks of that antiquity which has something stately in the lowest types of the Jew, and in this one an almost Mosaic might, were softened to a magnanimity where death had nothing to contribute but its silence and respect. Laying them together, the fishermen and idlers looked at them with a superstition partly of remorse and mild remembrance, and·the star of Christmas twinkled over them in the sky. None felt that they were other than father and son, and black men and white, indifferent that day to social prejudices, followed the child of Hagar and the Hebrew patriarch to the grave.

HAUNTED PUNGY.

THEY hewed the pines on Haunted Point
  To build the pungy boat,
And other axes than their own
  Yet other echoes smote ;
They heard the phantom carpenters,
  But not a man could see ;
And every pine that crashed to earth
  Brought down a viewless tree.

They launched the pungy, not alone ;
  Another vessel slipped
Down in the water with their own,
  And ghostly sailors shipped ;
They heard the rigging flap and creak,
  And hollow orders cried,
But not a living man could seek,
  And not a boat beside.

They sailed away from Haunted Point,
  Convoyed by something more :
A boatswain's whistle answered back,
  And oar replied to oar.
No matter where the anchor dropped,
  The fiends would not aroint,
And every morn the pungy boat
  Still lay off Haunted Point.

They hailed ; and voices as in fog
  Seemed half to speak again—
A devilish chuckling rolled afar,
  And mutiny of men.
The parson of the islands said
  It was the pirate band,
Whose gold was lost on Haunted Point
  And hid with bloody hand,

Until what time a kidnapped boy,
  By ruffians whipped and stole,
Should in the groves of Haunted Point
  Convert his stealer's soul !
They stole the island parson's child,
  He said a little prayer:
Down sank the ground ; a gliding sound
  Went whispering through the air.

And in the depths the pungy sank ;
  And, as the divers told,
They sought the wreck to lift again,
  And found the pirates' gold.
And in a chapel close at hand
  The pious freedmen toil ;
No slaves are left in all the land,
  Nor any pirates' spoil.

TICKING STONE.

PEOPLE say that a certain tombstone in the London Tract "Hardshell" Baptist graveyard, near Newark, Delaware, will give to the ear placed flat upon it the sound of a ticking like a watch. The London Tract Church, as its name implies, was the worshipping place of certain settlers who either came from London, or chose land owned by a London company. It is a quaint edifice of hard stone, with low-bent bevelled roof, and surrounded by a stone wall, which has a shingle coping. The wall incloses many gravestones, their inscriptions showing that very many of the old worshippers of the church were Welsh. Some large and healthy forest trees partly shade the graveyard and the grassy and sandy cross-roads where it stands, near the brink of the pretty White Clay Creek.

I climbed over the coping of the graveyard wall last spring, and followed my companion, the narrator of the following story, to what appeared to be the very oldest portion of the inclosure. The tombstones were in some cases quite illegible as to inscriptions, worn bare and smooth by more than a century's rains and chipping frosts, and others were sunken deep in the grass so as to afford only partial recompense for the epitaph hunter.

"This is the Ticking Stone," said my companion, pointing to a recumbent slab, worn smooth and scarcely showing a trace of former lettering; "put your ear upon it while I pull away the weeds, and then note if you hear any thing."

1 laid my ear upon the mossy stone, and almost im-

mediately felt an audible, almost tangible ticking, like that of a lady's watch.

"You are scratching the stone, Pusey," I cried to my informant.

"No! Upon my honor! That is not the sound of a scratch that you hear. It cannot be any insect nor any process of moving life in the stone or beneath it. Can you liken it to any thing but the equal motion of a rather feeble timepiece?"

I listened again, and this time longer, and a sort of superstition grew over me, so that had I been alone, probably I would have experienced a sense of timid loneliness. To stand amidst those silent memorial stones of the early times and hear a watch beat beneath one of them as perfectly as you can feel it in your vest pocket, and then to feel your heart start nervously at the recognition of this disassociated sound, is not satisfying, even when in human company.

"This is the best ghost I have ever found," I said. "Perhaps some one has slipped a watch underneath, for it is somebody's watch; there *is* something real in it."

"I took the stone up once myself," said Pusey, "and the ticking then seemed to come up from the ground. While I deliberated, an old man came out of yonder old sexton-looking house, and warned me not to disturb the dead. He crossed the wall, and assisted me to replace the stone, and then bade me sit down upon it, ancient mariner-like, while he disclosed the cause of the phenomenon."

Here my companion stopped a minute—and in the pause we could hear the old trees wave very solemnly above us, and a nut, or burr, or sycamore ball, came rattling down the old kirk roof as we stood there in the graves, to startle us the more, and then he said:

"It is just as queer as the tale he told me—the disappearance of that old man. Nobody about here can recognize him from my descriptions. He walked toward the old mill down the Newark road, and the next time I looked up he was gone. The people in the house there think I am flighty in my mind for insisting upon his appearance to me at all."

" Go on with the tale right here, my flesh-creeping friend," I said. " It will do us good to feel occasionally solemn."

" This stone, young man," said my Quakerly re-buker, in a hard, country farmer's voice ; " this stone is the London Tract Ticking Stone. It is the oldest preacher and admonitor in this churchyard. It is older than the graves of any of the known pastors or communicants round about it.

" In the year 1764 the comparative solitude of this region was broken by a large party of chain-bearers, rod-men, axe-men, commissaries, cooks, baggage-carriers, and camp-followers. They had come by order of Lord Baltimore and William Penn, to terminate a long controversy between two great landed proprietors, and they were led by Charles Mason, of the Royal Observatory, at Greenwich, England, and by Jeremiah Dixon, the son of a collier discovered in a coalpit. For three years they continued westward, running their stakes over mountains and streams, like a gypsy camp in appearance, frightening the Indians with their sorcery. But, near this spot, they halted longest, to fix with precision the tangent point, and the point of intersection of three States—the circular head of Delaware, the abutting right angle of Maryland, and the tiny pan-handle of Pennsylvania.

" The people of this region were sparse in number, but of strong, sober, and yet wild characteristics. The long boundary quarrel had made them predatory, and though God-fearing people, they would fight with all their religious intensity for their right in the land and the dominion of their particular province. They suspended their feuds when the surveying battalion came into their broken country, and looked with curi-

ous interest upon all that pertained to the distinguished
foreign mathematicians. Around the camp of tents
and pack-mules, pedlers and preachers called together their motley congregations, and the sound of
axes clearing the timber was accompanied by fiddling
and haranguing, the fighting of dogs, and the coarse
tones of religious or business oratory. It was in the
height of the era of the great period of the Dissenters
in England, and Methodist, Baptist, and Calvinistic
zealots were piercing to the boundaries of English-
speaking people, wild forerunners of those organized
bands of clergy which were speedily to make our colo-
nies sober-minded, and prepare them for self-govern-
ment.

"Charles Mason was the scientific spirit of the party
—a cool, observing, painstaking, plodding man, slow
in his processes and reliable in his conclusions, and
the bond of friendship between himself and Dixon
was that of two unequal minds admiring the superiorities
of each other. They had already proceeded together
to the Cape of Good Hope on two occasions to study
an eclipse and an occultation. Mason liked Dixon for
his ready spirits, almost improvident courage, speed
with details, and worldly bearing. Though little is
known of their memories now, because they left us
no prolific records and spent much of the period of
service among us in the midst of the wilderness or
in the reticence required for mathematical calculation,
yet they were the successors of Washington in the surveying of the Alleghany ridges. Their survey was reliable ; the line was true. How much superior does it
stand to-day to the line of thirty degrees thirty minutes,
which is the next great political parallel below it, and
was partly run only a few years afterwards ! Up to
their line for the next hundred years flowed the waters
of slavery, but sent no human drop beyond, which did
not evaporate in the free light of a milder sun. God
speed the surveyor, whoever he be, who plants the
stakes of a tranquil commonwealth and leaves them to

be the limit of bad principles, the pioneer line of good ones !

"Charles Mason had spent many years of his life, up to his old age, experimenting with timepieces of his own invention. Many years before, Sir Isaac Newton had called the attention of the British Government to the necessity for an accurate portable time-keeper at sea, to determine longitude, and in 1714 Parliament offered a reward of 20,000 pounds sterling for such a chronometer. Thenceforward for fifty years the inventive spirits of England and the Continent were secretly at work to produce a timepiece which would deserve the large reward, amongst them Charles Mason, who labored with such perfect discretion and uncommunicative self-reliance that none knew, none will ever know, the motive principle he employed or the enginery he devised. While he was working at this survey, near the spot at which we stand, the Board of Award gave the £20,000 to one John Harrison, almost at the very instant when Mason and Dixon's line was begun. This you can confirm by any history of Horology. Charles Mason lived down to the year 1787, surviving Dixon, who had died in England ten years previously, and he was known to say to the end of his days, to people resident in Philadelphia, that a child had eaten up £20,000 belonging to him at a single mouthful.

"The child whom the neighborhood at that time accused of this act was known in later life as Fithian Minuit, babe of a woman of mixed English and Finnish-Dutch descent, who came from the fishermen's town of Head of Elk, a few hours' jog to the southward, to sell fish to the surveying camp. She was a woman of mingled severity of features and bodily obesity, uniting in one temper and frame the Scandinavian and the Low Dutch traits, ignorant good-humor, grim commerce, and stolid appetite. Her baby was the fattest, quaintest, and ugliest in the country ; ready to devour any thing, to grin at any thing, go to the arms of everybody, and, in short, it represented all the traits of the Middle State races—the government of the members, including the brain, by the belly.

"One day this Finnish-Dutch baby—aged perhaps two years—was picked up by one of the assistant surveyors and carried into the tent of Charles Mason. The great surveyor was at that instant bending down over a small metallic object which he was examining through the medium of a lens. He recognized the child, and seemed glad of the opportunity to dismiss more serious occupation from his mind, so he instantly leaped up and poked the fat urchin with his thumb, tempting the bite of its teeth with his forefinger, and was otherwise reducing his tired faculties to the needs of a child's amusement, when suddenly the voice of its mother at the tent's opening drew him away.

"'Fresh fish, mighty surveyor! Fall shad, and the most beautiful yellow perch. Buy something for the sake of Minuit's baby!'

"The celebrated surveyor, who seemed in an admirable humor, stepped just outside the tent to look at the fish, and in that little interval his assistant, seized with inquisitiveness, stole up to his table, and picked up the tiny object lying there under the magnifying glass.

"'This is the little ticking seducer which absorbs my master's time,' he said. 'Why, it isn't big enough for an infant to count the minutes of its life upon it!'

"At this the fat, good-humored baby, anticipating something to eat, reached out its hands. The surveyor's assistant, in a moment of mischief, put the object in the child's grasp. The child clutched it, bit at it, and swallowed it whole in an instant.

"Before the assistant surveyor could think of any other harm done than the possible choking of the child, the child's mother and the great surveyor entered the tent. The arms of the first reached for her offspring, and of the second for the subject of his experiment.

"'My chronometer!'

" ' The child of the fish-woman ate it ! '

" The fish-woman screamed, and reversed the urchin after the manner of mothers, and swung him to and fro like a pendulum. He came up a trifle red in the face, but laughing as usual, and the ludicrous inappositeness of the great loss, the unconscious cause of it, the baby's wonderful digestion, the assistant's distress, and the surveyor's calm but pallid self-control, made Jeremiah Dixon, dropping in at the minute, roar with laughter.

" ' Dixon,' said Mason, ' the work of half my life, my everlasting timepiece, just completed and set going, has found a temperature where· it requires no compensation balance.'

" ' I am glad of it,' said his associate, ' for now we can proceed with Mason and Dixon's line, and nothing else ! '

" A look, more of pity than of reproach, passed over Mason's scarcely ruffled face—the pity of one man solely conscious of a great object lost, for another, indifferent or ignorant both of the object and the loss. He took the smiling urchin in his hands, and raising it upon his shoulder, placed his ear to its side. Thence came with faint regularity the sound of a simple, gentle ticking. They all heard it by turns, and, while they paused in puzzled wonder and humor, the undaunted infant looked down as innocent as a chubby, cheery face painted on some household clock. The innocent expression of the child touched the mathematician's heart. He filled a glass with good Madeira wine, and drank the devourer's health in these benignant words :

" ' May Minuit's baby run as long and as true as the article on which he has made his meal ! '

" Next day they set the great stone in the corner of the State of Maryland, and, breaking camp, vanished westward through the cleft of light opened by their pioneers, pursued yet for many miles by a motley multitude.

" Before many years this fertile country filled up with

hamlets, mills, and churches ; the War of Independence
scarcely interrupted its prosperity, because the Quaker
element adhered with constancy to neither side, and
only one campaign was fought here.   The story of the
boy who ate a watch passed out of general knowledge
and remark ; he was known to have been a drummer
at the battle of Chadd's Ford, and to have buried his
mother before the close of the war, at the Delaware
fishing hamlet of Marcus Hook, amongst her Finnish
progenitors.

"But soon after the peace, the short, fat body and
queer, merry Dutch face of Fithian Minuit were known
all along the roads of Chester, Cecil, and Newcastle
counties, by parts of the people of three States, as com-
ponents of one of the least offensive, most industrious,
and most lively and popular young chaps around the
head of the Chesapeake.

"He was respectful with the old and congenial with
the young—always going and never tired, up early and
late, of a chirruping sort of address and an equal temper, and while he appeared to be thrifty and money-
making, he did all manner of good turns for the high
and the humble ; and, although everybody said he
was the homeliest young man in the region, yet more
village girls went to their front doors to see him than
if he had been a showman coming to town to do feats
of magic.   He was not unintelligent either, and could
play on the violin, compute accounts equal to the best
country book-keeper, and as he was of religious turn,
although attached to no particular denomination, the
meeting-houses on every side, hardly excepting the
Quakers themselves, delighted to see him drive up on
Sundays and tell an anecdote to the children and sing
a little air, half-hymn sort, half stave, but always
given with a good countenance, which apologized for
the worldly notes of it.   If any severe interpreter of
Christian amusements took the people to task for toler-
ating such a universal and desultory character, there
were others to rise up and ask what evil or passionate

word or act of sorry behavior in Fithian Minuit could be instanced. The severe Francis Asbury himself raised the question once on the Bohemia Manor amongst the Methodists, and got so little support that he charged young Minuit with the possession of some devilish art or spell to entrap the people ; but Fithian once, when the good itinerant's horse broke down on the road, met Mr. Asbury, won his affections, and mended his big silver watch.

" This mending of clocks, watches, and every description of time-keepers was the occupation of Minuit. He had picked up the art, some said, from a Yankee in the army at the close of the war, and certainly no man of his time or territory had such good luck with time-pieces. Residing in the little village of Christina (by the pretentious called Christi-anna, and by the crude, with nearer rectitude, called Cris*tene*), Fithian kept a snug little shop full of all manners and forms of clocks, dials, sand-glasses, hour-burning candles, water-clocks, and night tapers. He had amended and improved the new Graham clock, called the ' dead scapement,' or ' dead-beat escapement ' ,the origin of our modern word *dead-beat*, signifying a man who does not meet his engagements, whereas the original ' dead-beat ' was the most faithful engagements-keeper of its time. Perhaps a dead-beat nowadays is a time-server ; for this would be a correct derivation). From this shop the young Minuit, in a plain but reliable wagon, with a nag never fast and never slow, and indifferent to temperatures, travelled the country for a radius of forty miles—not embarrassed even by the Delaware, which he crossed once a month, and attended fully to the temporal and partly to the spiritual needs of all the Jerseymen betwixt Elsinborough and Swedesboro.

" Over the door of Minuit's whitewashed cabin on the knoll of Christina was the sign of a jovial, fat person, bearing some resemblance to himself, in the centre of whose stomach stood a clock inscribed, ' My time

is everybody's.' Past this little shop went the entire
long caravan and cavalcade by land between the North
and South, stage-coaches, mail-riders, highwaymen,
chariots, herdsters, and tramps ; for Christina bridge
was on the great tide-water road and at the head of
navigation on the Swedish river of the same name, so
that here vessels from the Delaware transferred their
cargo to wagons, and a portage of only ten miles to
the Head of Elk gave goods and passengers reship-
ment down the Chesapeake. This village declined only
when the canal just below it was opened in 1829 and
a little railway in 1833. It was nearly a century and
a half old when Minuit set his sign there, before General Washington went past it to be inaugurated. From
Fithian's window the pleasant land was seen spread
out below him beyond the Christina ; and the Swedish,
Dutch, and English farms smiled from their loamy
levels on sails which moved with scarcely perceptible
motion through the narrow dykes planted with greenest
willows. Before his door the teamsters, ill-tempered
with lashing and swearing at their teams in the ruts of
Iron Hill, schoolboys from Nottingham, millers' men
from Upper White Clay, and bargemen and stage passengers, recovered temper to see the sign of the great
paunch with a timepiece set so naturally in it indicating the hour of dinner. Within they found the
clock-maker, with face beaming as if reflected from a
watch-case, working handily amongst a hundred ticking pieces, of which he looked to be one. There were
large sundials for the outer walls of barns and farm-
houses, very popular in the Pennsylvania hills ; sand-
glasses for the Peninsula, where it cost nothing to fill
them ; and hour-burning candles, much affected by the
Chesapeake gentry, which gave at once light and time.
There were ancient striking clocks, such as the monks
may have used to disturb them for early prayers,
which, with a horrible rattle of wheels and clash of
heavy weights, hammered the alarm. There were the
tremendous watches of river captains who had aspired

to go to sea, and old crutch escapement watches which Huygens himself had perhaps handled in Holland. The window was filled with trains of wheels and pinions, snails and racks, crystals, and faces and watches, cackling at each other. There were striking clocks which rung chimes or rocked like little vessels on apparent billows, or started off with notes like grasshoppers. A hundred of the most musical tree-frogs shut up in a piano might give a feeble notion of the tunes and thrummings assembled in this shop. It was the same day or night, and the power of Fithian Minuit over time-keepers was nearly miraculous. He appeared to be able to smile an old watch into action. Transferred to his hand, some spent and rusty sentinel, long silent and useless, seemed to feel the warmth of the mender and resumed the round of duty. He would buy from the old estate halls on the Sassafras and the Chester rivers, tall, solemn clocks, dead to the purpose of their creation, their stately learned faces lost to former automatic expressions or waggery, and when exposed to the infectious influences of his shop, a gurgle of sound as of the inhalation of air into their lungs had been heard, according to some people, and next day the carcass of the clock would be found resonant and its faculties recovered. One day the great patriots, John Dickinson and Cæsar Rodney, riding past Christina together, stopped for dinner, and sent their watches in to be cleaned meantime.

" ' Minuit,' said Rodney, ' you are a devil with a time-keeper !'

" ' Nay, Minuit,' said Dickinson, ' thou art the gentlest custodian of time in our parts. I would some one could regulate these States and times like thee.'

" The country round resorted to Minuit for repairs, but he generally came himself along the roads fortuitously about the time anybody's dials stood still. He was almost equal as a weather prophet to his fame as a mechanic, and as his broad, fat face, blue eyes, and portly body passed some farmer's gate, the cheery cry would go up, perhaps :

" ' Make hay—the wind's right ! ' or again : ' Time enough, farmer, with another pair of hands. But it's coming from the east ! '

" Had it been possible to suggest any superstition about a man universally popular, people would have said that this henchman of time and minute-hand of diligence drew his power from doubtful sources. Further north, where there was less superstition than amongst these mingled unspiritualized populations, Minuit might have been burnt as a wizard. A little doctor in the Deutsch hills, who once prescribed for the clock-mender, reported that his pulse had a metallic beat, and, looking suddenly up, he saw, where Minuit's face had been, a round clock face looking down and ticking at him. This doctor was a worthless fellow, however, and loose of tongue. Minuit, it was observed, never used a tuning-fork in church, like all leaders of religious music, but cast his eyes down a moment towards his heart, and tapped his foot, and then, as if catching the pitch somewhere from within, he raised the tune and carried it forward with an exquisite sense of rhythm.

" A very old man and a cripple, who lived across the way from Minuit's, affected to observe extraordinary changes in his stature according to the weather changes, elongating as the temperature rose, and in very cold weather sinking into himself ; this man also observed, on the day of a solar eclipse, that for the period there was nothing at all in the place where the clock-mender's head had been except a ring of light which enlarged as the disk of the sun was released. But who could rely upon the vagaries of an old man, who could do nothing but make memoranda out of his window upon the doings of his neighbors ?

" If anybody knew more than that Fithian Minuit was an obliging, neighborly man, and a model for mechanics, it must have been the subject of his romance.

He was related to have told all that he knew upon the mystery of his being to his clergyman, and there is nothing now to confirm the gossip ; for the preacher himself has gone to sleep in the old Shrewsbury grave-yard in Maryland.

" At Port Penn, where the last island in the channel of the lower Delaware now raises its flaming beacon, and the belated collier steers safely by Reedy Island light, lived the daughter of an old West India and coasting captain, who would permit his chronometers to be repaired and cleaned by nobody but Minuit. His cottage stood where now there is a broad and sandy street leading to a wooden pier and to bathing-houses on a pleasure beach. The few people near at hand were pilots, captains of bay craft, and grain-buyers ; although the Dutch and Swedish farms, alter-nating with long marshes, musical with birds, had lined the wide Delaware at this point many a year. In calm, sunny weather, the broad beauty of the river and its low gold and emerald shores, with bulky ves-sels swinging up on the slow full tide, combined the sceneries of America and the Netherlands ; but when a gale blew over the low shores, scattering the reed-birds like the golden pollen of the marsh lilies, and cold white gulls succeeded, diving and careening like sharks of the sky, the ships and coasters felt no se-renity in these wide yeasty reaches of the Delaware bay, and they labored to drop anchor behind the natural breakwater of Reedy Island. There, clustering about as thickly in that olden time as they now seek from all the ocean round the costly shelter of Henlopen break-water, coaster and pirate, fisherman and slaver, sent up the prayer a beneficent government has since granted in the fullest measure, for a perfect Coast Survey and a vigilant Lighthouse Board.

" The daughter of Captain Lum was named Lois, and she was the junior of Fithian Minuit by several years, a slender, beautiful girl, with hair and eyes of the softest brown, and household ways, daughterly and endearing. .

"The old sea-captain, who made five voyages a year to the nearer Indies, and sent ashore to Port Penn as he passed, returning, the best of rum and the freshest of tropical fruits, looked with a jealous eye upon any possible suitor to his daughter, and had, perhaps, embarrassed her prospects for a younger protector, if such she had ever wished. But he loved to see the clockmaker come to the cottage, who had never shown partiality for any woman, while popular with all.

"'Minuit,' he used to say, 'the best man on watch by land or sea, thou North Star! look to my girl as to my chronometer, and I'll pay thee twice the cost of thy time!'

"It was the captain's delight, while ashore, to have every timepiece, stationary or portable, taken apart in the presence of his daughter and himself, while he told his sailor yarns, and Lois stood ready to serve his punch, or pass to the fat, smooth-faced, cheerful Minuit the pieces of mechanism: brass gimbals, chronometer-boxes, wheels and springs, ship-glasses, compasses, the manifold parts of little things by which men grope their way out of sight of land, hung between a human watch and the crystal shell of the embossed heaven. Chronometers were with Minuit attractive and yet awe-giving subjects. The legend of his childhood, well forgotten by all else, said that he had swallowed a chronometer, so small that a sea-captain could swim with it in his mouth. And now the sailors of all the navies cruised by the aid of clumsy watches, big as house-clocks, which to look at made Minuit smile with pity.

"'Captain Lum,' he said aloud, on the eve of a voyage in the winter season, 'I have often yearned to go to sea. The sight of it makes me a little wild. I think I could guess my way over it and about it, by inherent reckoning.'

"He saw the pair of white hands holding something before him tremble a little, and he looked up. The spiritual face of Lois was looking at his with wistful apprehension and interest. If ever his pulse beat out of time it was now—for in that exchange of glances he felt what she did not understand—that he was beloved.

"Pain and joy, not swiftly, but softly, filled Minuit —pain, because he had loved this girl and wished never to have her know it, but would keep it an unbreathed, a holy mystery ; and joy, like any lover's recognizing himself in the dear heart he had never importuned.

"Next day the good ship Chirpland came off Port Penn. The jolly captain saying adieu to Minuit, clasped his hand.

"'I saw thy look and my daughter's yesterday,' he said. 'It is weak of me to deny her a man like thee, thou sailor's friend. My ship is old. These coasts are dangerous. Nights and days come when we get no sight of lights ashore or in heaven. If thy chronometer fail, fail not thou, but be to her repairer and possessor !'

"The discovery and the trust embarrassed Minuit, but he had never denied the request of any man. His time, as his sign affirmed, was everybody's. Yet a thrill, a twang, a twinge of delicious fear passed through him now. He loved this girl dearly, but he feared to love at all. He had now both the parental and the womanly recognition, and his days were lonely even with his garrulous timepieces, but he felt a lonelier sense of the possibility of turning her affection to awe. Those queer legends of his birth, his affinity for fixed luminaries and motions, and his conscious knowledge that he stood in some way related to spheres and orbits, and the laws of revolution and period, had never disturbed his mind in its calculations. But if he did stand exceptional in these respects to his fellowmen, might another and a beloved one comprehend what he himself did not? Yet the kindly regard of his neighbors, the composure of a conscience well consulted, and the hope that he was worthy of human love, made him resolve to keep the captain's admoni·

tion, though he hoped the occasion to obey it might never arrive.

"In the absence of the good ship, however, love could not be deceived. It spoke in waitings and longings, and in tender glances and considerateness. She knew the rattle of his carriage-wheels, and he could feel her in the air like the breath of a beautiful day soon to appear in distance. Time, toward which he stood in such natural harmony, was dearer that it contained this passion and life more exquisite, and himself more questionable for it all.

"It was a stormy winter. Ships strewed the coast between Hatteras and Navesink, and the capes of the Delaware received many a tattered barque. The ice poured down and wedged itself between Reedy Island and the shores, and crushed to pieces many that had escaped the ocean gales. One night in a raging storm the door of Captain Lum's cabin was thrown open, and a sailor appeared fresh from the water. He bore in his hand a chronometer, which Minuit recognized in a moment, and he drew his arm for the first time around the maiden's form.

"'The Chirpland went down on Five Fathom Shoal, and the captain stood by her. He bade us return his chronometer, and say that he perished in the assurance that his daughter was left to the guidance of another fully as sure.'

"'My child,' said Minuit, 'I accept thee wholly, sharing thy griefs! Weep, but on the breast of one who loves thee!'

"The village of Christina rejoiced when its broad-faced, dimpled friend came home with a bride so fair and well-descended. They dressed the sign before his door with flowers. Only the groom wore an anxious face as he led her into his tidy home, now for the first time blessed with a mistress.

"The night of the nuptials came softly down, as nowhere else except upon the skies of the Delaware and Chesapeake, and Minuit was happy. The thrumming clocks in the shop below mingled their tones and tickings in one consonant chorus, scarcely heard above the long drone and low monotonies of the insects in the creeks and woods, which assisted silence. The husband slept, how well beloved he could not know.

"In the dreams of the night he was awakened. In the pale moonshine he saw his wife, clad in her garments of whiteness, standing by his bed all trembling.

"'Tell me,' she said, 'what it is that I hear? I have listened till I am afraid. As I lay in this room perfectly silent, with my head, my husband, nearest your heart, I felt the ticking of a watch. At first it was only curious and strange. Now it haunts me and terrifies me. I am a simple girl, new and nervous to this wedded life. Is this noise natural? What is it?'

"Minuit trembled also.

"'Lois, my bride, my heaven!' he said. 'Oh! pity me, who have tried to pity all and make all happy, if I cannot myself explain away the cause of your alarm. I have kept myself lonely these many years, aware that I was not like other men, but that my heart—no evil monitor to me—gave a different sound. There is nothing in its beat, my wife, to make you fear it. Return and lay your head upon it, and you will hear it say this only, if you listen with faith : *love!*'

"Thus the watch-maker turned superstition to assurance, and the admonition of his heart was a source of joy instead of fear to the listener at its side. It ticked a few bright years with constancy, and was the last benediction of the world to her ere she was ushered into that peace which passeth understanding.

"At the death of his wife Minuit felt a deeper sense of his responsibility to time, and the finite uses of it expanded to a cheerful conception of the infinite. The country round was generally settled by a religious people, and the many meeting-houses of different sects had his equal confidence and sympathy. Pursuing his craft with unwearied diligence, and delighting the homestead with his violin as of old, a more pensive and wistful expression replaced his smile, and love withdrawn beckoned him toward it beyond the boundaries of period. Hard populations, which would not listen to preachers, heard with delight the amiable warnings of this friendly man, and as his own generation grew older, a new race dawned to whom he appeared in the light of a pure-spirited evangelist. ' Improve the time! watch it! ennoble it! It is a part of the beautiful and perpetual circle of everlasting duty. It is to the great future only the little disk of a second-hand, traversed as swiftly, while the great rim of heaven accepts it as a part of the eternal round!' Such was the burden of his sermon.

"He could ride all along the roads, and hear his missionaries preaching for him wherever a clock struck, or a dial on the gable of a great stone barn propelled its shadows. His tracts were in every farmer's vest pocket. Whatever he made he consecrated with a paragraph of counsel.

"The old sign faded out. The clock-maker's sight grew dim, but his apprehensions of the everlasting love and occupation were clearer and more confident to the end.

"One day they found him in the graveyard of the London Tract, by the side of the spot where his wife was interred, worn and asleep at the ripe age of three-score.

"The mill teams and the farm wagons stopped in the road, and the country folks gathered round in silence.

"' Run down at last,' said one. ' If there are heavenly harps and bells, he hears them now!' "

And there they hear the ticking, the preaching of this faithful life, under the old stone, sending up its pleasant message yet. The stone is perishing like a broken crystal, but the memory of the diligent and useful man beneath it rings amongst the holy harmonies of the country. Though dead, he yet speaketh!

THE IMP IN NANJEMOY.

DULL in the night, when the camps were still,
Thumped two nags over Good Hope Hill ;
The white deserter, the passing spy,
Took to the brush as the pair went by ;
The army mule gave over the chase ;
The Catholic negro, hearing the pace,
Said, as they splashed through Oxon Run :
" Dey ride like de soldiers who speared God's Son !"
But when Good Friday's bells behind
Died in the capital on the wind,
He who rode foremost paused to say :
  " Herold, spur up to my side, scared boy !
A word has rung in my ears all day—
  Merely a jingle, 'Nanjemoy.' "

" Ha !" said Herold, " John, why that's
A little old creek on the river.   Surratt's
Lies just before us.   You halt on the green
While I slip in the tavern and get your carbine !"
The outlaw drank of the whiskey deep,
Which the tipsy landlord, half asleep,
Brought to his side, and his broken foot
He raised from the stirrup and slashed the boot.
" Lloyd," he cried, " if some news you invite—
Old Seward was stabbed in his bed to-night.
Lincoln *I* shot—that long-lived fox—
As he looked at the play from the theatre box ;
And it seemed to me that the sound I heard,
  As the audience fluttered, like ducks round decoy,
Was only the buzz of a musical word
  That I cannot get rid of—' Nanjemoy.' "

" Twenty miles we must ride before day,
Cross Mattawoman, Piscataway,
If in the morn we would take to the woods
In the swamp of Zekiah, at Doctor Mudd's !"

" Quaint are the names," thought the outlaw then,
" Though much I have mingled with Maryland men !
I have fever, I think, or my mind's o'erthrown.
Though scraped is the flesh by this broken bone,
Every jog that I take on this road so lonely,
    With thoughts, aye bloody, my mind to employ,
I can but say, over and over, this only—
    The drowsy, melodious ' Nanjemoy.' "

Silent they galloped by broken gates,
By slashes of pines around old estates ;
By planters' graves afield under clumps
Of blackjack oaks and tobacco stumps ;
The empty quarters of negroes grin
From clearings of cedar and chinquopin ;
From fodder stacks the wild swine flew,
The shy young wheat the frost peeped through,
And the swamp owl hooted as if she knew
    Of the crime, as she hailed : " Ahoy ! Ahoy !"
And the chiming hoofs of the horses drew
    The pitiless rhythm of " Nanjemoy."

So in the dawn as perturbed and gray
They hid in the farm-house off the way,
And the worn assassin dozed in his chair,
A voice in his dreams or afloat in the air,
Like a spirit born in the Indian corn—
Immemorial, vague, forlorn,
And disembodied—murmured forever
The name of the old creek up the river.
" God of blood !" he said unto Herold,
As they groped in the dusk, lost and imperilled,
In the oozy, entangled morass and mesh
Of hanging vines over Allen's Fresh :
" The chirp of birds and the drone of frogs,
The lizards and crickets from trees and bogs
Follow me yet, pursue and ferret
    My soul with a word which I used to enjoy,
As if it had turned on me like a spirit
    And stabbed my ear with its ' Nanjemoy.' "

Ay ! Great Nature fury or preacher
Makes, as she wists, of the tiniest creature—
Arming a word, as it floats on the mind,
With the dagger of wrath and the wing of the wind.

What, though weighted to take them down,
Their swimming steeds in the river they drown,
And paddle the farther shore to gain,
Chased by gunboats or lost in rain ?
Many a night they try the ferry
    And the days in haggard sleep employ,
But every raft, or float, or wherry,
    Drifts up the tide to Nanjemoy.

" Ho ! John, we shall have no more annoy,
We've crossed the river from Nanjemoy.
The bluffs of Virginny their shadows reach
To hide our landing upon the beach !"
Repelled from the manse to hide in the barn,
The sick wretch hears, like a far-away horn,
As he lies on the straw by the snoring boy,
The winding echo of " N-a-n-j-e-m-o-y."
All day it follows, all night it whines,
From the suck of waters, the moan of pines,
And the tread of cavalry following after,
The flash of flames on beam and rafter,
The shot, the strangle, the crash, the swoon,
Scarce break his trance or disturb the croon
Of the meaningless notes on his lips which fasten,
    And the soldier hears, as he seeks to convoy
The dying words of the dark assassin,
    A wandering murmur, like " Nanjemoy."

THE FALL OF UTIE.

THE reception at Secretary Flake's was at its height. Bland Van, the President of the nation, had departed with his boys ; the punch-bowl had been emptied nine times ; and still the cry from our republican society was, " Fill up ! "

A pair of young men, unacquainted with each other, pressed at the same time to the punch-bowl, and Jack, the chief ladler, turning from the younger, a clerk in civil dress, helped the elder, a tall naval officer, to a couple of glasses. The clerk, young Utie, who was somewhat flushed, addressed the chief ladler and remarked :

" You dam nigger, didn't you see my glass ? "

" See it, sah ? Yes ! I've seen it seval times afo, dis evening."

Black Jack then received the current allowance of curses for his color and his impudence, all of which he took meekly, till the officer, Lieutenant Dibdo, interrupted on the negro's behalf.

" It's none o' yo affair, I reckon ! " cried Utie sullenly.

" The man had no intention of slighting you," said Dibdo. " You have been drinking too much, boy, and your coarseness is coming out."

A fresh crowd of thirsty people pressing up at this point gave Jack his opportunity to cry : " Room around de punch-bowl ! "

And the disputants were separated and squeezed by the promenading tides into different rooms.

The officer presently forgot all about it, but not so young Utie, who was partly drunk, entirely vain, not a

gentleman by nature, and outraged that anybody had
dubbed him '' a boy.'' He sought the side of a fine
young girl, the daughter of the chief of the bureau
where he was employed, and with whom he was in love.
She was attired in the free costume of republican re-
ceptions—bare arms, a low dress giving ample display
to the whitest shoulders in the room, and fine natural
hair dressed with flowers. Every gentleman who
passed her during the evening had looked his homage
freely—old beaux, dignitaries, officers, foreign deputies,
roués—and as she had been two or three winters in
that kind of society, nothing discomposed her.

'' Robert,'' she said, with part of a glance, as Utie
rejoined her, '' you go to the punch-bowl too much.
You rèflect upon me, sir. Besides, I heard you quar-
relling with that handsome officer. I am dying to
know him. Who is he ?''

Utie looked viciously up, anger and jealousy inflam-
ing his heated face, for, although he had no engagement with Miss Rideau, he conceived himself her
future suitor. But some rash words that he said
against the officer were scarcely heard by the self-pos-
sessed beauty of official society, because, just then, the
young officer and a friend were approaching them. She
dropped her eyes when she met Lieutenant Dibdo's bold
glance of admiration, perhaps in order not to be privy
to the more searching look with which, like a gentleman
of the world, he ran over the fine points of her plump
body as he passed. But young Utie, seeing the offender of a moment ago taking such ardent and leisurely
survey of the girl under his care, turned pale with
hate. The officer did not notice him at all, absorbed
in the fine colors, eyes, and proportions of Miss
Rideau, and this further outraged Utie who—to his
credit be it said—had only modest thoughts for her.
When he saw, however, that she looked after the manly figure and naval gilt of him of the profane eyes, as
if to return his admiration, the intoxicated boy dropped
an oath.

" I will horsewhip that powder-monkey !" he said.

" Robert," said the girl placidly, " you won't.
You have no horse and no horse-whip, but you have
been drinking. Go from me, sir ! Some one else
shall see me home to-night."

" I will kill the man who takes my place ! Do you
dare to speak that way to me ?"

He had raised his voice, in his rage, so that some
others heard it. There was a little pause of pressing
people, for that was a chivalrous age as to the manner
of men to women, and the young officer, just then returning, availed himself of a pretty girl's dilemma to
say :

" May I assist you, miss ? I presume you are not
in very agreeable company."

" Thank you, sir," answered Miss Rideau. " I
would be obliged to have some one find my aunt for
me ; she is here somewhere."

" Will you accept a stranger's arm ?"

" In this misfortune, I will."

Dibdo took off the pretty girl, and one of his naval
companions, looking after him, exclaimed, " What a
genius Dib. is with the ladies !" But the companion,
feeling a trembling, unsteady hand upon his arm,
turned about and met young Utie's desperate face.
" I want to know the name of that fellow !" said
Utie.

" That is Charles Dibdo," said the naval companion, " lieutenant of the United States frigate Fox,
and I recommend you, my boy, to address *him* in a
civil tone. For me, I never mind a drunken man."

Thoroughly demonized now, young Robert Utie
turned blindly about for some implement of revenge.
He found it in Tiltock, a fellow-clerk, a novitiate and
a ninny, who was visible in the crowd.

" Tiltock, are you a man of honor ?"

" I hope so, Bob."

" Can you carry a challenge ?"

" Oh yes ! 1 guess so, to 'blige a ole friend."

" Can you write it ?"

" I'm afraid not."

" Then take it by word of mouth. That scoundrel there, Lieutenant Dibdo, has insulted a lady, and me too. I must have his blood. Follow him up, and meet me at Gadsby's with his answer."

Full of self-importance at this first and safe opportunity to stand upon what is known as " the field of honor," Tiltock kept the lieutenant in his eye, and took him finally aside and demanded a meeting in the name of Utie. The naval officer answered that he had simply relieved a lady from a drunken boy ; but Tiltock, in the dramatic way common to halcyon old times, refused to accept either " drunken" or " boy" as terms appropriate to " the code," and pressed for an answer. In five minutes the naval officer replied, through his naval companion, that having ascertained Mr. Utie to be a gentleman's son, and he as an United States officer not being able to decline a challenge, the latter was accepted. The weapons were to be pistols, the place the usual ground at Bladensburg, and the time the afternoon of the next day.

There was a good deal of drinking and boasting at the hotels that night, Utie and Tiltock telling everybody, as a particular secret, that there was to be " an 'fah honah," otherwise a ' " juel," at " Bladensburg, sah !" The gin-drinking, cock-fighting, sporting element of the town was aroused, and Utie and Tiltock were invited on all sides to imbibe to the significant toast of " The Field." Very noisy, very insolent, nuisances indeed, these two mere lads—the offspring of a vain and ignorant social period of which some elements yet remain—borrowed the money to hire a carriage, and at midnight they set out with some associates by the old, rutty, clay road for the Maryland village of Bladensburg. That night they caroused until Nature, despite her revolt, put them to bed. In the morning, with a swollen and sallow face, dry hair, unsteady hands, aching eyes and dim vision, Robert

Utie awoke to the recollection of his folly and his rash-
ness, and he realized the critical period which he had
provoked.   His clerkship lost, his self-pride poignant,
his pockets nearly empty, his respectable career irre-
trievably terminated, his sweetheart insulted, and his
life in danger ! There was no escape either from despair
or fate.   Tiltock was strutting about below stairs with
a drunken old doctor, misnamed a surgeon, who deposited behind the bar a rusty case of surgical instruments, and who took a deep potation to the toast of
" The fawchuns of waw."   The Bladensburg people
were well aware of the occasion, and the old tavern was
surrounded by loafers and gossips, many of whom were
boys who had walked out from the city as we go to
prize-fights in our day.   To fill up the time a dog-fight
and a chicken-fight were improvised by the enterprising stable-boys in the back yard, on the green slopes
of the running Branch.   While Tiltock strutted out of
town at an imposing pace to examine " The Field,"
Robert Utie retired to his room, sought with an emetic
to relieve his stomach, and then sat down to write
some letters and an epitaph.   The paper was thin, and
the pen and ink matched it, but the drunken boy's
eyes marred more than all ; for suddenly the secret
fountains of his lost youth were touched as by the
prick of his pen, and the drops gushed out upon the
two words he had written :
    " Dear mother—"
    Not his sweetheart, who was nothing to him now ;
not his " honor," which had been only vain-glory and
deceit ; not any thing but this earliest, everlasting faith
which is ours forever, whether we be steadfast or go
astray : the tie of home, of childhood, and of our
mother's prayer and kiss—this was the soft reproach
which glided between a wasted youth and the " field
of valor" he had tempted.   He wept.   He sobbed.
He threw himself upon the bed, and pressing his
temples into the ragged quilt, felt the panorama of
childhood pass across his mind like something cool,

sorrowful, and compassionate. The sickness *she* had
cured, the bad words *she* had taken from his undutiful
lips, the whipping she had saved him from at the cost
of her deceit, the lie she had never told *him*, the tears
he had found her shedding upon her knees when first
he had been drinking, the money he had never given
her out of his salary but had spent with idlers, his
ruined soul which to that mother's thought was pure as
a baby's still, and watched by all the angels of God :
these were admonitions from the green meadows of
childhood. Before was the barren field of honor.

How short is the struggle betwixt youth and selfishness, that sum of all diseases and crimes ; that selfishness out of which wars arise and hell is habitated !

A poor, overworked Christian negro, a slave in the
tavern, hearing the sobbing of Robert Utie and aware
that one of the duellists occupied that room, lifted the
latch, and wakened the wretched boy from his remorse.

" Young moss," he said, " doan you fight no juels !
Oh ! doan do it, for de bressed Lord's sake ! It's
nuffin but pride and sin. Yo's only a pore, spilt boy,
but you got a soul, young moss ! Doan you go git kilt
in dat ar bloody gully wha' so many gits hurt amoss to
deff !"

Utie arose from the dream of home, and kicked the
poor slave out of the room. He then drank, speculat-
ed upon his chances, practised with an imaginary pistol
at the wall, and meditated running away, alternately,
until Tiltock's business-step rang in the hall.

" Bob," he said, " we've picked you a beautiful
piece of ground, and the other party's waiting. It's
the most popular juel of the season."

They walked up the sandy village street, under the
old hip-roofed houses, crossed the Branch bridge, and
proceeded a quarter of a mile on the road to Washington. There, where a rivulet crossed the road amongst
some bushes, they descended by a path into a copse,
and on to a green meadow-space cleared away by
former rain freshets. Farm boys, town boys, and in-

truders of all sorts were lurking near. The field of
honor resembled a gypsy camp.

Lieutenant Dibdo's companion came up to Tiltock
and said that his friend did not wish to fight, and
would make any manly apology, even though unconscious of offence, if the challenge was withdrawn. The
crowd was ardent for the fight, and Tiltock, who was
punctilious about honor, particularly where he could
cut a safe figure, repelled the compromise, as " un-
warranted by the code." He knew as much about the
code as about honor, and more about both than about
getting a living.

" Then," said the lieutenant, " I am authorized to
say that my principal will take Mr. Utie's first fire.
Let him improve the generous chance as he will. The
second time we will make business of it."

The interlopers fell back. The word was given :
" Ready—Aim—Fire !" Robert Utie, sustained by
braggadocio, that quality which makes murderers die
on the scaffold heroically, fired full at the body of
Lieutenant Dibdo. That officer fired into the air and
remained unmoved and unharmed.

" Is another shot demanded ?"

" Yes," said Tiltock, " our honor is not yet satisfied."

He waved the crowd back in an imperious way—
they having rushed in after the first shot—and he gave
the word himself like a dramatic reading.

Robert Utie looked, and this time with a livid, sob-
ered face, into the open pistol of the man he had provoked, the professional officer of death. The fine,
cool face behind the pistol was concise, grave, and eloquent now as a judge's pronouncing the last sentence
of the law. The next instant the boy was biting and
clawing at the ground in mortal agony. The impatient
crowd rushed in. A faint voice was heard to gasp for
what some said was " water" and some thought was
" mother." Then a figure with a dissipated face a
little dignified by death, and with some of the softness

of childhood glimmering in it, like the bright foot-fall of the good angel whose mission was done and whose flight was taken—this figure lay upon its back amongst the bushes, under the sunshine, peeped at by distant hills, contemplated by idlers as if it were the body of a slain game-chicken, and the drunken "surgeon" was idiotically feeling for its heart.

"Gentlemen," said Tiltock with a flourish, "we are all witnesses that every thing has been honorably conducted."

The city had its little talk. The newspapers in those days were models of what is called high-toned journalism, and printed nothing on purely personal matters like duels when requested to respect the feelings of families. As if "the feelings of families" were not the main cause of duels! There was a mother somewhere, still clinging with her prayers to the footstool of God, hoping for the soul of her boy even after death and wickedness. This was all, except the revolution of the world, and the wedding in due time upon it of Lieutenant Dibdo and Miss Rideau. It was what was called a romantic wedding.

LEGEND OF FUNKSTOWN.

I.

NICK HAMMER sat in Funkstown
  Before his tavern door—
The same old blue-stone tavern
  The wagoners knew of yore,
When the Conestoga schooners
  Came staggering under their load,
And the lines of slow pack-horses
  Stamped over the National Road.

Nick Hammer and son together,
  Both blowing pipe-smoke there,
Like a pair of stolid limekilns,
  In the blue South Mountain air;
And the mills of the Antietam,
  Grinding the Dunker's wheat
So oldly and so slowly,
  Groaned up the deserted street.

" What think'st thou, Nick, my father?
  Said Nick, the old man's twin,
" This whole year thou art silent.
  Let a little speech begin.
Thou think'st the bar draws little ;
  That the stables are empty yet,
And the growing pride of Hagerstown,
  Thou can'st not that forget."

" Thou liest, Nick, my little boy ;
  For Hager's bells I hear
Like the bells of olden travel,
  Forgot upon mine ear.
In a wonderful thing once asked him
  Thy dear old daddy is sunk—
I have sot here a year and wondered
  Who the devil was Mr. Funk !

II.

" A year ago I was smoking,
    When a strange young fellow came by.
He was taking notes on paper,
    And the rum in his'n was *rye*.
Says he : ' I'm a writin' a hist'ry '—
    'Twas then I thought he was drunk-
' And I want to see your graveyard,
    And the tomb of your founder, Funk ! '

" I think if he'd sot there, sonny,
    I'd looked at him a week ;
But he wanished tow'rd the graveyard,
    Before your daddy could speak.
Directly back he tumbled,
    Before I had quit my stare,
And he says : ' I'm disappinted !
    No Funk is buried in there.'

" ' The Funks is all up-country '—
    That's all I could think to say,
' There never was Funks in Funkstown,
    And there ain't any Funks to-day.'
' Why man,' he says, ' the city
    That stands on Potomac's shores
Was settled by Funk, the elder,
    Who afterward settled yours !

' The Carrols, they bust him yonder ;
    Old Hager, he bust him here ;
But my heart will bust till I find him,
    And make a sketch of his bier.
Oh shame on the Funkstown spirit
    That in Maryland does dwell !
He wouldn't consent to be buried
    Where you can keep a hotel.' "

III.

" There's John Stocklager, daddy,"
    Said young Nick, thinking much ;
" A hundred years he's settled
    Amongst the mountain Dutch.

Ask *him !*''   '' Nay, young Nick Hammer,
  You young fellows run too fast :
I shall set out here a thinking,
  And maybe Funk'll go past !''

IV.

He drank and smoked and pondered,
  And deep in the mystery sunk ;
And the more Nick Hammer wondered
  The duller he grew about Funk.
The wagoners talked it over,
  And a new idea to trace
Enlivened the dead old village
  Like a new house built in the place.

V.

One day in June two wagons
  Came over Antietam bridge
And a tall old man behind them
  Strode up the turnpike ridge.
His beard was long and grizzled,
  His face was gnarled and long,
His voice was keen and nasal,
  And his mouth and eye were strong.

One wagon was full of boxes
  And the other full of poles,
As the weaver's wife discovered
  While the weaver took the tolls.
Two young men drove the horses,
  And neither the people knew ;
But young Nick asked a question
  And that old man looked him through.

A little feed they purchased,
  And their teams drank in the creek,
And to and fro they travelled
  As silently for a week—
Went southward laden heavy,
  And northward always light,
And the gnarled old man aye with them,
  With the long beard flowing white.

From Sharpsburg up to Cavetown
  The story slowly rolled—
That old man knew the mountains
  Were filled with ore of gold.
The boxes held his crucibles ;
  'Twas haunted where he trod ;
And every shafted pole he brought
  Was a divining rod !

And none knew whence he came there,
  Nor they his course who took,
Down the road to Harper's Ferry,
  In a shaggy mountain nook ;
But Nick the Sire grew certain,
  While from his eye he shrunk,
That old man was none other
  Than the missing Mr. Funk :

The famous city-builder
  Who once had pitched upon
The sunny ledge of Funkstown,
  And the site of Washington.
Again he was returning
  To the Potomac side,
To found a temple in the hills
  Before he failed and died !

And Nick laughed gently daily
  That he alone had guessed
The mystery of the elder Funk
  That had puzzled all the rest.
And younger Nick thought gently :
  " Since that chap asked for Funk
There's been commotion in this town,
  And daddy's always drunk."

VI.

But once the ring of rapid hoofs
  Came sudden in the night,
And on the Blue Ridge summits flashed
  The camp-fire's baleful light.
Young Nick was in the saddle,
  With half the valley men,
To find that old man's fighting sons
  Who kept the ferry glen.

And like the golden ore that grew
  To his divining rod,
The shining, armèd soldiery
  Swarmed o'er the clover sod ;
O'er Crampton's gap the columns fought,
  And by Antietam fords,
Till all the world, Nick Hammer thought,
  At Funkstown had drawn swords.

VII.

Together, as in quiet days
  Before the battle's roar,
Nick Hammer and his one-legg'd son
  Smoked by the tavern door.
The dead who slept on Sharpsburg Heights
  Were not more still than they ;
They leaned together like the hills,
  But nothing had to say ;

Save once, as at his wooden stump
  The young man looked awhile,
And damned the man who made that war--
  He saw Nick Hammer smile.
My little boy," the old man said,
  " Think long as I have thunk—
You'll find this war rests on the head
  Of that 'air Mister Funk !''

JUDGE WHALEY'S DEMON.

In the little town of Chester, near the Bay of Chesapeake, lived an elegant man, with the softest manners in the world and a shadow forever on his countenance. He bore a blameless character and an honored name. He had one son of the same name as his own, Perry Whaley. This son was forever with him, for use or for pleasure ; they could not be happy separated, nor congenial together. A destiny seemed to unite them, but with it also a baleful memory. The negroes whispered that in the boy's conception and birth was a secret of shame ; he was not this father's son, and his mother had confessed it.

That mother was gone—fled to a distant part of the world with her betrayer—and the divorce was recorded while yet young Perry Whaley was a babe. But the boy never knew it : his origin reposed in the sensitive memory of his father only, and every day the father looked at the son long and distantly, and the son at the father with a most affectionate longing.

"Papa," he would say, "can't you try to love me ? Do I disobey you ? I am sure I am always unhappy out of your sight."

The father could not do without that boy, but could only hate him. "My son," he would reply, "you are obedient, but a demon ! I could not love you if I would !

"Never mind then, father, I can wait. There is plenty of time in life to make you love me !"

Judge Whaley—for he had been on the bench—was the highest example in Maryland of honor and pride. A General of militia, often in the Legislature, and once

or twice a Senator at Washington, he had all the shattered sensibilities of a proud man wounded in the soul.
Age was coming untimely upon his high temples and
shadowed countenance, and as he walked along the
market-place and green court-house yard, polite to
men, boys, and negroes, they said in low tones, " Pity
such a real gentleman can't be happy !''

In public affairs Judge Whaley was not silent : he
led his party with intrepid utterances, and his prejudices, like his intellect, were strong ; but though the
election sometimes hung by a few votes, and his influence then gave every temptation on the part of low
speakers and writers to allude to his domestic dishonor,
the vile reminiscence was never mentioned. A profound respect for the man permeated society, and in
his unsmiling way he was kind to whites and blacks.
A slaveholder, and at the head of the principal slave-
holding connection, and the particular champion in
that region of slavery privileges, he would take his
Bible and visit the cottages of his negroes and read to
them even when sick of contagious fevers. He de-
fended poor clients freely in the courts, and fought for
the lives of free negroes under capital indictments.
He was of the vestry of the aged Episcopal Church,
which dominated the social influence of the town, and
never omitted attendance on all the services, but with
the shadow forever on his brow. Young Perry went
everywhere with his father, and chattered and was active to oblige him, and sometimes by his boyish humor
made a little light weaken the strong edges of that paternal shadow ; but in a few minutes, looking up into
the Judge's face, he would see that distant, accusing
look returned again.

A great desire sprang up in the boy's heart to be
fully loved by his father. He looked at other boys
and saw that they received from their fathers a treatment not more gentle, but more real, as if a deep well
of feeling lay in those parents which could send up
cool water or tears, either in disagreement or sympa-

thy. Young Perry had his own horse and his negro, and was the only inhabitant, besides the Judge, of the old black brick, square, colonial house on the brink of the river—that house whence the light had gone in lurid flight when the young wife, in the bravado of her shame, departed forever.

Judge Whaley was able, with his intellectual sympathy, to observe that his boy was apt and right-minded.

Perry read law precociously, and liked it. He was the best juvenile debater in the little old college on the slight hill overlooking the town. His appearance was good, and he had a cheerful nature ; yet nowhere, among beautiful girls or riding companions, gunning on the river, crabbing on the bridge, or skating on the meadows, was he half so happy as with his father.

" Well, Perry," the Judge would say, " how is my demon to-day—what is he studying now ?"

" Studying you, papa ; I don't understand you."

" The time will come, alas for you !" exclaimed the Judge

" Do I displease you in any thing I do ?"

" No, my son."

" Do you believe I love you ?"

" Yes, I do believe it. I wish, Perry, it could be returned."

The son, under the influence of this discouraging confidence, became serious and melancholy. He would take his gun on his shoulder and wade out into the meadow marshes, as if for game, and there would be seen by other gunners sitting on some old pier or perched on some worm fence, looking straight up at the sky, as if it might answer the riddle of his father's hate and his own unreciprocated affection. He would also, on rainy or cold days, when the inmates could not stir abroad, mount his horse and ride to the alms-house beyond the town mill, and, taking a pleasant story or ballad from his pocket, read to the huddled paupers, as well as to the keeper's family, attracted by

his pleasant condescension.   By degrees the boy's face
also took the shadow worn by his father.

" Oh, if they could only love !" remarked the old
people around the court-house ; " or if they only could
admit the real love between them !"

The Judge never admitted it ; that seemed to be a
part of his religion, a duty to himself, if painful, and
the son never woke nor retired to rest without searching in that paternal shadow for the kindly gleam of
awakened love, yet ever kissed the shadow only, and a
brow that was cold.

One Christmas Day the river was frozen—a rare event
in that genial latitude, and hearing that wild geese were
flying down toward the bay creeks and coves, the
Judge took his gun and a negro and set off, without
waiting for Perry, who was not immediately to be
found.   An hour later the boy returned and heard of
his father's departure, and started on horseback to
overtake the carriage.   He followed the track beyond
the mill and almshouse, and across the heads of several
peninsulas or necks leading into the wide tidal river.
A few frosted persimmons hung yet to their warty
branches ; the hulls of last autumn's black walnuts
were beneath the spreading boughs ; old orchards of
peach-trees where the tints of green and bud smoul-
dered in pink contrast to the oft-blackened and sapless
branches, set off the purple beads of the haw on the
bushes along the lanes.   Fish-hawks, flying across the
sky, felt the shadow of the flocks of wild ducks flying
higher ; and rabbits crossed the road so boldly in the face
of Perry Whaley, that once a raccoon, limping across a
cornfield like a lame spaniel, turned too and took both
barrels of Perry's gun without other fright or injury
than slightly to hurry its pace.   As the young man
heard the crows chatter around the corn-shocks and
the mocking-bird in some alder-thicket answer and
sauce the catbird's scream, he said to himself :

" Every thing is attached by an inner chord to something else, and that other thing, free-hearted, carols or

quarrels back—except father to me. Can I not, too, find something to love me? There is Marion, the Doctor's daughter, with the chestnut curls falling all round her neck—she loves me, I know ; but until I gain my father's love I cannot think of woman !"

The pine-trees above his head murmured rather than moaned, as if they strongly sympathized with him and would presently make loud and angry cause against his enemies. " What is it," asked Perry of his unsuspecting mind, " which makes my father so unappeasable ? What is there in me which broods upon his just and honorable life, and which he cannot drive away though he tries ? Has he some learned superstition, some religious vow or mistaken sacrifice ?"

Perry turned down a lane and then into the bed of a frozen brook, and coming in sight of the broad river, espied his father, gun in hand, stealthily creeping under a load of brush and twigs which the Judge's negro had piled about his back and head, to conceal his figure from a flock of ducks that were bathing and diving in an open place of deep water, to which the ice had not extended.

The gliding brush heap, by slow and flitting advances, had progressed about to within gunshot of the scarce suspecting fowls, and Perry and the negro, from different sides of the cove, watched with the keenest interest—when suddenly, with very little noise, the ice gave way and Judge Whaley had sunk in deep water, loaded down with heavy gunning boots, shot-belt, overcoat and gun. The negro stood paralyzed a minute and then fell upon his knees, unknowing what to do. A sense of joy started in Perry Whaley's breast as strong as his apprehensive fears. He might be made the instrument of saving that beloved life, and dissipating the spell of its indifference !

Nothing but this ardent passion saved Perry himself from drowning. He had crossed the cove ere yet the impulse of parental recognition had taken form, and throwing a rein from the carriage around the negro man's armpits, and seizing a long fence-rail, ran rapidly across, pulling both toward the point of danger.

Judge Whaley had been a powerful man and an accomplished sportsman ; and still as resolute as in youth, struggled with all intelligence for his life.   He sank to the bottom on first breaking through the ice, then reaching upward made two or three powerful efforts to catch the rim of the ice-field and sank again in each endeavor, weighted down with leather and iron. He had sunk to rise no more when Perry reached the edge of the field, placed the end of the rail over the abyss and planted the negro's weight upon it, and then he dived, head foremost, into the freezing salt depths— where the tide was running—and with the carriage rein looped in his right hand.   Before he could lay hand upon his father, that desperate man had seized him by the hair and drawn his head to the bottom, and every instant Perry felt that his remainder of breath was almost run unless he could break that iron hold.   Even in that instant of agony, with death painting its awful pageantry on his interior sight, Perry felt a gladder kind of destiny ; that perhaps the arms of a father's love were around him, and in another sphere, already about to dawn, the shadow might depart from that kind face and unyearning heart.

But with a sense of mere human dutifulness, Perry recalled his residuum of perception.   It was necessary to break that drowning man's grapple upon his hair, and taking the only way, if cruel, to assist his father, the young man struck the elder's knuckles with his clinched fist.   As they released the rein was thrown about Judge Whaley's shoulders and run through the buckle, and as his rescuer, almost exhausted, swam upward, he made the rein fast to his ankle and seized hold of the rail.   Here occurred another agonizing delay.   The negro could not pull the rail in, between his own fears and the double burden ; the young man was exhausted and cramped with cold, and every instant his father, still submerged, was drowning.   At this moment

when the renewed probability of death brought no com-
pensations of a tender sentiment, it pleased the tide to
whirl Judge Whaley's body inwards, directly beneath
the ice-field, and he being now insensible, if alive at
all, the negro clutched it effectually. In the awakened
pain and hope of that minute, Perry Whaley supported
himself along the piece of rail to the solid ice, and assisted to draw his father from the water, and then
swooned dead. They lay together, the unwelcome son
and the repelling father, under the universal pity of the
great eye of Heaven, on the natal day of Him who came
into the world also fatherless, but not disowned.

A neighboring farmer sent one of his boys to Chester
for the doctor, and by rubbing and restoratives, both
the Judge and his son were brought back to circulation
and pulsation. Perry soon recovered, but Judge
Whaley was saved only with the greatest difficulty. It
was nightfall in the hospitable farm-house before he was
able to see or speak, and then, a little drunken with
the spirits which had been administered, he asked in a
whisper :

" Who saved my life ?"

" Who but your son Perry ?" answered the cheerful
Doctor Voss. " You were both wrapped together for
a long while in the bottom of the cove !"

" My son !" exclaimed Judge Whaley, scarcely understanding the reply. " Who is my son ?"

" Here, father ! We are both alive. Thank God !"

" *My* son ?" muttered Judge Whaley. " Brave son !
Who is it ?"

" Why, Perry Whaley !" answered the good house-
wife. " His arms are around your neck. Those warm
kisses were his !"

The sick man glared about him till his eye fell on the
boy.

" Ha !" he whispered. " By you ? Had I awakened
in heaven would you have been there, too ?"

The Judge sank back into a moment's insensibility,
and the son sat there, sobbing piteously.

Though saved from the wave Judge Whaley had a long following spell of fever, in which his son nursed him for many weeks, and once the spark of life seemed to have fled ; the Judge's pulse stopped still, and while they were at solemn prayer—the rector of the Episcopal Church reading from his book—Perry cried : " He still lives.   It is the medicine he needs !''

After the second resuscitation Dr. Voss remarked : " It is not often, Judge Whaley, that a man's life is twice saved by his son !''

Tears were no longer in Perry's eyes ; he had heard his father in delirium constantly repeat his name. After the Judge's recovery he placed in Perry's pocket a fine English watch, and gave him a pair of horses and a stylish wagon.

" Hereafter," he said, " you shall take charge of the property.   My son, look about you and find a wife ! In your character you are deserving of a good one, for I fear the affection you are seeking can never arise in my heart enough to satisfy you.   Gratitude and respect are always here, my son, but love has been a stranger to me these many years.   I wish you to marry while I live, and be happy in some good woman's affection.   I may die and you may not become my heir !   There is the doctor's beautiful daughter ; she has my decided approval !''

" If it is your wish, father, I will marry.''

The day Perry Whaley was admitted to the bar of Kent County on motion of his father, he stopped with his pair of horses at Doctor Voss's house, and asked Miss Marion to take a drive.   She was a peerless brunette, whose dark brown curls taking the light upon their luxuriance seemed the rippling of water from the large amber wells of her eyes.   In childhood she had looked with admiration on his straight, trim figure and manly courtesy, and hoped that she might find favor in his sight.   For this she had put by the scant opportunities in a small, old, unvisited town, to be wedded to her equals, and the whispered imputation that there

was a taint in Perry Whaley's blood made no impression
upon her wishes.   Her younger sisters were gone before her, but true to the impetuous tendencies of her
childhood she waited for Perry, indulging the dream
that she was destined to be his wife.

The happy, supreme opportunity had come.   They
took the road over the river drawbridge into another
county ; the frost was out of the ground, and the loamy
road invited the horses to their speed until the breath
of spring raised in Marion's cheeks the color that
dressed the budding peach orchards which spread over
the whole landscape, as if Nature was in maternity and
her rosy breasts were full of milk.

" Do you like these horses, Marion ?" said Perry
Whaley, when they had gone several miles.   " If you
do you can drive them as long as you live."

She laughed, more because it was the feminine way
than in her feeling.

" Drive them alone ?"

" Only when you do not want me to go."

" Then it will seldom be alone, Perry."

They both breathed short in silence, the happy
silence of youth's desire and assent, until Perry said,
" You are sure you love me, then ?"

" Must I be frank, Perry ?"

" As much as ever in your life !"

" I am very sure.   I loved you in my childhood—no
more now than then, except that the growth of love has
strengthened with my strength."

" Marion," said the young man with a thoughtful
face, " if I have not long ago recognized this fidelity,
which, to be also frank with you, I have suspected—
not because of any desert of mine, but love is like the
light which we distinctly feel even with our eyes shut—
it has been because with all my soul I was laboring for
my father's love first.   You have seen the shadow on
his brow ?   How it came there I do not know.   I have
thought that with my wife to light the dark chambers
of our old house, a triple love would bloom there, and

what he has called the demon in me would disappear
beneath your beautiful ministrations.   Be that angel to
both of us, and as my wife touch the fountain of his
tears and make his noble heart embrace me !''

Marion Voss felt a great sense of trouble.   '' Is it
possible,'' she thought, '' that Perry has never suspected the cause of that shadow on the Judge's life ?   Perhaps not !   It would have been cruel to tell Perry, but
crueller, perhaps, to let him grow to manhood in un-
challenged pride and find it out at such a critical time.''
The rest of the ride passed in endearments and the engagement vow was made.

'' My dear one,'' said Marion, as they rolled on the
bridge at Chester, and the few lights of the town and
of the vessels and the single steamboat descended into
the river, '' had you not better have an understanding
with your father on the subject of his affection ?   Perhaps you have talked in riddles.   Something far back
may have disturbed your mutual faith.   Whatever it is,
nothing shall break my promise to you.   I will be your
wife, or no man's.   But the shadow that is on Judge
Whaley's face I fear no wife can drive away.''

These words disturbed young Perry Whaley, as he
drove his horses into the hotel stable and slowly pursued his way across the public plot or area, past the
old square brick Methodist church, already lighted
brightly for a special evening service, though it was a
week-day.   He passed next the small, echoing market-
house and the Episcopal church, and court-house
yard.   Every thing he saw had at that moment the appearance of something so very vivid and real that it
frightened him.   Yonder was the spot where, with
other boys, he had burned tar-barrels on election
nights ; up a lane the jail where he had seen the pris-
oners flatten their noses against the bars to beg tobacco ; a tall Lombardy poplar at a corner stood stolid
except at its summit, where a portion of the foliage
whispered with a freshening sound.   How still ; as if
every thing was in suspense like him—the favorite of the

old town for so many years, and soon to become the possessor of its most beautiful and virtuous woman !

He sounded the knocker at the door of the square, solid brick mansion, built while all acknowledged the King of Britain here, and in whose threshold General Washington had stood more than once. His father admitted him directly into a prim, wainscoted room with a square-angled stairway in the corner leading above ; a thick rag carpet was on the floor ; the furniture was mahogany and hair-cloth ; on the wall were portraits of the Whaleys or Whalleys, back to that regicide who fled from the vengeance of King Charles's sons, and, escaping many perils in New England, lived unrecognized on this peninsula.

Judge Whaley had lighted a large oil lamp, and its shade threw the flame upon his strong magisterial face, wherein grief and righteousness seemed as highly blent as in some indigent republican Milton or Pym.

" My father," said Perry Whaley with the tender tone habitual to him, " I have consulted your wishes as well as my desire. Marion Voss will be my wife."

" It is well, my son," replied Judge Whaley, placing upon his nose his first pair of silver spectacles. " You are entitled to so much beauty and grace on every ground of a dutiful youth and agreeable person, and of talents which will make both of you a comfortable livelihood."

" Father, with so great a change of relations before me, I desire to obtain your whole confidence."

Perry's voice trembled ; the Judge sat still as one of the brazen andirons where the wood burned with a colorless flame in the fireplace. The father took off the spectacles and laid them down.

" Confidence in what respect, Perry ?"

The young man walked to his father and knelt at his knee and clasped his hand. Even then Perry saw the shadow gather in that kind man's brow, as if he perceived the demon in his son.

" Before I make a lady my wife, father, I want every

mystery of my life related. I have always heard that
my mother died. Where is she buried?"

There was à long pause.

" She is not dead," said Judge Whaley, without any
inflection, " except to me."

" Not dead, father?" asked the son, with throbbing
temples. " Oh, why have I been so deceived? Were
you unhappy?"

" I thought I was happy," said the Judge huskily;
" that was long my impression."

" And my mother—was she, too, happy when you
were so?"

" No."

The young man rose and walked to the wainscot and
back again. " Dear father, I see the origin of the
shadow upon your brow. Why was I not told before?
Perhaps the son of two unhappy parents might have
brought them together again, if for no other congenial
end, than that he was their only son!"

The Judge raised his eyes to the imploring eyes of
the younger man. The shadow never was so deep
upon his brow as Perry saw it now; it was the shadow
of a long inured agony intensified by a dread judicial
sympathy.

" You are not my son!" he said.

Perry's mouth opened, but not to articulate. He
stretched out his hands to touch something, and that
only which he could not reach struck and stunned him;
he had fallen senseless to the floor.

When Perry returned to knowledge he was lying upon
the carpet, a cloak under his head, and his father,
walking up and down, stooped over him frequently to
look into his face with a tender, yet suffering interest.
The young man did not move, and only revealed his
wakefulness at last by raising his hand to check a re-
lieving flow of tears.

" My dear boy," finally said Judge Whaley, himself
shedding tears, " I had supposed that you already
knew something of the tragedy of my life."

"Never," moaned Perry.

"Then, forgive me ; I should myself have gradually told you the tale ; it might have come up with your growth, inwoven like a mere ghost story. Did no playmate, no older intimate, not one of your age striving for the bar, ever whisper to you that I had been deceived, and that you, my only comfort, were the fruit of the deception ?"

"No, sir." Perry's tears seemed to dry in the recollection. "We were both gentlemen—at least, after we reached this world. No one ever insulted me nor you ! I humbly thank God that, discredited as I may have been, my conduct to all was so considerate that no one could obtrude such a truth upon me. Is it the truth ? O father !—I must call you so ! it is the only word I know—is this, at last, one of the dreadful visions of diseased sleep or of insanity ? Who am I ? What was my mother ? I can bear it all, for now I have seen why you never loved me."

Perry, pale as death and still of feeble brain, had arisen as he spoke and made this imploration with only the eloquence of haggard forgetfulness. The Judge took Perry's hands and supported him.

"My son, have I not earned the name of father ? Yes, I have plucked the poison-arrow from my heart and sucked its venom. I have taken the offspring of my injurer and warmed it in my bosom. Every morning when you arose I was reminded of my dishonor. Every night when we kissed good-night, I felt, God knows, that I had loved my enemies and done good to them which injured me !"

The young man, looking up and around in the impotence of expression, saw the portraits of the dead Whaleys in unbroken lineal respectability, bending their eyes upon him—the one, the only impostor of the name !

"Perry," continued the Judge, "I am not wholly guilty of keeping you blind. I have told you many times that between us was a gap, a rift of something.

I have sometimes said, as your artless caresses, mixed with the bitter recollection of your origin, almost dispossessed my reason, that you were ' my demon.' "

" Yes, father ; but I was so anxious to love you that I never brooded on that. I see it all ! Every repulse comes back to me now. You have suffered, indeed, and been the Christian. But I must hear the tale before I depart."

" Depart ! Where ?"

" To find my mother, if she lives. To find my name ! I cannot bear this one. It would be deceit."

" Not even the name of My Son ?"

" Alas ! no. Just as I am I must be known. My putative father, if he lives, must give me another name."

" Thank God, Perry, he is dead !"

" But not his name. I can make honorable even my—"

" Say it not !" exclaimed the Judge, placing his hand upon Perry's mouth. " Pure as all your life has been, you shall not degrade it with such a word. Oh, my son ! — my orphan son ! — dear faithful prattler around my feet for all these desolate and haunted years, I have doubted for your sake every thing—that wedlock was good, that pride of virtuous origin was wise, that human jealousy was any thing but a tiger's selfishness. I did not sow the seed that brought you forth ; too well I know it ! Yet grateful and fair has been the vine as if watered by the tears of angels ; and when I sleep the demon in you fades, and then, at least, your loving tendrils find all my nature an arbor to take you up !"

" Would to God !" said Perry bitterly, " that in the sleep of everlasting death we laid together. O my God ! how I have loved you—father !"

The Judge enfolded the young man in his arms and like a child Perry rested there. The lamp, previously burning very low, went out for want of oil, as the old man nursed like his own babe the serpent's offspring,

not his own but another's untimely son, bred on the
honor of a husband's name. As they sat in the perfect darkness of the old riverside mansion, Judge
Whaley told his tale.

He had neglected to marry until he had become of
settled legal and business habits, and more than forty-
five years of age when he chose for a wife a young lady
who professed to admire and love him. They had no
children. The wife was a coquette, and began to woo
admiration almost as soon as the nuptials were done.
Judge Whaley thought nothing ill of this ; he was in the
heyday of his practice and willing to let one so much
his junior enjoy herself. Among his law students was
a young man from South Carolina, of brilliant manners
and insidious address. This person had already become so intimate with Mrs. Whaley as to draw upon
the Judge anonymous letters notifying him that he was
too indifferent, to which letters he gave no attention,
only bestowing the more confidence and freedom upon
her, when, happily, as it was thought, the wife showed
signs of maternity. Perry was born, to the joy of his
father. The young mother, however, hastened to recover her health and gayety. The favor she expressed
for the student's society was revived and not opposed
by her husband. Judge Whaley returned unexpectedly
one day to his residence ; he came upon a scene that in
an instant destroyed faith and rendered explanation im-
possible. His wife was false. The student passion-
ately avowed himself her seducer. The Judge went
through the ordeal like a magistrate.

" Take her away with you," he said. " That is the
only reparation you can do her, until she is legally
divorced, and after that, if necessary, I will give her an
allowance, but she cannot rest under this roof another
night. It has been the abode of chaste wives since it
was builded. My honor is at stake. This day she
must go. Make her your wife and let neither ever
return." •

They departed by carriage, unknown to any, and

never had returned.   But a few weeks after they disappeared a letter was received by Judge Whaley, admonishing him that his son was the offspring of the same illegal relations.   It was signed and written by his wife.   The wretched man debated whether he should send the infant to an asylum or keep it upon his premises.   Through procrastination, continued for twenty years, the child had derived all the advantages of legitimacy, and still the demon of the husband's peace was the test of the gentleman's religion.

As this story had proceeded toward its final portions, the young man had detached himself from his father's arms.   When Judge Whaley concluded in the darkness he waited in vain for a response.   The old man lighted the lamp and peered about the room wistfully.   Perry was gone.

That night, in the happiness of her engagement, Marion Voss had a glad unrest, which her mother noticed.   " Dear," said the mother, " let us go over to the Methodist church.   It is one of their protracted meetings or revivals, as they call it.   If Perry comes he will know where to find us, as I will leave word."

The Methodists were second in social standing, but a wide gap separated them from the slave-holding and family aristocracy, who were Episcopalians.   The sermon was delivered by one of their most powerful proselytizers, an old man in a homespun suit, high shoulders, lean, long figure, and glittering eyes.   He was a wild kind of orator, striking fear to the soul, dipping it in the fumes of damnation, lifting it thence to the joys of heaven.   Terrible, electrical preaching !   It was the product of uncultured genius and human disappointment.   Marion sat in awe, hardly knowing whether it was impious or angelic.   In a blind exordium the old zealot commanded those who would save their souls to walk forward and kneel publicly at the altar, and make their struggle there for salvation.

The first whom Marion saw to walk up the dimly lighted aisle and kneel was Perry Whaley.   All in the

church saw and knew him, and a thunderous singing
broke out, in which religious and mere denominational
zeal all threw their enthusiasm.

" Judge Whaley's son—Episcopalian—admitted to
the bar to-day—wonderful !''

Marion heard these whispers on every hand ; and as
the singing ceased, and the congregation knelt to pray,
Marion's mother saw her turning very pale, and silently and unobserved led her out of the meeting-house.

It was one o'clock in the morning when Judge Whaley heard Perry enter the door. He was preceded by
the beams of a lamp, as his step came almost trippingly
up the stairs. The Judge looked up and saw the face
of his demon, streaked with recent tears and shaded
with dishevelled hair, but on it a look like eternal sunshine.

" Glory ! glory ! glory !'' exclaimed the young man
hoarsely. He rushed upon his aged friend, and kissed
him in an ecstacy almost violent.

" My boy ! Perry ! What is it ? You are not out
of your mind ?''

" No ! no ! I have found my father, *our* father !''

" Who is it ?'' asked the Judge, with a rising superstition, as if this were not his orphan, but its preternat-
ural copy ; " you have found your father ? What
father ?''

" God !'' exclaimed young Perry, his countenance
like flame. " My father is God and He is love !''

The town of Chester and the whole country had now
a serious of rapid sensations. Judge Whaley and his
son were turned lunatics, and behaved like a pair of
boys. Marion Voss had broken her engagement with
Perry Whaley because he insisted that he was not the
Judge's son. Young Perry was exhorting in the Methodist church, and studying and starving himself to be
a preacher. The Methodists were wild with social and
denominational triumph : the Episcopalians were outraged, and meditated sending Perry to the lunatic
asylum. Finally, to the great joy of nervous people,

the last sensation came—Perry Whaley had left Chester to be a preacher.

Judge Whaley now grew old rapidly, and meek and careless of his attire. In an old pair of slippers, gloveless and abstracted, he crossed the court house green, no longer the first gentleman in the county in courteous accost and lofty tone. He read his Bible in the seclusion of his own house, and fishermen on the river coming in after midnight saw the lamp-light stream through the chinks of his shutters, and said : " He has never been the same since Perry went away." But he read in the religious papers of the genius and power of the absent one, roving like a young hermit loosened, and with a tongue of flame over the length and breadth of the country, producing extraordinary excitement and adding thousands to his humble denomination.

On Christmas Day the Judge was sitting in his great room reading the same mystic book, and listening, with a wistfulness that had never left him, to every infrequent footfall in the street. There came a knock at the door. He opened it, and out of the darkness into which he could not see came a voice altered in pitch, but with remembered accents in it, saying :

" Father, mother has come home !"

Stepping back before that extraordinary salutation, Judge Whaley saw a man come forward leading a woman by the hand. The Judge receded until he could go no farther, and sank into his chair. The woman knelt at his feet ; older, and grown gray and in the robes of humility, yet in countenance as she had been, only purified, as it seemed, by suffering and repentance, he saw his wife of more than twenty years before.

Looking up into the face of the son he had watched so long for, the old man saw a still more wonderful transformation. The elegant young gentleman of a few months before was a living spectre, his bright eyes standing out large and consumptive upon a transparent skin, and glittering with fanaticism or excitement.

"Perry Whaley," said the woman firmly, but with sweetness, "it is twenty-two years, since I left this house with hate of me in your heart and a degraded name ; I was in thought and act a pure woman, though the evidence against me was mountain-high. My sin was that of many women—flirtation. Nothing more, before my God ! I trifled with one of your students, a reckless and hot-blooded man, and inspired him with a tyrannous passion. He swore if I would not fly with him to destroy me. One day, the most dreadful of my life, he heard your foot upon the stairs ascending to my chamber, and threw himself into it before you and avowed himself your injurer. Then rose in confirmation of him every girlish folly ; I saw myself in your mild eyes condemned, in this community long suspected, and by my own family discarded for your sake. Where could I go but to the author of my sorrows ? He became my husband and I am a widow."

Judge Whaley stretched out his hand in the direction of his eyes, not upon the old wife at his feet, but toward his son, who had settled into a chair and closed his eyes as if in tired rapture.

"Hear me but a moment more," said the kneeling woman. "I was the slave of an ever-jealous maniac ; but my heart was still at this fireside with your bowed spirit, and this our son. My husband told me that the way to recover the child was to claim it as his. His motive, I fear, was different—to place me on record as confessedly false and prevent our reunion forever. But I was not wise enough to see it. I only thought you would send my son to me. I waited in my lonely home in Charleston years on years. He came at last, but not too late ; my frivolous soul, grown selfish with vanity and disappointment, bent itself before God through the prayers of our son. I am forgiven, Perry Whaley. *I have felt it !*"

The old man did not answer, but strained his eyes upon his son. "See there !" he slowly spoke, "Perry is dying. Famished all these years for human love,

this excess of joy has snapped the silver cord. Wife,
Mary, we have martyred him.''

It was the typhoid fever which had developed from
Perry's wasting vitality. He sank into delirium as they
looked at him, and was carried tenderly to his bed.
Marion Voss came to nurse him with his mother. She,
too, after Perry's departure, had grown serious and
followed his example, and was a Methodist. The
young zealot sank lower and lower, despite science or
prayers. Both churches prayed for him. Negroes and
whites united their hopes and kind offices. One morning he was of dying pulse, and the bell in the Episcopal church began to toll. At the bedside all the little
family had instinctively knelt, and Perry's mother was
praying with streaming eyes, committing the worn-out
nature to Heavenly Love, when suddenly Judge Whaley,
who had kept his hand on Perry's pulse, exclaimed :

" It beats ! He lives again. The stimulant,
Marion !''

Father and son had rescued each other's lives. One
day as Perry had recovered strength, Judge Whaley
said :

" My son, are you a minister, qualified to perform
marriages ?''

" Yes.''

" When you are ready and strong, will you marry
your mother and me again ?''

" Very soon,'' said Perry ; " but not too soon.
Here is Marion waiting for me, as she has waited, like
Rachel for Jacob, these many years. I shall preach
no more, dear father, except as a layman. I see by
your eyes that the demon is no longer in our home, and
the remainder of my life will be spent in returning to
you the joy my presence for years dispelled.''

" O Perry, my patient son,'' exclaimed the father,
" they who entertain angels unawares have nothing to
look to with regret—except unkindness.''

A CONVENT LEGEND.

THE General Moreau, that pure republican,
   Who won at Hohenlinden so much glory,
And by Bonaparte hated, crossed the sea to be free,
   And brought to the Delaware his story.
World-renowned as he was, unto Washington he strayed.
   Where Pichegru, his friend, had contended,
And to Georgetown he rode, in search of a church,
   To confess what of good he offended.

The Jesuits' nest beckoned up to the height
   Where pious John Carroll had laid it,
And the General knelt at the cell but to tell
   His offence ; yet or ever he said it,
A voice in the speech of his Bretagny home,
   From within, where the monk was to listen,
Exclaimed like a soldier : " Ah me ! *mon ami*,
   Take my place and a sinful one christen !

" For mine was the band that brought exile to you ;
   Cadoudal, the Chouan, my master,
Broke my sword and my heart, and I lost when I crost,
   Both honor and love to be pastor.
A knight of the king and my lady at court,
   At the call of Vendée the despisèd,
Into Paris I stole with a few, one or two,
   As assassins, to murder disguised.

" On the third of Nivose, in the narrowest street,
   And never a traitor one to breathe it,
We prepared to blow up Bonaparte with a cart,
   And a barrel of powder beneath it.
He came like a flash, dashing by, but behind,
   Poor folks and his escort in feather,
And the child that we put, *sans* remorse, by the horse,
   Were torn all to pieces together.

" To the guillotine both of my comrades were sent,
  But the Church, saving me for the tonsure,
Hid me off in the wilds, and my dame, to her shame,
  To be *Père* sold me out from a *Monsieur ;*
And now she is clad in the silk of the court,
  And I in the wool of confessor,—
Hate me not, ere hence you go, Jean Victor Moreau !
  And with France be my fame's intercessor !"

" Limoelan ! priest ! is it you that I hear
  In this convent by Washington's river ?
Ah ! France, how thy children are hurled round the world,
  Like the arrows from destiny's quiver !
Take shrift for thy crime !   Be thou pardoned with peace,
  Poor exile of Breton, my brother !"
And the cannon of Dresden Moreau gave release,
  The bells of the convent the other.

CRUTCH, THE PAGE.

THE Honorable Jeems Bee, of Texas, sitting in his committee-room half an hour before the convening of Congress, waiting for his negro familiar to compound a julep, was suddenly confronted by a small boy on crutches.

" A letter !" exclaimed Mr. Bee, " with the frank of Reybold on it—that Yankeest of Pennsylvania Whigs ! Yer's familiarity ! Wants me to appoint one U—U— U, what ?"

" Uriel Basil," said the small boy on crutches, with a clear, bold, but rather sensitive voice.

" Uriel Basil, a page in the House of Representatives, bein' an infirm, deservin' boy, willin' to work to support his mother. Infirm boy wants to be a page, on the recommendation of a Whig, to a Dimmycratic committee. I say, gen'lemen, what do you think of that, heigh ?"

This last addressed to some other members of the committee, who had meantime entered.

" Infum boy will make a spry page," said the Hon. Box Izard, of Arkansaw.

" Harder to get infum page than the Speaker's eye," said the orator, Pontotoc Bibb, of Georgia.

" Harder to get both than a 'pintment in these crowded times on a opposition recommendation when all ole Virginny is yaw to be tuk care of," said Hon, Fitzchew Smy, of the Old Dominion.

The small boy standing up on crutches, with large hazel eyes swimming and wistful, so far from being cut down by these criticisms, stood straighter, and only his narrow little chest showed feeling, as it breathed quickly under his brown jacket.

"I can run as fast as anybody," he said impetuously. "My sister says so. You try me!"

"Who's yo' sister, bub?"

"Joyce."

"Who's Joyce?"

"Joyce Basil—*Miss* Joyce Basil to you, gentlemen. My mother keeps boarders. Mr. Reybold boards there. I think it's hard when a little boy from the South wants to work, that the only body to help him find it is a Northern man. Don't you?"

"Good hit!" cried Jeroboam Coffee, Esq., of Alabama. "That boy would run, if he could!"

"Gentlemen," said another member of the committee, the youthful abstractionist from South Carolina, who was reputed to be a great poet on the stump, the Hon. Lowndes Cleburn—"gentlemen, that boy puts the thing on its igeel merits and brings it home to us. I'll ju my juty in this issue. Abe, wha's my julep?"

"Gentlemen," said the Chairman of Committee, Jeems Bee, "it 'pears to me that there's a social p'int right here. Reybold, bein' the only Whig on the Lake and Bayou Committee, ought to have something if he sees fit to ask for it. That's courtesy! We, of all men, gentlemen, can't afford to forget it."

"No, by durn!" cried Fitzchew Smy.

"You're right, Bee!" cried Box Izard. "You give it a constitutional set."

"Reybold," continued Jeems Bee, thus encouraged, "Reybold is (to speak out) no genius! He never will rise to the summits of usefulness. He lacks the air, the swing, the *pose*, as the sculptors say; he won't treat, but he'll lend a little money, provided he knows where you goin' with it. If he ain't open-hearted, he ain't precisely mean!"

"You're right, Bee!" (General expression.)

"Further on, it may be said that the framers of the

govment never intended *all* the patronage to go to one side. Mr. Jeffson put *that* on the steelyard principle : the long beam here, the big weight of being in the minority there. Mr. Jackson only threw it considabul more on one side, but even he, gentlemen, didn't take the whole patronage from the Outs ; he always left 'em enough to keep up the courtesy of the thing, and we can't go behind *him*. Not and be true to our traditions. Do I put it right ?"

" Bee," said the youthful Lowndes Cleburn, extending his hand, " you put it with the lucidity and spirituality of Kulhoon himself !"

" Thanks, Cleburn," said Bee ; " this is a compliment not likely to be forgotten, coming from you. Then it is agreed, as the Chayman of yo' Committee, that I accede to the request of Mr. Reybold, of Pennsylvania ?"

" Aye !" from everybody.

" And now," said Mr. Bee, " as we wair all up late at the club last night, I propose we take a second julep, and as Reybold is coming in he will jine us."

" I won't give you a farthing !" cried Reybold at the door, speaking to some one. " Chips, indeed ! What shall I give you money to gamble away for ? A gambling beggar is worse than an impostor ! No, sir ! Emphatically no !"

" A dollar for four chips for brave old Beau !" said the other voice. " I've struck 'em all but you. By the State Arms ! I've got rights in this distreek ! Everybody pays toll to brave old Beau ! Come down !"

The Northern Congressman retreated before this pertinacious mendicant into his committee-room, and his pesterer followed him closely, nothing abashed, even into the privileged cloisters of the committee. The Southern members enjoyed the situation.

" Chips, Right Honorable ! Chips for old Beau. Nobody this ten-year has run as long as you. I've laid for you, and now I've fell on you. Judge Bee, the fust business befo' yo' committee this mornin' is a assessment for old Beau, who's away down! Rheumatiz, bettin' on the black, failure of remittances from Fauqueeah, and other casualties by wind an' flood, have put ole Beau away down. He's a institution of his country and must be sustained!''

The laughter was general and cordial amongst the Southerners, while the intruder pressed hard upon Mr. Reybold. He was a singular object; tall, grim, half-comical, with a leer of low familiarity in his eyes, but his waxed mustache of military proportions, his patch of goatee just above the chin, his elaborately oiled hair and flaming necktie, set off his faded face with an odd gear of finery and impressiveness. His skin was that of an old *roué's*, patched up and calked, but the features were those of a once handsome man of style and carriage.

He wore what appeared to be a cast-off spring over-coat, out of season and color on this blustering winter day, a rich buff waistcoat of an embossed pattern, such as few persons would care to assume, save, perhaps, a gambler, negro buyer, or fine '' buck'' barber. The assumption of a large and flashy pin stood in his frilled shirt-bosom. He wore watch-seals without the accompanying watch, and his pantaloons, though faded and threadbare, were once of fine material and cut in a style of extravagant elegance, and they covered his long, shrunken, but aristocratic limbs, and were strapped beneath his boots to keep them shapely. The boots themselves had been once of varnished kid or fine calf, but they were cracked and cut, partly by use, partly for comfort; for it was plain that their wearer had the gout, by his aristocratic hobble upon a gold-mounted cane, which was not the least inconsistent garniture of his mendicancy.

'' Boys,'' said Fitzchew Smy, '' I s'pose we better come down early. There's a shillin', Beau. If I had one more sech constituent as you, I should resign or die premachorely!''

"There's a piece o' tobacker," said Jeems Bee languidly, "all I can afforde, Beau, this mornin'. I went to a chicken-fight yesterday and lost all my change."

"Mine," said Box Izard, "is a regulation pen-knife, contributed by the United States, with the regret, Beau, that I can't 'commodate you with a pine coffin for you to git into and git away down lower than you ever been."

"Yaw's a dollar," said Pontotoc Bibb; "it'll do for me an' Lowndes Cleburn, who's a poet and genius, and never has no money. This buys me off, Beau, for a month."

The gorgeous old mendicant took them all grimly and leering, and then pounced upon the Northern man, assured by their twinkles and winks that the rest expected some sport.

"And now, Right Honorable from the banks of the Susquehanna, Colonel Reybold—you see, I got your name; I ben a layin' for you!—come down handsome for the Uncle and ornament of his capital and country. What's yore's?"

"Nothing," said Reybold in a quiet way. "I cannot give a man like you any thing, even to get rid of him."

"You're mean," said the stylish beggar, winking to the rest. "You hate to put your hand down in yer pocket, mightily. I'd rather be ole Beau, and live on suppers at the faro banks, than love a dollar like you!"

"I'll make it a V for Beau," said Pontotoc Bibb, "if he gives him a rub on the raw like that another lick. Durn a mean man, Cleburn!"

"Come down, Northerner," pressed the incorrigible loafer again; "it don't become a Right Honorable to be so mean with old Beau."

The little boy on crutches, who had been looking at this scene in a state of suspense and interest for some time, here cried hotly:

"If you say Mr. Reybold is a mean man, you tell a story, you nasty beggar! He often gives things to me and Joyce, my sister. He's just got me work, which is the best thing to give ; don't you think so, gentlemen ?''

" Work," said Lowndes Cleburn, " is the best thing to give away, and the most onhandy thing to keep. I like play the best—Beau's kind o' play !'

" Yes," said Jeroboam Coffee ; " I think I prefer to make the chips fly out of a table more than out of a log."

" I like to work !" cried the little boy, his hazel eyes shining, and his poor, narrow body beating with unconscious fervor, half suspended on his crutches. as if he were of that good descent and natural spirit which could assert itself without bashfulness in the presence of older people. " I like to work for my mother. If I was strong, like other little boys, I would make money for her, so that she shouldn't keep any boarders —except Mr. Reybold. Oh ! she has to work a lot ; but she's proud and won't tell anybody. All the money I get I mean to give her ; but I wouldn't have it if I had to beg for it like that man !"

" O Beau," said Colonel Jeems Bee, " you've cotched it now ! Reybold's even with you. Little Crutch has cooked your goose ! Crutch is right eloquent when his wind will permit."

The fine old loafer looked at the boy, whom he had not previously noticed, and it was observed that the last shaft had hurt his pride. The boy returned his wounded look with a straight, undaunted, spirited glance, out of a child's nature. Mr. Reybold was impressed with something in the attitude of the two, which made him forget his own interest in the controversy.

Beau answered with a tone of nearly tender pacification :

" Now, my little man ; come, don't be hard on the old veteran ! He's down, old Beau is, sence the time he owned his blooded pacer and dined with the *Corps Diplomatique ;* Beau's down sence then ; but don't call

the old feller hard names. We take it back, don't we?
—we take *them* words back?"

" There's a angel somewhere," said Lowndes Cleburn, " even in a Washington bummer, which responds
to a little chap on crutches with a clear voice. Whether
the angel takes the side of the bummer or the little
chap, is a p'int out of our jurisdiction. Abe, give
Beau a julep. He seems to have been demoralized by
little Crutch's last."

" Take them hard words back, Bub," whined the
licensed mendicant, with either real or affected pain ;
" it's a p'int of honor I'm a standin' on. Do, now,
little Major !"

" I shan't !" cried the boy. " Go and work like
me. You're big, and you called Mr. Reybold mean.
Haven't you got a wife or little girl, or nobody to work
for? You ought to work for yourself, anyhow.
Oughtn't he, gentlemen ?"

Reybold, who had slipped around by the little cripple and was holding him in a caressing way from behind, looked over to Beau and was even more impressed with that generally undaunted worthy's expression. It was that of acute and suffering sensibility,
perhaps the effervescence of some little remaining
pride, or it might have been a twinge of the gout.
Beau looked at the little boy, suspended there with the
weak back and the narrow chest, and that scintillant,
sincere spirit beaming out with courage born in the
stock he belonged to. Admiration, conciliation, and
pain were in the ruined vagrant's eyes. Reybold felt
a sense of pity. He put his hand in his pocket and
drew forth a dollar.

" Here, Beau," he said, " I'll make an exception.
You seem to have some feeling. Don't mind the
boy !"

In an instant the coin was flying from his hand
through the air. The beggar, with a livid face and
clinched cane, confronted the Congressman like a
maniac.

" You bilk !" he cried.   " You supper customer !
I'll brain you !   I had rather parted with my shoes at a
dolly shop and gone gadding the hoof, without a doss
to sleep on—a town pauper, done on the vag—than to
have made been scurvy in the sight of that child and
deserve his words of shame !"

He threw his head upon the table and burst into
tears.

II.—HASH.

Mrs. Tryphonia Basil kept a boarding-house of the
usual kind on Four-and-a-Half Street.   Male clerks—
there were no female clerks in the Government in 1854
—to the number of half a dozen, two old bureau officers, an architect's assistant, Reybold, and certain temporary visitors made up the table.   The landlady was
the mistress ; the slave was Joyce.

Joyce Basil was a fine-looking girl, who did not know
it—a fact so astounding as to be fitly related only in
fiction.   She did not know it, because she had to work
so hard for the boarders and her mother.   Loving her
mother with the whole of her affection, she had suffered
all the pains and penalties of love from that repository.
She was to-day upbraided for her want of coquetry and
neatness ; to-morrow, for proposing to desert her
mother and elope with a person she had never thought
of.   The mainstay of the establishment, she was not
aware of her usefulness.   Accepting every complaint
and outbreak as if she deserved it, the poor girl lived
at the capital a beautiful scullion, an unsalaried domestic, and daily forwarded the food to the table, led in
the chamberwork, rose from bed unrested and retired
with all her bones aching.   But she was of a natural
grace that hard work could not make awkward ; work
only gave her bodily power, brawn, and form.
Though no more than seventeen years of age, she was
a superb woman, her chest thrown forward, her back
like the torso of a *Venus de Milo*, her head placed on
the throat of a Minerva, and the nature of a child

moulded in the form of a matron. Joyce Basil had
black hair and eyes—very long, excessive hair, that in
the mornings she tied up with haste so imperfectly, that
once Reybold had seen it drop like a cloud around her
and nearly touch her feet. At that moment, seeing
him, she blushed. He pleaded, for once, a Congressman's impudence, and without her objection, wound
that great crown of woman's glory around her head,
and, as he did so, the perfection of her form and skin,
and the overrunning health and height of the Virginia
girl, struck him so thoroughly that he said :

" Miss Joyce, I don't wonder that Virginia is the
mother of Presidents."

Between Reybold and Joyce there were already the
delicate relations of a girl who did not know that she
was a woman, and a man who knew she was beautiful
and worthy. He was a man vigilant over himself, and
the poverty and menial estate of Joyce Basil were
already insuperable obstacles to marrying her, but still
he was attracted by her insensibility that he could ever
have regarded her in that light of marriage. " Who
was her father, the Judge ?" he used to reflect. The
Judge was a favorite topic with Mrs. Basil at the
table.

" Mr. Reybold," she would say, " you commercial
people of the Nawth can't hunt, I believe. Jedge
Basil is now on the mountains of Fawquear hunting
the plova. His grandfather's estate is full of plova."

" If, by chance, Reybold saw a look of care on Mrs.
Basil's face, he inquired for the Judge, her husband,
and found he was still shooting on the Occequan.

" Does he never come to Washington, Mrs. Basil ?"
asked Reybold one day, when his mind was very full
of Joyce, the daughter.

" Not while Congress is in session," said Mrs. Basil.
" It's a little too much of the *oi polloi* for the Judge.
His family, you may not know, Mr. Reybold, air of the
Basils of King George. They married into the Tay-
loze of Mount Snaffle. The Tayloze of Mount Snaffle

have Ingin blood in their veins—the blood of Poky-
huntus. They dropped the name of Taylor, which had
got to be common through a want of Ingin blood, and
spelled it with a E. It used to be Taylor, but now it's
Tayloze."

On another occasion, at sight of Joyce Basil cooking
over the fire, against whose flame her moulded arms
took momentary roses upon their ivory, Reybold said
to himself : "Surely there is something above the
common in the race of this girl." And he asked the
question of Mrs. Basil :

"Madame, how was the Judge, your husband, at
the last advices ?"

"Hunting the snipe, Mr. Reybold. I suppose you
do not have the snipe in the North. It is the aristocratic fowl of the Old Dominion. Its bill is only
shorter than its legs, and it will not brown at the fire,
to perfection, unless upon a silver spit. Ah ! when
the Jedge and myself were young, before his land
troubles overtook us, we went to the springs with our
own silver and carriages, Mr. Reybold."

Looking up at Mrs. Basil, Reybold noticed a pallor
and flush alternately, and she evaded his eye.

Once Mrs. Basil borrowed a hundred dollars from
Reybold in advance of board, and the table suffered in
consequence.

"The Judge," she had explained, "is short of
taxes on his Fawquear lands. It's a desperate moment
with him." Yet in two days the Judge was shooting
blue-winged teal at the mouth of the Accotink, and his
entire indifference to his family set Reybold to thinking whether the Virginia husband and father was any
thing more than a forgetful savage. The boarders,
however, made very merry over the absent unknown.
If the beefsteak was tough, threats were made to send
for "the Judge," and let him try a tooth on it ; if
scant, it was suggested that the Judge might have paid
a gunning visit to the premises and inspected the
larder. The daughter of the house kept such an even

temper, and was so obliging within the limitations of
the establishment, that many a boarder went to his department without complaint, though with an appetite
only partly satisfied. The boy, Uriel, also was the
guardsman of the household, old-faced as if with the
responsibility of taking care of two women. Indeed,
the children of the landlady were so well behaved and
prepossessing that, compared with Mrs. Basil's shabby
hauteur and garrulity, the legend of the Judge seemed
to require no other foundation than offspring of such
good spirit and intonation.

Mrs. Tryphonia Basil was no respecter of persons.
She kept boarders, she said, as a matter of society, and
to lighten the load of the Judge. He had very little
idea that she was making a mercantile matter of hospitality, but, as she feelingly remarked, " the old families
are misplaced in such times as these yer, when the departments are filled with Dutch, Yankees, Crackers,
Pore Whites, and other foreigners." Her manner was,
at periods, insolent to Mr. Reybold, who seldom protested, out of regard to the daughter and the little Page ;
he was a man of quite ordinary appearance, saying
little, never making speeches or soliciting notice, and
he accepted his fare and quarters with little or no complaint.

" Crutch," he said one day to the little boy, " did
you ever see your father ?"

" No, I never saw him, Mr. Reybold, but I've had
letters from him."

" Don't he ever come to see you when you are
sick ?"

" No. He wanted to come once when my back was
very sick, and I laid in bed weeks and weeks, sir,
dreaming, oh ! such beautiful things. I thought mamma and sister and I were all with papa in that old
home we are going to some day. He carried me up
and down in his arms, and I felt such rest that I never
knew any thing like it, when I woke up, and my back
began to ache again. I wouldn't let mamma send for

him, though, because she said he was working for us
all to make our fortunes, and get doctors for me, and
clothes and school for dear Joyce. So I sent him my
love, and told papa to work, and he and I would bring
the family out all right."

" What did your papa seem like in that dream, my
little boy ?

" Oh ! sir, his forehead was bright as the sun.
Sometimes I see him now when I am tired at night after
running all day through Congress."

Reybold's eyes were full of tears as he listened to
the boy, and, turning aside, he saw Joyce Basil weeping also.

" My dear girl," he said to her, looking up significantly, " I fear he will see his great Father very soon."

Reybold had few acquaintances, and he encouraged
the landlady's daughter to go about with him when she
could get a leisure hour or evening. Sometimes they
took a seat at the theatre, more often at the old Ascen-
sion Church, and once they attended a President's reception. Joyce had the bearing of a well-bred lady,
and the purity of thought of a child. She was noticed
as if she had been a new and distinguished arrival in
Washington.

" Ah ! Reybold," said Pontotoc Bibb, " I understand, ole feller, what keeps you so quiet now. You've
got a wife onbeknown to the Kemittee ! and a happy
man I know you air."

It pleased Reybold to hear this, and deepened his
interest in the landlady's family. His attention to her
daughter stirred Mrs. Basil's pride and revolt together.

" My daughter, Colonel Reybold," she said, " is designed for the army. The Judge never writes to me
but he says : ' Tryphonee, be careful that you impress
upon my daughter the importance of the military profession. My mother, grandmother, and great-grandmother
married into the army, and no girl of the Basil stock
shall descend to civil life while I can keep the Fawquear estates.' "

"Madame," said the Congressman, "will you permit me to make the suggestion that your daughter is already a woman and needs a father's care, if she is ever to receive it. I beseech you to impress this subject upon the Judge. His estates cannot be more precious to his heart, if he is a man of honor ; nay, what is better than honor, his duty requires him to come to the side of these children, though he be ever so constrained by business or pleasure to attend to more worldly concerns."

" The Judge," exclaimed Mrs. Basil, much miffed, " is a man of hereditary ijees, Colonel Reybold. He is now in pursuit of the—ahem !—the Kinvas-back on his ancestral waters. If he should hear that you suggested a pacific life and the grovelling associations of the capital for him, he might call you out, sir !"

Reybold said no more ; but one evening when Mrs. Basil was absent, called across the Potomac, as happened frequently, at the summons of the Judge—and on such occasions she generally requested a temporary loan or a slight advance of board—Reybold found Joyce Basil in the little parlor of the dwelling. She was alone and in tears, but the little boy Uriel slept before the chimney-fire on a rug, and his pale, thin face, catching the glow of the burning wood, looked beautified as Reybold addressed the young woman.

" Miss Joyce," he said, " our little brother works too hard. Is there never to be relief for him ? His poor, withered body, slung on those crutches for hours and hours, racing up the aisles of the House with stronger pages, is wearing him out. His ambition is very interesting to see, but his breath is growing shorter and his strength is frailer every week. Do you know what it will lead to ?"

" O my Lord !" she said, in the negrofied phrase natural to her latitude, " I wish it was no sin to wish him dead."

" Tell me, my friend," said Reybold, " can I do nothing to assist you both ? Let me understand you.

Accept my sympathy and confidence. Where is Uriel's father? What is this mystery?"

She did not answer.

"It is for no idle curiosity that I ask," he continued. "I will appeal to him for his family, even at the risk of his resentment. Where is he?"

"Oh, do not ask!" she exclaimed. "You want me to tell you only the truth. He is *there!*"

She pointed to one of the old portraits in the room—a picture fairly painted by some provincial artist—and it revealed a handsome face, a little voluptuous but aristocratic, the shoulders clad in a martial cloak, the neck in ruffles and ruffles, also and a diamond in the shirt bosom. Reybold studied it with all his mind.

"Then it is no fiction," he said, "that you have a living father, one answering to your mother's description. Where have I seen that face? Has some irreparable mistake, some miserable controversy, alienated him from his wife? Has he another family?"

She answered with spirit:

"No, sir. He is my father and my brother's only. But I can tell you no more."

"Joyce," he said, taking her hand, "this is not enough. I will not press you to betray any secret you may possess. Keep it. But of yourself I must know something more. You are almost a woman. You are beautiful."

At this he tightened his grasp, and it brought him closer to her side. She made a little struggle to draw away, but it pleased him to see that when the first modest opposition had been tried she sat quite happily, though trembling, with his arm around her.

"Joyce," he continued, "you have a double duty: one to your mother and this poor invalid, whose journey toward that Father's house not made with hands is swiftly hastening; another duty toward your nobler self—the future that is in you and your woman's heart. I tell you again that you are beautiful, and the slavery to which you are condemning yourself forever is an

offence against the creator of such perfection.   Do
you know what it is to love?''

" I know what it is to feel kindness," she answered
after a time of silence.   " I ought to know no more.
You goodness is very dear to me.   We never sleep,
brother and I, but we say your name together, and ask
God to bless you."

Reybold sought in vain to suppress a confession he
had resisted.   The contact of her form, her large dark
eyes now fixed upon him in emotion, the birth of the
conscious woman in the virgin and her affection still in
the leashes of a slavish sacrifice, tempted him onward
to the conquest.

" I am about to retire from Congress," he said.
" It is no place for me in times so insubstantial.
There is darkness and beggary ahead for all your
Southern race.   There is a crisis coming which will be
followed by desolation.   The generation to which your
parents belong is doomed !   I open my arms to you,
dear girl, and offer you a home never yet gladdened by
a wife.   Accept it, and leave Washington with me and
with your brother.   I love you wholly."

A happy light shone in her face a moment.   She
was weary to the bone with the day's work, and had
not the strength, if she had the will, to prevent the
Congressman drawing her to his heart.   Sobbing
there, she spoke with bitter agony :

" Heaven bless you, dear Mr. Reybold, with a wife
good enough to deserve you!   Blessings on your generous heart.   But I cannot leave Washington.   I love
another here !''

III.—DUST.

The Lake and Bayou Committee reaped the reward
of a good action.   Crutch, the page, as they all called
Uriel Basil, affected the sensibility of the whole committee to the extent that profanity almost ceased there,
and vulgarity became a crime in the presence of a
child.   Gentle words and wishes became the rule ; a

glimmer of reverence and a thought of piety were not unknown in that little chamber.

"Dog my skin !" said Jeems Bee, " if I ever made a 'pintment that give me sech satisfaction ! I feel as if I had sot a nigger free !"

The youthful abstractionist, Lowndes Cleburn, expressed it even better. " Crutch," he said, " is like a angel reduced to his bones. Them air wings or pinions, that he might have flew off with, being a pair of crutches, keeps him here to tarry awhile in our service. But, gentlemen, he's not got long to stay. His crutches is growing too heavy for that expandin' sperit. Some day we'll look up and miss him through our tears."

They gave him many a present ; they put a silver watch in his pocket, and dressed him in a jacket with gilt buttons. He had a bouquet of flowers to take home every day to that marvellous sister of whom he spoke so often ; and there were times when the whole committee, seeing him drop off to sleep as he often did through frail and weary nature, sat silently watching lest he might be wakened before his rest was over. But no persuasion could take him off the floor of Congress. In that solemn old Hall of Representatives, under the semicircle of gray columns, he darted with agility from noon to dusk, keeping speed upon his crutches with the healthiest of the pages, and racing into the document-room ; and through the dark and narrow corridors of the old Capitol loft, where the House library was lost in twilight. Visitors looked with interest and sympathy at the narrow back and body of this invalid child, whose eyes were full of bright, beaming spirit. He sometimes nodded on the steps by the Speaker's chair ; and these spells of dreaminess and fatigue increased as his disease advanced upon his wasting system. Once he did not awaken at all until adjournment. The great Congress and audience passed out, and the little fellow still slept, with his head against the Clerk's desk, while all the other pages were grouped around him, and they finally bore him off to the committee-room in their arms, where, amongst the sympathetic watchers, was old Beau. When Uriel opened his eyes the old mendicant was looking into them.

" Ah ! little Major," he said, " poor Beau has been waiting for you to take those bad words back. Old Beau thought it was all bob with his little cove."

" Beau," said the boy, " I've had such a dream ! I thought my dear father, who is working so hard to bring me home to him, had carried me out on the river in a boat. We sailed through the greenest marshes, among white lilies, where the wild ducks were tame as they can be. All the ducks were diving and diving, and they brought up long stalks of celery from the water and gave them to us. Father ate all his. But mine turned into lilies and grew up so high that I felt myself going with them, and the higher I went the more beautiful grew the birds. Oh ! let me sleep and see if it will be so again."

The outcast raised his gold-headed cane and hobbled up and down the room with a laced handkerchief at his eyes.

" Great God !" he exclaimed, " another generation is going out, and here I stay without a stake, playing a lone hand forever and forever."

" Beau," said Reybold, " there's hope while one can feel. Don't go away until you have a good word from our little passenger."

The outstretched hand of the Northern Congressman was not refused by the vagrant, whose eccentric sorrow yet amused the Southern Committeemen.

" Ole Beau's jib-boom of a mustache 'll put his eye out," said Pontotoc Bibb, " ef he fetches another groan like that."

" Beau's very shaky around the hams an' knees," said Box Izard ; " he's been a good figger, but even figgers can lie ef they stand up too long.

The little boy unclosed his eyes and looked around on all those kindly, watching faces.

"Did anybody fire a gun?" he said. "Oh! no. I was only dreaming that I was hunting with father, and he shot at the beautiful pheasants that were making such a whirring of wings for me. It was music. When can I hunt with father, dear gentlemen?"

They all felt the tread of the mighty hunter before the Lord very near at hand; the hunter whose name is Death.

"There are little tiny birds along the beach," muttered the boy. "They twitter and run into the surf and back again, and am I one of them? I must be; for I feel the water cold, and yet I see you all, so kind to me! Don't whistle for me now; for I don't get much play, gentlemen! Will the Speaker turn me out if I play with the beach birds just once? I'm only a little boy working for my mother."

"Dear Uriel," whispered Reybold, "here's Old Beau, to whom you once spoke angrily. Don't you see him?"

The little boy's eyes came back from far-land somewhere, and he saw the ruined gamester at his feet.

"Dear Beau," he said, "I can't get off to go home with you. They won't excuse me, and I give all my money to mother. But you go to the back gate. Ask for Joyce. She'll give you a nice warm meal every day. Go with him, Mr. Reybold! If you ask for him it will be all right; for Joyce—dear Joyce!—she loves you."

The beach birds played again along the strand; the boy ran into the foam with his companions and felt the spray once more. The Mighty Hunter shot his bird —a little cripple that twittered the sweetest of them all. Nothing moved in the solemn chamber of the committee but the voice of an old forsaken man, sobbing bitterly.

IV.—CAKE.

The funeral was over, and Mr. Reybold marvelled much that the Judge had not put in an appearance. The whole committee had attended the obsequies of Crutch and acted as pall-bearers. Reybold had escorted the page's sister to the Congressional cemetery, and had observed even Old Beau to come with a wreath of flowers and hobble to the grave and deposit them there. But the Judge, remorseless in death as frivolous in life, never came near his mourning wife and daughter in their severest sorrow. Mrs. Tryphonia Basil, seeing that this singular want of behavior on the Judge's part was making some ado, raised her voice above the general din of meals.

"Jedge Basil," she exclaimed, "has been on his Tennessee purchase. These Christmas times there's no getting through the snow in the Cumberland Gap. He's stopped off thaw to shoot the—ahem !—the wild torkey—a great passion with the Jedge. His half-uncle, Gineral Johnson, of Awkinso, was a torkey-killer of high celebrity. He was a Deshay on his Maw's side. I s'pose you haven't the torkey in the Dutch country, Mr. Reybold ?"

"Madame," said Reybold, in a quieter moment, "have you written to the Judge the fact of his son's death ?"

"Oh yes—to Fawquear."

"Mrs. Basil," continued the Congressman, "I want you to be explicit with me. Where is the Judge, your husband, at this moment ?"

"Excuse me, Colonel Reybold, this is a little of a assumption, sir. The Jedge might call you out, sir, for intruding upon his incog. He's very fine on his incog., you air awair."

"Madame," exclaimed Reybold straightforwardly, "there are reasons why I should communicate with your husband. My term in Congress is nearly expired. I might arouse your interest, if I chose, by recalling to your mind the memorandum of about seven hundred dollars in which you are my debtor. That would be a reason for seeing your husband anywhere north of the Potomac, but I do not intend to mention it. Is he aware—are you?—that Joyce Basil is in love with some one in this city?"

Mrs. Basil drew a long breath, raised both hands, and ejaculated : " Well, I declaw !"

" I have it from her own lips," continued Reybold. " She told me as a secret, but all my suspicions are awakened. If I can prevent it, madame, that girl shall not follow the example of hundreds of her class in Washington, and descend, through the boarding-house or the lodging quarter, to be the wife of some common and unambitious clerk, whose penury she must some day sustain by her labor. I love her myself, but I will never take her until I know her heart to be free. Who is this lover of your daughter?"

An expression of agitation and cunning passed over Mrs. Basil's face.

" Colonel Reybold," she whined, " I pity your blasted hopes. If I was a widow, they should be comfoted. Alas ! my daughter is in love with one of the Fitzchews of Fawqueeah. His parents is cousins of the Jedge, and attached to the military."

The Congressman looked disappointed, but not yet satisfied.

" Give me at once the address of your husband," he spoke. " If you do not, I shall ask your daughter for it, and she cannot refuse me."

The mistress of the boarding-house was not without alarm, but she dispelled it with an outbreak of anger.

" If my daughter disobeys her mother," she cried, " and betrays the Jedge's incog., she is no Basil, Colonel Reybold. The Basils repudiate her, and she may jine the Dutch and other foreigners at her pleasure."

" That is her only safety," exclaimed Reybold. " I hope to break every string that holds her to yonder barren honor and exhausted soil."

He pointed toward Virginia, and hastened away to the Capitol. All the way up the squalid and muddy avenue of that day he mused and wondered : " Who is Fitzhugh ? Is there such a person any more than a Judge Basil ? And yet there *is* a Judge, for Joyce has told me so. *She*, at least, cannot lie to me. At last," he thought, " the dream of my happiness is over. Invincible in her prejudice as all these Virginians, Joyce Basil has made her bed amongst the starveling First Families, and there she means to live and die. Five years hence she will have her brood around her. In ten years she will keep a boarding-house and borrow money. As her daughters grow up to the stature and grace of their mother, they will be proud and poor again and breed in and out, until the race will perish from the earth."

Slow to love, deeply interested, baffled but unsatisfied, Reybold made up his mind to cut his perplexity short by leaving the city for the county of Fauquier. As he passed down the avenue late that afternoon, he turned into E Street, near the theatre, to' engage a carriage for his expedition. It was a street of livery-stables, gambling dens, drinking houses, and worse ; murders had been committed along its sidewalks. The more pretentious *canaille* of the city harbored there to prey on the hotels close at hand and aspire to the chance acquaintance of gentlemen. As Reybold stood in an archway of this street, just as the evening shadows deepened above the line of sunset, he saw something pass which made his heart start to his throat and fastened him to the spot. Veiled and walking fast, as if escaping detection or pursuit, the figure of Joyce Basil flitted over the pavement and disappeared in a door about at the middle of this Alsatian quarter of the capital.

" What house is that ?" he asked of a constable passing by, pointing to the door she entered.

" Gambling den," answered the officer. " It used to be old Phil Pendleton's."

Reybold knew the reputation of the house : a resort for the scions of the old tidewater families, where hospitality thinly veiled the paramount design of plunder. The connection established the truth of Mrs. Basil's statement. Here, perhaps, already married to the dissipated heir of some unproductive estate, Joyce Basil's lot was cast forever. It might even be that she had been tempted here by some wretch whose villainy she knew not of Reybold's brain took fire at the thought, and he pursued the fugitive into the doorway.   A negro steward unfastened a slide and peeped at Reybold knocking in the hall ; and, seeing him of respectable appearance, bowed ceremoniously as he let down a chain and opened the door.

" Short cards in the front saloon," he said ; " supper and faro back.   Chambers on the third floor. Walk up."

Reybold only tarried a moment at the gaming tables, where the silent, monotonous deal from the tin box, the lazy stroke of the markers, and the transfer of ivory " chips" from card to card of the sweat-cloth, impressed him as the dullest form of vice he had ever found.   Treading softly up the stairs, he was attracted by the light of a door partly ajar, and a deep groan, as of a dying person.   He peeped through the crack of the door, and beheld Joyce Basil leaning over an old man, whose brow she moistened with her handkerchief.   " Dear father," he heard her say, and it brought consolation to more than the sick man.   Reybold threw open the door and entered into the presence of Mrs. Basil and her daughter.   The former arose with surprise and shame, and cried :

" Jedge Basil, the Dutch have hunted you down. He's here—the Yankee creditor."

Joyce Basil held up her hand in imploration, but Reybold did not heed the woman's remark.   He felt a weight rising from his heart, and the blindness of many months lifted from his eyes.   The dying mortal upon the bed, over whose face the blue billow of death was rolling rapidly, and whose eyes sought in his daughter's the promise of mercy from on high, was the mysterious parent who had never arrived—the Judge from Fauquier. In that old man's long waxed mustache, crimped hair, and threadbare finery the Congressman recognized Old Beau, the outcast gamester and mendicant, and the father of Joyce and Uriel Basil.

"Colonel Reybold," faltered that old wreck of manly beauty and of promise long departed, "Old Beau's passing in his checks. The chant coves will be telling to-morrow what they know of his life in the papers, but I've dropped a cold deck on 'em these twenty years. Not one knows Old Beau, the Bloke, to be Tom Basil, cadet at West Point in the last generation. I've kept nothing of my own but my children's good name. My little boy never knew me to be his father. I tried to keep the secret from my daughter, but her affection broke down my disguises. Thank God! the old rounder's deal has run out at last. For his wife he'll flash her diles no more, nor be taken on the vag."

"Basil," said Reybold, "what trust do you leave to me in your family?"

Mrs. Basil strove to interpose, but the dying man raised his voice:

"Tryphonee can go home to Fauquier. She was always welcome there—without me. I was disinherited. But here, Colonel! My last drop of blood is in the girl. She loves you."

A rattle arose in the sinner's throat. He made an effort, and transferred his daughter's hand to the Congressman's. Not taking it away, she knelt with her future husband at the bedside and raised her voice:

"Lord, when Thou comest into Thy kingdom, remember him!"

HERMAN OF BOHEMIA MANOR.

(See note at end of poem.)

I.—THE MANOR.

" MY corn is gathered in the bins,"
  The Lord Augustin Herman said ;
" My wild swine romp in chincapins ;
  Dried are the deer and beaver skins ;
    And on Elk Mountain's languid head
    The autumn woods are red.

" So in my heart an autumn falls ;
  I stand a lonely tree unleaved ;
And to my hermit manor walls
The wild-goose from the water calls,
  As if to mock a man bereaved :
  My years are nearly sheaved.

" Go saddle me the Flemish steed
  My brother Verlett gave to me,
What time his sister did concede
Her dainty hand to hear me plead !
  Poor soul ! she's mouldering by the sea
  And I with misery."

The slave man brought the wild-maned horse—
  All wilder that with stags he grazed—
Bred from the seed the knightly Norse
Rode from Araby.   Like remorse
  The eyes in his gray forehead blazed,
  As on his lord he gazed.

" Now guard ye well my lands and stock ;
  Slack not the seine, ply well the axe ;
The eagle circles o'er the flock ;
The Indian at my gates may knock :
  The firelock prime for his attacks ;
  I ride the sunrise tracks."

Swift as a wizard on a broom,
　The strong gray horse and rider ran,
Adown the forest stripped of bloom.
By stump and bough that scarce gave room
　To pass the woodman's caravan,
　Rode the Bohemian.

" Lord Herman, stay," the brewer cried,
　" And Huddy's friendly flagon clink !"
And martial Hinoyóssa spied
The horseman, moving with the tide
　That ebbed from Appoquininiink,
　Nor stopped to rest or drink.

" Where rides old Herman ?" Beekman mused ;
　" That railing wife has turned his head."
" He keeps the saddle as he used,
In younger days, when he infused
　Three provinces," Pierre Alricks said,
　" And mapped their landscapes spread."

Broad rose Zuydt River as the sail
　Above his periauger flew ;
Loud neighed the steed to snuff the gale ;
But Herman saw not, swift and pale,
　Two carrier pigeons, winging true
　North-east, across the blue.

They quit the cage of Stuyvesant's spy,
　And lurking Willems' message bore :
(" This morn rode Herman rapid by,
Tow'rd Amsterdam, to satisfy
　Yet wider titles than he tore
　From shallow Baltimore !")

II.—REPLEVIN.

The second sunset at his back
　From Navesink Highlands threw the shade
Of horse and Herman, long and black,
Across the golden ripples' track,
　Where with the Kills the ocean played
　A measured serenade ;

There where to sea a river ran,
  Between tall hills of brown and sand,
A mountain island rose to span
The outlet of the Raritan,
  And made a world on either hand,
  Soft as a poet planned :

Fair marshes pierced with brimming creeks,
  Where wild-fowl dived to oyster caves ;
And shores that swung to wooded peaks,
Where many a falling water seeks
  The cascade's plunge to reach the waves,
  And greenest farmland laves ;

Deep tide to every roadstead slips,
  And many capes confuse the shore,
Yet none do with their forms eclipse
Yon ocean, made for royal ships,
  Whose swells on silver beaches roar
  And rock forevermore.

Old Herman gazed through lengthening shades
  Far up the inland, where the spires,
Defined on rocky palisades,
Flung sunset from their burnished blades,
  And with their bells in evening choirs
  Breathed homesick men's desires :

" New Amsterdam ! 'tis thine or mine—
  The foreground of this stately plan !
To me the Indian did assign—
Totem on totem, line on line—
  Both Staten and the groves that ran
  Far up the Raritan.

" By spiteful Stuyvesant long restrained,
  Now, while the English break his power,
Be Achter Kill again regained
And Herman's title entertained,
  Here float my banner from my tower,
  Here is my right, my hour !"

III.—THE SQUATTERS.

He scarce had finished, when a rush,
   Like partridge through the stubble, broke,
And armèd men trod down the brush ;
A harsh voice, trembling in the hush,
   As it must either stab or choke,
   Imperiously spoke :

" Ye conquered men of Achter Kill,
   Whose farms by loyal toil ye got,
True Dutchmen ! give this traitor will—
And he is yours to loose or kill—
   All that ye have he will allot
   Anew—field, cradle, cot.

" Years past, beyond our Southern bounds,
   On States' commission sent by me,
He mapped the English papists' grounds,
And like a Judas, o'er our wounds,
   Our raiment parted openly :
   This is the man ye see !

' Yet followed by my sleepless age,
   Fast as he rode my pigeons sped—
Straight as the ravens from their cage,
Straight as the arrows of my rage,
   Straight as the meteor overhead
   That strikes a traitor dead."

They bound Lord Herman fast as hate,
   And bore him o'er to Staten Isle ;
Behind him closed the postern gate,
And round him pitiless as fate,
   Closed moat and palisade and pile :
   " Thou diest at morn," they smile.

IV.—STUYVESANT.

Morn broke on lofty Staten's height,
   O'er low Amboy and Arthur Kill ;
And ocean dallying with the light,
Between the beaches leprous white,
   And silent hook and headland hill,
   And Stuyvesant had his will ;

One-legged he stood, his sharp mustache
　　Stiff as the sword he slashed in ire ;
His bald crown, like a calabash,
Fringed round with ringlets white as ash,
　　And features scorched with inner fire ;
　　　Age wore him like a briar.

" Bring the Bohemian forth !" he cried ;
　　" Old man, thy moments are but few."
" So much the better, Dutchman ! bide
Thy little time of aged pride,
　　Thy poor revenges to pursue—
　　　Thy date is hastening, too.

" No crime is mine, save that I sought
　　A refuge past thy jealous ken,
And peaceful arts to strangers taught,
And mine own title hither brought,
　　Before the laws of Englishmen,
　　　A banished denizen.

" Yet that thy churlish soul may plead
　　A favor to a dying foe,
I'll ask thee, Stuyvesant, ere I bleed,
Let me once more on my gray steed
　　Thrice round the timbered *enceinte* go :
　　　Fire, when I tell thee so !"

" What freak is this ?" quoth Stuyvesant grim.
　　Quoth Herman, " 'Twas a charger brave—
Like my first bride in eye and limb—
A wedding-gift ; indulge the whim !
　　And from his back to plunge, I crave,
　　　A bridegroom, in her grave."

Then muttered the uneasy guard :
　　" We rob an old man of his lands,
And slay him.　Sure his fate is hard,
His dying plea to disregard !"
　　" Ride then to death !" Stuyvesant commands ;
　　　" Unbind his horse, his hands !"

The old steed darted in the fort,
  And neighed and shook his long gray mane ;
Then, seeing soldiery, his port
Grew savage.   With a charger's snort,
  Upright he reared, as young again
  And scenting a campaign.

Hard on his nostrils Herman laid
  An iron hand and drew him down,
Then, mounting in the esplanade,
The rude Dutch rustics stared afraid :
  " By Santa Claus ! he needs no crown,
  To look more proud renown !"

Lame Stuyvesant, also, envious saw
  How straight he sat in courteous power,
Like boldness sanctified by law,
And age gave magisterial awe ;
  Though in his last and bitter hour,
  Of knightliness the flower.

His gray hairs o'er his cassock blew,
  And in his peak'd hat waved a plume ;
A horn swung loose and shining through
High boots of buckskin, as he drew
  The rein, a jewel burst to bloom :
  The signet ring of doom.

' Thrice round the fort !   Then as I raise
  This hand, aim all and murder well !"
His head bends low ; the steed's eyes blaze,
But not less bright do Herman's gaze,
  As circling round the citadel,
  He peers for hope in hell.

Fast were the gates ; no crevice showed.
  The ramparts, spiked with palisades,
Grew higher as once round he rode ;
The arquebusiers prime the load,
  And drop to aim from ambuscades ;
  No latch, no loophole aids.

But one small hut its chimney thrust
　　Between the timbers, close as they ;
Twice round and with a desperate trust
Lord Herman muttered : " die I must :
　　There, CHARGE !" and spurred through beam
　　　　and clay—
　　" By heaven ! he is away !"

VI.—THE KILLS.

In clouds of dust the muskets fire,
　　And volleying oaths old Stuyvesant from :
" Turn out !   In yonder Kills he'll mire,
Or drown, unless the fiends conspire.
　　" Mount !   Follow !   Still he must succumb—
　　That tide was never swum."

Through hut and chimney, down the ditch
　　And up the bank, plunge horse and man ;
And down the hills of bramble pitch,
Oft-stumbling, those old gray knees which,
　　Hunting the raccoon, led the van ;
　　Now, limp yet game he ran.

But cool and supple, Herman sat,
　　His mind at work, his frame the horse's,
And knew with each pulsation, that
Past foe and fen, past crag, and flat,
　　And marsh, the steed he nearer forces
　　To the broad sea's recourses.

" Old friend," he thought, " thou art too weak
　　To try the Kills and drown, or falter,
The while from shore their marksmen seek
My heart.   (Once o'er the Chesapeake
　　I paddled oarless.)   Lest the halter
　　Be mine, I must not palter—

" Thou diest, though my marriage-gift :
　　I still can swim.   Poor Joost, adieu !"
Ere ceased the heartfelt sigh he lift,
The prospect widened : all adrift,
　　The salty sluice burst into view,
　　Where grappling tides fought through,

And sucked to doom the venturous bear,
  And from his ferry swept the rower—
How wide, how terrible, how fair !
Yet how inspiriting the air—
  How tempts the long salt grass the mower !
  How treacherous the shore !

Far up the right spread Newark Bay,
  To lone Secaucus wooded rock ;
Nor could the Kill von Kull convey
Passaic's mountain flood away :
  In Arthur Kill the surges choke,
  The wild tides interlock.

O'er Arthur Kill the Holland farms
  Their gambril roofs, red painted, show ;
Beyond the newer Yankee swarms—
His cider-presses spread their arms.
  Before, the squatter ; back, the foe :
  And the dark waters flow.

As that salt air the stallion felt,
  He whimpers gayly, as if still is
Upon his sight his native Scheldt,
Or Skagger Rack, or Little Belt,—
  Their waving grass and silver lilies,
  Where browsed the amorous fillies.

And o'er the tide some lady nags
  Blew back his challenge. Scarce could Herman
Hold in his seat. " By John of Prague's
True faith !" he thought, " thy spirit lags
  Not, Joost ! Thy course thyself determine !"
  And plunges like a merman.

Leander's spirit in the steed
  Inspired his stroke, not Herman's fear ;
And fast the island shores recede,
Fast rise the rider's spirits freed,
  The golden mainland draws more near—
  " O gallant horse ! 'tis here :"

VII.—ELUSION.

Across the Kills the muskets crack—
  " Ha ! ha !" Lord Herman waves his beaver :
" Die of thy spleen ere I come back,
Old Stuyvesant !"   With a noise of wrack
  The fort blew up of his aggriever !—
  But not without retriever.

For from the smoke two pigeons fly,
  One south, one westward, separating,
And straight as arrows crossed the sky,
With silent orders ("*He must die
  Who comes hereafter.   Lie in waiting !*")
  Their snowy pinions freighting.

They warn the men of Minisink ;
  They warn the Dutchmen of Zuydt River.
Now speed to Jersey's farther brink,
Old horse, old master, ere ye shrink !—
  Or ambushed fall ere moonrise quiver,
  On paths where ye shall shiver.

On went the twain till past the ford
  That red-walled Raritan led over,
And lonely woodland shades explored.
Unarmed with firelock or with sword,
  Free-hearted rode the forest rover,
  Of all wild kind the drover :

Fled deer and bear before his coming,
  The wild-cat glared, the viper hissed ;
And died the long day's insect-drumming.
Where things of night began their humming,
  And witchly phantoms went to tryst,
  Was Herman exorcist.

' No land so tangled but my eye
  Can map its confines and its courses ;
Yet on life's map who can espy
Where hides his foe—where he shall die ?"
  So Herman said, and his resources
  Resigned unto his horse's.

All night the steed instinctive travelled—
  His weary rider wept for him—
Through unseen gulfs the whirlwind ravelled,
Up moonlit beds of streamlets gravelled,
  Till halting every bleeding limb,
  He stands by something dim,

And will not stir till morning breaks.
  " What is't I see, low clustering there,
Beyond those broadening bays and lakes,
That yonder point familiar makes ?—
  Is it New Amstel, lowly fair,
  And this the Delaware ?"

VIII.—THE ECHO.

Lord Herman hugged his horse with pride :
  He raised his horn and blew so loudly,
That more than echoes back replied :
Horns answered louder ; horsemen cried,
  And muskets banged, as if avowedly
  On Stuyvesant's errand proudly !

" Die, traitor ! fleér ! though thou 'scape
  Our ambush on thy devil's racer,
Caught here upon this marshy cape,
Thy bones the muskrat's brood shall scrape,
  The sturgeon suck—Death thy embracer !"
  So shouts each sanguine chaser.

To die in sight of Amstel's walls,
  And gallant Joost to die beside him ?—
O foolish blast, such fate that calls !
O river that the heart appalls !
  Dear Joost may live.   And *they* bestride him ?
  " By hell ! none else shall ride him !

" My steed, thy limbs like mine are sore !
  Few years are left us ere the billows
Roll over both.   Come but once more,
And to the bottom or the shore,
  Bear me and thee to happy pillows,
  Or 'neath the water willows !"

He strokes old Joost.   He bends him low.
  He winds his horn and laughs derision.
One spring !—they've cleared the bog and sloe,
And down the ebb tide buoyant go—
  That stately tide.   So like a vision
  Of home, to Norse and Frisian,

Where full a league spread Maas and Rhine,
  And in the marsh the rice-birds twitter ;
The long cranes pasture and the kine
Loom lofty in the misty shine
  Of dawn and reedy islands glitter :
  Yet death all where is bitter.

Ere out of range a volley peals,
  But greed too great made aye a blunder.
His horse Lord Herman's self conceals,
Yet once his horse and he go under,
  And rise again.   No wound he feels.
  They hold their fire in wonder !

Short of the mark the bullets splash :
  " Now drown thee, wizard ! at thy pleasure,"
The Dutchmen hiss through teeth they gnash.
He answers not ; for o'er the plash
  Of waves he hears Joost's gasping measure
  Of breath's fast wasting treasure.

IX.—PEGASUS.

The sighs when dying comrades fall,
  Struck by the foe, are only sad ;
They leaped the ditch and climbed the wall,
And shared the purpose of us all ;
  The fame they have ; the joy they had :
  " Rest in thy tracks, brave lad !"

But thou, poor beast ! unknown to fame,
  Whose heart is reached while ours is bounding,
Amidst the victory's acclaim—
By thee we kneel with more of shame,
  That bore us through the fight resounding,
  And dumbly took our wounding !

Lord Herman saw the blood drops seethe,
  The nag's neck droop, the nostril bubble,
And loosed the bridle from his teeth ;
Yet swam the old legs underneath,
  Invincibly.   The gap they double ;
  But further swim in trouble.

And lovely Nature stretched her aid,
  Her sympathetic tow and eddy ;
The oars of air with azure blade,
And silent gravities persuade
  And waft them onward, slow and steady—
  On duteous deeds aye ready.

High leaped the perch.   The hawk screamed joy.
  Under Joost's belly musically
The ripples broke.   Bright clouds convoy
The brute that man would but destroy,
  And all instinctive agents rally
  Strong and medicinally.

In vain !   The gurgling waters suck
  That old life under.   Herman swimming
Seized but the horse tail.   Like a buck
Breasting a lake in wild woods' pluck,
  Joost rose, the glaze his bright eyes dimming,
  And blood his sockets brimming.

Then voices speak and women cry.
  The treading feet find soil to stand.
Above them the green ramparts lie,
And twixt their shadows and the sky,
  The wondering burghers crowd the strand,
  And Herman help to land :

" Now to Newcastle's English walls,
  Hail, Herman ! and thy matchless stud !"
Joost staggers up the bank and falls,
And dying to his master crawls.
  Yields up his long solicitude,
  And spills his veins of blood.

In Herman's arms his neck is prest,
  With martial pride his dark eye glazes ;
He feels the hand he loves the best
Stroke fondly, and a chill of rest,
  As if he rolled in pasture daisies
  And heard in winds his praises :

" O couldst thou speak, what wouldst thou say ?
  I who can speak am dumb before thee.
Thine eyes that drink Olympian day
Where steeds of wings thy soul convey,
  With pride of eagles circling o'er thee :
  Thou seest I adore thee !

" Bound to thy starry home and her
  Who brought me thee and left earth hollow !
An honored grave thy bones inter,
And painting shall thy fame confer,
  Ere in thy shining track I follow,
  Thou courser of Apollo !"

The singular incident of this poem was published in 1862. in Rev. John Lednum's " Personal Rise of Methodism," and in the following words :

" It is said that the Dutch had him (Herman) a prisoner of war, at one time, under sentence of death, in New York. A short time before he was to be executed, he feigned himself to be deranged in mind, and requested that his horse should be brought to him in the prison. The horse was brought, finely caparisoned. Herman mounted him, and seemed to be performing military exercises, when, on the first opportunity, he bolted through one of the large windows, that was some fifteen feet above ground, leaped down, swam the North River, ran his horse through Jersey, and alighted on the bank of the Delaware, opposite Newcastle, and thus made his escape from death and the Dutch. This daring feat, tradition says, he had transferred to canvas—himself represented as standing by the side of his charger, from whose nostrils the blood was flowing."—Page 277.

Such a singular and improbable story attracted great local attention, and in 1870, Francis Vincent, publishing his " History of Delaware," wrote : " The author found this incident in both Lednum and Foot, and has seen a copy of this painting. It is in the possession of James R. Oldham, Esq., of Christiana Bridge, the only male descendant of Herman in Delaware State. He is the seventh in descent from Augustin Herman."—Page 469.

In 1875, Rev. Charles P. Mallery, of Chesapeake City, a part of the Bohemia Manor, wrote in the Elkton (Md.) *Democrat* as follows : " Herman resided on the Manor for more than twenty years, during which time he once rode to New York on the back of his favorite horse, to reclaim his long-neglected possessions there. He found his land occupied by squatters. . . . They secured him, as they thought, for the night ; but he soon found means to escape by leaping his horse through a forced opening, swimming the North River, and continuing his flight through New Jersey until he reached the shore opposite Newcastle, where he swam his horse across the Delaware and was safe. . . . Dr. Spotswood, of Newcastle, told me that there was a tradition in his town that the horse was buried there." Augustin Herman made the first drawing of New Amsterdam, and

---

* The Bohemia Manor is a tract of 18,000 acres of the best land on the Delaware peninsula. It was granted to Augustine Herman, Bohemian, whose tombstone, now lying in the yard of Richard Bayard, on the site of Herman's park, bears date 1651. He received the manor for making an early map of Maryland, and granted a part of the land to the sect of Labadists. In the course of a century it became the homestead of Senator Richard Bassett, heir of the last lord of the manor, and of his son-in-law, Senator James A. Bayard, the first. Herman was the principal historic personage about the head of the Chesapeake, and was Peter Stuyvesant's diplomatist to New England as well as Maryland. The argument he made for the priority of the Dutch settlement on the Delaware was the basis of the independence of Delaware State. The legend of his escape from New York is told in several local books and newspapers, and it was the subject of one of his paintings, as he was both draughtsman and designer G A. T.

early maps of Maryland and New England. He was the first specu-
lator in city real estate in America.

In 1876 I visited the relics of Herman on the Manor, and observed
the topography and foliage. I then undertook to put this legend into
verse, but struck a short, ill-accommodating stanza, in which I never-
theless persevered until the tale was told. I found that Herman had
bought, in 1652, " the Raritan Great Meadows and the territory along
the Staten Island Kills from Ompoge, or Amboy, to the Pechciesse
Creek, and a tract on the south side of the Raritan, opposite Staten
Island " (see Broadhead, page 537). It at once occurred to me to
put the seat of Herman's capture by squatters on this property, and
to take Staten Island's bold scenery as a contrast to that of the head
of the Chesapeake, whence Herman had ridden. He could, besides,
more reasonably swim the Kills than the North River with a horse, as
a gentle prelude to swimming the Delaware.

One year before buying the above property (see Broadhead's
" History of New York," page 526), Peter Stuyvesant vindictively
persecuted Herman, Lockerman, and others, who retired to Staten
Island to brood. These men belonged to " the popular party." I
therefore had a hint to make Stuyvesant himself the incarcerator of
Herman in a fort, and the most available period seemed to be subsequent to the capture of Dutch New York by the English, but before
the Dutch settlements on the Delaware were yielded. Stuyvesant
surrendered New York September 8th, 1664. It was not until October
10th that Newcastle on the Delaware surrendered. The theory of
the poem is that Herman, hearing New York to be English, like
Maryland where he resided, repaired to his possessions. Stuyvesant
rallies the squatters against him and makes use of a fort on Staten
Island, not yet noticed by the English, as Herman's place of punishment. On Herman's escape this fort is blown up. When Herman
returns to Newcastle, it is no longer Dutch, but English. Four days
is the time of the action. The device of the carrier pigeons is possibly
an anachronism, and also the age of Herman. I have aimed to make
the story reasonable, if not creditable.

KIDNAPPED.

A CELEBRATED apostle of the Methodist sect, on the Eastern shore of Maryland, was the Rev. Titus Bates. He had been twenty-six years engaged in the ministry, and was now a bronzed, worn, failing man, consumed by the zeal of his order, but still anxious to continue his work and die at his post. Like all his tribe, he was an itinerant, moving from town to town every second year—these towns being his places of abode, while his fields of labor were called "circuits," and comprised many houses of worship scattered through the surrounding district. He had chosen his wife with reference to his vocation, and she was equally earnest with himself. She attended the sick, prayed with the dying, taught Sabbath-schools, and organized religious meetings among the women. They had but one son, Paul, an odd, silent little fellow, who was thought to be more bashful than bright ; but his parents loved him tenderly, and argued the highest usefulness from his still, sober, thoughtful habits. He was of a singularly dark complexion, with fine black eyes and curling hair, and he was now old enough to ride to and fro with his father upon the long pastoral journeys.

Paul's sixth birthday occurred on a raw Sunday in December. He had been promised, as a special treat on that occasion, a visit to Hogson's Corner, an old meeting-house near the bay-side, twenty miles distant. His mother woke him at an early hour, and, while he breakfasted, the gray pony Bob came to the door in the "sulky." His mother bade him to be a good boy, and kissed him ; he took his seat upon a stool at his father's feet, and watched the stone parsonage fade

quickly out of sight. The last houses of the town vanished ; they passed some squalid huts of free negroes ;
and when, after an hour, they came to a grim, solitary
hill, the snow began to fall. It beat down very fast,
whitening the frozen furrows in the fields, making pyra-
mids of the charred stumps, and bleaching the sinuous
" worm-fences" which bordered the road. After a
while, they found a gate built across the way, and Paul
leaped out to open it. The snow was deep on the
other side, and the little fellow's strength was taxed to
push it back ; but he succeeded, and his father applauded him. Then there were other gates ; for there
were few public highways here, and the routes led
through private fields. It seemed that he had opened
a great many gates before they came to the forest, and
then Paul wrapped his chilled wet feet in the thick
buffalo hide, and watched the dreary stretches of the
pines moan by, the flakes still falling, and the wheels
of the sulky dragging in the drifts. The road was
very lonely ; his father hummed snatches of hymns as
they went, and the little boy shaped grotesque figures
down the dim aisles of the woods, and wondered how
it would be with travellers lost in their depths. He
was not sorry when they reached the meeting-house—
a black old pile of planks, propped upon logs, with a
long shelter-roof for horses down the side of the graveyard. A couple of sleighs, a rough-covered wagon,
called a " dearbourn," and several saddled horses, were
tied beneath the roof. Two very aged negroes were
seen coming up one of the cross-roads, and the shining, surging Chesapeake, bearing a few pale sails, was
visible in the other direction. Some boors were gos-
siping in the churchyard, slashing their boots with
their riding-whips ; one lean, solemn man came out to
welcome the preacher, addressing him as " Brother
Bates ;" and another led the sulky into the wagon-
shed, and treated Bob to some ears of corn, which he
needed very much.

Then they all repaired to the church, which looked

inside like a great barn. The beams and shingles were bare ; some swallows in the eaves flew and twittered at will ; and a huge stove, with branching pipes, stood in the naked aisle. The pews were hard and prim, and occupied by pinch-visaged people ; the pulpit was a plain shelf, with hanging oil-lamps on either side ; and over the door in the rear projected a rheumatic gallery, where the black communicants were boxed up like criminals. A kind old woman gave Paul a ginger-cake, but his father motioned him to put it in his pocket ; and after he had warmed his feet, he was told to sit in the pew nearest the preacher on what was called the "Amen side." Then the services began, the preacher leading the hymns, and the cracked voices of the old ladies joining in at the wrong places. But after a while a venerable negro in the gallery tuned up, and sang down the shrill swallows with natural melody. The prayers were long, and broken by ejacu-lations from the pews. The text was announced amid profound silence, after everybody had coughed several times, and then the itinerant launched into his sermon. At first it was dry and argumentative, then burdened with divisions and quotations, but in the end he closed the great book, and made one of those fierce, feeling appeals—brimming with promises of grace and threatenings of hell—in words so homely that all felt them true, while the wild, interpolated cries of the believers thrilled and terrified the young.

Little Paul heard with pale lips these grim, religious revelations, and his child's fancy conjured up awful pictures of worlds beyond the grave. He wondered that the birds dared riot in the roof : the sky in the gable window was full of cloudy marvels ; and the snow beat under the door, like a shroud blown out of one of the churchyard tombs. The closing prayer was said at last, the unconverted walked away, but five or six communicants remained to tell their experience in the class-meeting. Paul's father gave him permission to go into the yard if he liked, and the boy got into the sulky, beneath the buffalo, and heard the sobs and hymns floating dismally on the wind. Grim shapes thronged his mind again, wherein the Bible stories were mingled with tales of ghosts and strange nursery fables. They chased each other in and out, generating others as they went, and then came drowsiness, and Paul slept.

The class-meeting lasted an hour. It was very fervent and demonstrative; and when it was over the kind old lady who had given Paul the gingerbread asked the preacher home to dinner. She said that roasted turkey, wild duck, and pumpkin-pie were waiting for them; and Mr. Bates thought fondly what a treat it would be for Paul on his birthday. He was to preach again that afternoon, seven miles away, and so moved briskly toward the sulky.

"The poor fellow is asleep," said the preacher, seeing that the curling head was not thrust up at his approach. "I wonder of what he dreams?" He drew near as he spoke. Old Bob was munching his corn sedately; the sulky had a saucy air; the robe nestled in the front, with the tiny stool peeping from a corner; but Paul was not there. The preacher called aloud; the horses raised their ears in reply, and the wheels crackled in the frozen crust. He called again; some sleigh-bells jingled merrily, and then the pines moaned. He looked into the other vehicles; he watched for the little foot-tracks in the snow; he ran back to the old church, and searched beneath every pew.

"Brethren—sisters," he cried, "I cannot find my boy!" and his voice was tremulous. They gathered round him and some said that Paul had ridden away with the worldly lads; others, that he was hiding mischievously. But one silent bystander looked into the drifts, and traced four great boot-marks close to the sulky. He followed them across the road into the pines, and out into the road again, where they were lost in the multitude of impressions. "Brother," he faltered, " God give you strength ! your boy has been stolen—kidnapped !''

The old man staggered, but the kind old lady caught him, and as he leaned upon her shoulder his face grew hard and blanched ; then he removed his hat, and his gray hair streamed over his gaunt features. " Let us pray !'' he said.

The preacher plodded to his next appointment as if he had still a child, and his sermon was as full and straightforward. He announced his bereavement from the pulpit when he had done, and the whole country was alarmed and excited. He bore the tidings to his desolate home, and his stricken wife heard it with a stern resignation. Thenceforward he preached more of the burning pit, and less of the golden city ; his eyes were full of fierce light, and his visage grew long and ghastly. He denied himself all joys and comforts ; his prayers rang in the midnight through the gloomy parsonage ; and he toiled in the ministry as if reckless of life, and anxious to lose it in his Master's service. The end came at last ; the world closed over the grim couple, and they hoped through the grave's portal to find their child.

When Paul awoke from his nap in the sulky, he found himself far in the forest, and moving swiftly forward. A huge negro, with bloodshot eyes, was transferring him to an evil-looking white man, and he struggled in the latter's arms, crying for his papa.

The negro drew a long knife from his breast and flourished it before Paul's face. " Hold um jaw, or I kill um dead !'' he muttered. " Got um grave dug out yer.''

" O yer young yerlin !'' said the other man, boxing Paul's ears, " yer don't know yer own father, don't yer ? I'm yer parpa !''

" You are not,'' cried Paul. " Where are you taking me ? Where is the church, and the sulky, and old Bob ?''

The negro drove his knife so close to Paul's throat that the boy flinched and shrieked

" You dare to say fader to anybody," yelled the negro, " and I cut yo' heart out ! You dare to tell yer name, or yer fader's name, or wha yo come from, and I cut yo' eyes out ! I cut yo' heart and eyes out—do yo' yar ?"

The lad was cowed into cold, tearless terror ; he shrank from the glittering edge, and trembled at the giant's murderous expression. He thought they had brought him to this lonely spot to slay him, and he embraced silence as the only chance for his young life. He wondered if this were not one of his wild imaginings, or if it had not something to do with the punishment pronounced in the morning's fierce sermon.

The two men came to a ruined cabin after awhile ; it was buried in deep shade ; the logs were worm-eaten, and the clay chimney had fallen down. They climbed by a creaking ladder into the loft and laid Paul upon a ragged bed. A young negro woman and her child were there, and the boy saw that her foot was shackled to the floor, for the chain rattled as she moved. They gave him a piece of beef and a corn-cake, and stripping him of his tidy clothes, dressed him in the coarse blue drilling worn by slaves. The two men drank frequently from the same bottle, talking in low tones, and after a time both of them lay down and slept. The woman dandled her child to and fro, for it moaned painfully, and the pines without made a deep dirge. No birds trilled or screamed in this desert place, but a roaring as of loud waters was borne now and then on the twilight ; it was the bay close below them, making thunder upon the beach.

When Paul woke from his second sleep he was on the deck of a vessel. The shore lay beneath him, and the waves heaved behind. It was night ; the snow-flakes still filtered through the profound darkness, and the wind whistled in the rigging. A red lantern moved along the beach ; some voices were heard speaking

together, and one of them said : '' Don't be afraid of
the boy ; I have sold lots paler than him. Lick him
smartly if he gammons, and he'll tell no tales.''

Then they lifted the anchor aboard ; the tide floated
off the sloop ; they were soon scudding before the
wind under a freezing starlight. Two weary days
passed over Paul, of travel by land and water. They
came to the city of Richmond at last, and marched
him with five other unfortunates to the common slave-
pen. It was situated in a squalid suburb, surrounded
by a high spiked wall, and entered by an office from
which a watchman could observe the interior through
two grated doors. The pen consisted of a paved area
open to the sky, except on one side, where it was protected by a shelving roof, and of a jail or den. The
latter was walled up in a corner, but its inmates could
look out upon the area through a window in the door,
and their savage features revealed at the bars, so terrified Paul that he retreated to the opposite corner, afraid
to look towards them. Now and then they howled and
blasphemed ; for two were delirious from drunken-
ness and one was desperate from rage, and as they
moved like tigers to and fro, their irons clanked behind
them, dragging on the stone floor. A number of
women were huddled together beneath the roof, some
as fair as Paul, others as black as ebony. Some had
babes at their breasts, others had no regard for their
offspring, but sat stolidly apart while their children
cried for nourishment. In the open place a bevy of
the coarser inmates were holding a rude dance, a large
gray-haired man patted time or '' juber'' with his feet
and hands, calling the figures huskily aloud ; while the
women, with bright turbans tied around their heads,
grinned and screamed with glee as they followed the
measure with their large, heavy shoes.

Their efforts were directed not so much to grace
as to strength, for some kept up the dance for a whole
hour, divesting themselves of parcels of clothing as they
proceeded, and breathing hard as if weary to exhaustion.

The men applauded vociferously, coupling the names of the performers with wild ejaculations, but subsiding when the keeper appeared at the door occasionally to command less noise. Remote from the bacchanals crouched a serious group of negroes, who sang religious melodies, quite oblivious of their wild associates ; and in still another quarter a humorous fellow was enlivening his constituents with odd sayings and stories. Paul's heart sank within him as he looked upon these scenes. A sense of his degradation rushed over his young mind, and he threw himself upon the stones with his head in his hands, and wept hot tears of bitterness. Henceforth he should be a creature, a thing, a slave ! He must know no ambition but indolence, no bliss but ignorance, no rest but sleep, no hope but death ! Long leagues must interpose between himself and his home ; he should never kiss his mother again, or kneel with his father in the holiness of prayer. The recollections of his childhood would be crushed out by agonizing experiences of bondage ; he would forget his name and the faces of his friends, and at last preserve only the horrible consciousness that he was the chattel of his master !

The uproar continued far into the night ; one poor creature was delivered of a child in the hazy light of the morning. Paul was too young to think much of the matter, for his own sorrows engrossed him ; but he often recurred, in his subsequent career, to the romance of that bondwoman, and the soul which first felt the breath of life in the precincts of the slave shamble. What a childhood must it have had to look back upon—cradled in disgrace, sung to sleep with the simple melodies of grief, bred for no high purposes, but with the one distinct and dreadful idea of gain—to be filched from that dusky bosom when its little limbs had first essayed motion, that its feeble lips might lisp the accents of servility. Days and weeks passed over Paul, but he found no opportunity to tell his story. They kept him purposely that he might forget it, or feel the hopelessness of relating it. Other wretches came and went, till there remained none of the original inmates of his prison, and he learned to mingle with his coarse companions, joining sometimes in their gayety, and the high walls stood forever between his dreams and the sky till the sombre shadows were printed upon his heart.

The boy's turn came at length. He climbed the auction block before the gaping multitude, and leaped to show his suppleness. They were pleased with his still serious manner, the paleness of his skin, his thoughtful eyes, and the shining ringlets of his hair. Bids were bandied briskly upon him, and the auctioneer rattled glibly of the rare lot to be sold.

" Who owns the boy ?" cried a bystander.

" Colonel James Purnell, of the Eastern shore," answered the auctioneer. " His mother is a likely piece that will be in the market presently."

Tears came to Paul's eyes, but he held down the great sob that started to his throat, and called lustily : " It is a wicked story ! My father is white, and my mother is white ! I am not a slave, and they have stolen me !"

A loud, long laugh broke from the crowd, and the trader cracked a merry joke, which helped the pleasantry.

" We may call that a ' white lie,' " he said ; " but it is a peart lad, and the air with which he told it is worth a cool hundred ! Going at four hundred dollars—four hundred," etc.

The bidding recommenced. The article rose in esteem, and Paul was pushed from the block into the arms of a tall, angular person, who led him into the city. That afternoon he was placed in a railway carriage, and on the third night he was quartered in Mobile, at the dwelling of his purchaser. The tall person proved to be the agent of a rich old lady—a childless widow—who required a handsome, active lad, to wait upon her person, and make a good appearance in the drawing-room.

She had many servants ; but Paul was not compelled
to associate with them, and his duties were light,
though menial. When his mistress went out to walk,
he must carry her spaniel in his arms. He must stand
behind her at dinner, wielding a fly-brush of peacock's
feathers. He must run errands, and be equally ready
to serve her whims and satisfy her wants. She was
not harsh, but very petulant ; and had Paul been hasty
or high-tempered, his lot might have been a bitter one.
On the contrary, he was quiet, docile, and bashful,
and he pleased her marvellously. If he sometimes
wept for the happy past, or felt a child's strong yearn-
ing for something to love, he hid his grief from those
about him, and sought that consolation which the
world cannot take away in the simple prayers he had
conned from his mother. He was a slave, but not a
negro. His pleasures were not theirs, for he had
quick intelligence, and he shrank from their loud,
lewd glee. Their blood had thickened through generations of bondage, and trained in the harness of
beasts, they had become creatures of draught. His
had rippled bright and brisk through generations of
freedom, and a year could not drag him to their level.
He had learned to read and write, and it was his habit
to stand at the window in his leisure moments, adding
to his information from some pleasant book ; but his
mistress supposed that he was looking at the pictures
merely, till one day, entering the dining-room softly,
she heard him reading aloud. He had a sweet, boy's
voice, which somewhat pacified the anger she felt at
such presumption in a slave ; and though at first re-
buking him, she reconsidered the matter during the
evening, and bade him read to her from a new novel.
Henceforward Paul gained favor, and his mistress
found it convenient to employ him as an amanuensis.
She released him from menial duties, and gave him
neat attire, and it was wonderful how well these acces-
sories became him. He was unassuming, as before,
submitting with patience to his lot ; and at length he

became indispensable to Mrs. Everett. Her attach-
ment to books of fiction amounted to dissipation, and
the part that he bore in their perusal filled his warm
imagination till his fancies were brighter than romance
—they became poetry. The one great grief of his
life touched his whole face with a pensive melancholy,
but he forebore to tell them his true history again,
preferring to wait for some golden moment when he
might be believed and emancipated.

From the beginning Mrs. Everett's agent disliked
him. Wait was a Northern adventurer, cool, courageous, and ambitious, who had settled in the South with
the resolution of becoming rich, and he had pursued
his purpose with steady inflexibility. He was not a bad
man, but a bitter one, and Paul had in some sort divided Mrs. Everett's esteem from him. Previously he
had been her sole and undisputed adviser, and as she
was readily influenced, he hoped, in course of time, to
be acceptable as her second husband. He was young
and manly, and she was giddy and middle-aged. Her
relatives held him in contempt, but he had proved his
courage, and they did not care to cross him. But
with the coming of Paul he had lost somewhat of her
regard, and he had laid it to the boy's charge. Paul
read his calm purpose in his keen eyes, and he shuddered at the thought of some day falling into his relent-
less hands. He labored to conciliate his enemy, but
with little effect, until one afternoon, Wait told him to
obtain permission from Mrs. Everett and come to the
office. He dictated some ambiguous letters to Paul,
and gave him many papers to burn, meanwhile inspect-
ing a pair of long pistols which he took from a port-
manteau. It was late in the afternoon when he had
done, and then he bade Paul take the case of pistols,
slip quietly into the street, and walk straight on till he
was overtaken. He obeyed, not without suspicion,
and when he reached the city limits found the agent,
to his great surprise, seated in a carriage. Two other
persons attended him, and one, who was bald and

wore glasses, had a case of surgical instruments lying at his feet. Paul climbed to the driver's box, and they dashed along by the water-side, meeting a second carriage on their way. The last rays of sunset were streaming over the low landscape when both carriages stopped, their occupants dismounted, and Wait came to the front and reached up his hand to Paul.

" Good-by, boy," he said in a tone of unwonted tenderness; " remain here a moment and you will see me again !"

They filed along a dyke separating two swamps, and turning down to the beach, were hidden behind a line of cypress trees. For a few moments Paul only heard the roar of the surf, the noise of the distant town, and the short breathing of the sedate negro beside him. Then there were shouts, as of a person counting rapidly, and two reports so close that one seemed the echo of the other. A few minutes afterward the agent appeared, leaning upon the arms of his attendants. He was divested of coat and vest, and as he came nearer, bareheaded, Paul saw that his face was colorless and working as from deadly pain. His shirt was perforated close to the collar, and the blood flowing beneath had stained it to his waist, and dripped in a runnel from his boots. He fainted when he had taken his seat ; and as the carriage rolled away, Paul looked back toward the duelling-ground, and beheld two men bearing upon their shoulders a stiff, straight burden, wrapped in a cloak.

The second carriage passed him, driven swiftly, and it seemed to emit a chill draught upon Paul like the damp wind from a tomb ; it was the presence of death, at whose very mention we grow cold.

Wait had vindicated his courage, but at the expense of his life. He lingered on in agony many days ; and Paul so pitied him that he stole into his darkened chamber and begged to do him kindnesses. The grim man lay implacable, waiting for death ; but one night as he writhed with the dew upon his forehead, Paul heard him mutter, " My God ! my mother !"

The boy remembered a quaint text of Scripture : " Save me, O God ! for the waters have come in unto my soul :" and he repeated it in the strong man's ear. " Go on," cried Wait, rising upon his elbow ; " I . have heard that before : tell me the rest."

" I have the good book here," replied Paul. " I am sure it will be pleasant to you, sir, if you will let me read."

" Do so, boy ; I used to know it well. An old friend taught those strange words to me, but I have forgotten them now."

Paul read some soothing and beautiful Psalms, which took his companion's mind back to his native moun- tains, and the white spire of the village church where he had worshipped with his mother. The hard lines melted in his face as he listened, but Paul fall upon a bitter verse, and the agent's conscience began to trouble him. He could not look into the boy's eyes, for they seemed to rebuke him, and at last he com- manded Paul to stop.

It was midnight. They heard the great clock in the hall strike twelve, and all the household slumbered.

" Go to your mistress's room," said Wait ; " tell her that I must see her *now*—she must come at once. The morning may never come to me. Go ; God bless you !"

He called Paul back when he had got to the door, and added falteringly :

" My boy, do you say your prayers ?"

" Yes, sir."

" Would you mind thinking of me when you say them to-night ?"

" I do so every night, sir."

" Good-night !"

Paul heard the agent sobbing as he stole away ; but when he knocked at Mrs. Everett's door she answered petulantly, and at first she refused to rise. She had little self-denial ; it would pain her to enter a dying chamber ; and she would have left Wait to perish, had not some strange passage from the romance entered her head of dead folk, with secrets on their minds, haunting the living. It would be very terrible to be haunted, and the old woman was frightened into obedience. When she returned her mind was disquieted, and she made Paul stay in her room to compose her with cheerful talk. Finally she fell asleep, and he hastened to the agent's chamber. It was very dark within, and he waited a moment that the other might recognize him. Wait seemed to be in deep slumber, though Paul could not hear him breathe ; but as the lad ventured to place his head upon the quilt, it encountered a hand so cold and hard that it seemed to be marble. Paul knew that he need no longer remember his enemy in his prayers.

What transpired between his mistress and her agent at this dying interview Paul could not surmise, but he believed that it concerned himself. He perceived that Mrs. Everett treated him more considerately afterward ; and many times, as he looked up from a long silence, he found her regarding him inquisitively. She asked him strange questions once, bearing upon his early life, and he was almost encouraged to reveal the secret of his birth ; but she seemed to divine his purpose, and changed the theme. Something troubled her, he knew ; and when he applied himself to conciliate and cheer her, at those moments she suffered most. Had she loved the stern, ambitious man whose closed chamber still chilled her mansion ? Was it because she was childless, and travelling graveward ? Or did she cherish a mother's feeling for Paul, and wish that he was of her race, and worthy to be her son ? Toward each of these theories he inclined, favoring the last, and finally he concluded that she did not love, but feared him. He had grown tall and manly. An individual beauty, rather of mind than of face, developed in him, and his mistress had been prodigal of favors, so that

his dress and ornaments corresponded with his person.
He might have ruled, rather than served in her dwelling ; but content with the recognition of his equality,
he maintained the same modest guise, and his mistress
felt an uneasy pride in his promotion.   One day he
found her weeping, and when he spoke she answered
bitterly :

"Paul, you have ceased to love me ; you are ungrate-
ful ; you wish to be free—you would leave me !"

He responded pleasantly—for he had become familiar
with such moods—that he had found a new romance
which he would read.   It was not a long story, but a
thrilling one, and based upon the simple narrative of
Joseph in bondage.   The outline was true, the details
were fabulous, and the old lady marvelled that a theme
so trite could be so well embellished.   He read far
into the night, and she bade him leave the book upon
her table, that she might peruse it again.

"It is manuscript," he said, "and this is the only
copy."

"Why, Paul," she said, "how came you by it ?"

"I wrote it myself."

Paul was indeed the author, having filled in the sorrows of his hero from his own experiences.   Mrs.
Everett was loud in its praises ; she was sure that it
indicated genius, and she lay awake that night medi-
tating an act of charity and of justice.   She would
make a free man of Paul, and he should find in far
lands that equality which he could not obtain in his
own.   They would journey together.   He should
have means and advantages, and become her protégé
and heir.   But the strong self-love defeated this resolve.   If Paul were not bound to her by law, he might
forsake her, and she could not bear to lose him, for he
had become a part of her heart ; but when she broached
the matter, Paul gave his parole never to leave her
without consent.

He was still a slave, with the taint of a trampled
race in his blood, and he said nothing to Mrs. Everett

of his origin.   They crossed the seas ; they dwelt in pleasant places, beneath soft skies ; and Paul grew in knowledge.   But his patron was still harassed by some deep remorse.   She hurried him from city to city like the fabled apostate, and at length fell sick in London, on the eve of their return to America.   Paul gleaned from her ravings in delirium the cause of her unrest.   Wait had made known to her on the night of his decease the secret of the young man's origin, and had conjured her to do justice to the lad.   Her self-love had deterred her in consummating this duty, and conscience had therefore tortured her.   She was enabled to reach New York, where she left the preacher's son the bulk of her property, and received his gratitude and forgiveness before she died.

Paul was free—haunted no longer by premonitions of future suffering ; and his first impulse was to return to the Eastern shore and discover his desolate parents. His recollections of them were imperfect.   He preserved many trifling circumstances, though more important events were forgotten ; but as he made his way to the old village his heart beat high.   There were the negro quarters, the cornfields, the twisting fences, and, at last, the shady stone parsonage—recollections they seemed of objects beheld in a foggy dream.   They directed him to the Methodist Church—a prim, square structure in the centre of the village—a tavern on one side, a court-house and market on the other ; and when the sexton threw open a window, the bleared light fell upon a marble slab set in the wall :

" Near this spot lie the remains of
REV. TITUS BATES,
for two years Pastor of this Congregation,
and of PEGGY, his Wife.
' They have ceased from their labors, and their
works do follow them.' "

Paul's hopes fell.   He walked through the village friendless, and, impelled by his swift-coming fancies, strolled far into the suburbs. A crowd was collected round a squalid negro cabin, and, less by interest than by instinct, he bent his steps toward it.

" What is the matter, friend ?" he asked of a bystander.

" The boys hez scented kidnappers to this shanty," answered the man ; " and by doggy ! they going to trap 'em !"

The mob seemed to be fearfully incensed as Paul pushed close to the scene. There were said to be two of the man-stealers, both of whom had been very daring and successful. He heard their names called as Peter Gettis and Dave Goule, and the opinion was expressed that the first-named would not yield without a desperate struggle. The mob was hot and clamorous, and while a selected committee entered the den to search it, the rest brandished clubs and knives, and yelled for justice and blood. Word came at length that the kidnappers were concealed beneath the floor of the cabin ; and at the hint, a score of stalwart fellows began to pull up the planks, while their associates formed a wide circle around, prepared to prevent escape.

Finally, the cry arose : " Here they air ! This is them ! Drag 'em out ! Whoo-oop !"

The men within the cabin rushed through the doors and windows as if pursued, and a stalwart negro, with bloodshot eyes, almost naked, and flourishing a huge knife, staggered to the threshold, and glared fiercely round him.

The circle stood firm ; some were clubbing their cudgels, others lifting their blades, and here and there along the line rang out the click of a pistol.

" Come, Pete," cried one of the ringleaders ; " you're treed, Pete ! Don't be a fool, but give yourself in."

The negro gnashed his teeth, and his wild eyes glared like coals of fire.

" Do you give me faih-play ?" he bellowed, extending the knife.

"Yes, Pete, yes," answered the multitude.

"Then look heah," answered the wretch, drawing his knife across his throat. He staggered into the air like an ox, cursing as he came. They parted to avoid him, and as he reached a fence, a few rods from the cabin, he leaned upon it, and swaying to and fro, raised his horrible eyes to the sky.

Paul recognized his ancient captor with a thrill and a silent prayer. Vengeance had come in His own good time, and Paul felt no bitterness toward the poor fellow, but prayed forgiveness for his slipping soul.

The second offender burrowed so remotely that the mob could not drag him from his covert. They struck at him with knives, and hired dogs to creep beneath the logs and rend him, but in vain. At length one of the ringleaders obtained a torch, and the cabin was fired in several places. The flames spouted into the night, bursting from the small windows, and the roof fell in with a crash, scattering ashes and red-hot coals. They could hear the shriek of the victim now, and he was seen dancing among the fire-brands, for the blaze encircled him like an impassable wall. He made a desperate rush at length to overleap the fire, and his figure, magnified by the red light, looked gigantic as he sprang high in the air. A dozen pistols clattered together—the man fell heavily forward, tossing up his scorched hands, and the frizzing, cracking timbers closed darkly above him to the thunder of his executioners' huzzas.

Paul did not reveal himself. He left the village stealthily, and journeyed northward. Years afterwards a name was added to the tablet in the old church :

> "Here lie also the Remains of the
> REV. PAUL BATES.
> 'He went about doing good.'"

THE JUDGE'S LAST TUNE.

THE Judge took down his fiddle,
   And put his feet on the stove,
And heaved a sigh from his middle
   That might have been fat, or love ;
He leaned his head on the mantel,
   And bent his ear to the strings,
And the tender chords awakened
   The echoes of many things.

The Bar had enjoyed the measure,
   The Bench and Senate had been
Amused at the simple pleasure
   He drew from his violin ;
But weary of power and duty,
   He had laid them down with a sigh,
Exhausted of life the beauty,
   And he fiddled he knew not why.

In the days when passion budded,
   And she in the churchyard lain
Came over his books as he studied
   With an exquisite pang of pain.
He played to his sons their mother's
   Old favorites ere she wed ;
Those tunes, like hundreds of others,
   Were requiems of the dead.

They lay in the kirk's inclosure :
   All three, in the shadows dim,
In a cenotaph's cynosure
   That waited for only him.
Who sat with his fiddle tuning
   On the spot where his fame was won,
On the empty world communing,
   Without a wife or a son.

And he drew his bow so plaintive
  And loud, like a human cry,
That the light of the shutter darkened
  From somebody passing by.
A young man peeped at the pensive
  Great man, so familiar known ;
His features, if inoffensive,
  Were like to the judge's own.

" Come in," cried the politician —
  " Come not," his soul would have said—
" Thou bringest to me a vision
  Of a sin ere thy mother wed,
When I, wild boy from college,
  Her humble desert o'ercame,
And we hid the guilty knowledge
  Beneath thy father's name."

The youth delayed no longer,
  His sense of music strong,
Nor knew of his mother's wronger,
  Nor that she had known a wrong ;
Deep in the grave the secret
  Her husband might never guess,
He stood before his father
  With a loyal gentleness.

" What tune, fair boy, desirest
  My old friend's worthy son ?—
Say but what thou requirest,
  And for father's sake 'tis done."
" Oh ! Judge, our State's defender,
  Whose life has all been power,
Play me the tune most tender,
  When thou felt thy greatest hour !"

The old man thought a minute,
  Irresolutely stirred,
As if his fiddle's humor
  Changed like a mocking-bird ;
Then, as his tears came raining
  Upon the plaintive chords,
He played the invitation
  To the sinner, of his Lord's.

" Come, poor and needy sinners,
   And weak and sick, and sore,
The patient Jesus lingers
   To draw you through the door."
It was a tune remembered
   From old revival nights,
In crowded country churches,
   Where dimly blew the lights

And boys grew superstitious
   To hear the mourners wail.
The great man, self-degraded,
   So sighed his contrite tale
In notes that failed for sobbing,
   To feel Heaven's sentence well,
That took away his Isaac
   And blessed the Ishmael.

.   .   .   .   .   .

Low in the tomb of glory
   The old man's ashes lie—
Unuttered this my story,
   Unwritten to human eye ;
And the young man, blessed and blessing,
   Walks over the shady town,
The evil passions repressing,
   And his head bent humbly down.

Perhaps he marvels why treasure
   Of the judge to his credit is set,
And an old revival measure
   Should have been the statesman's pet.
But he hears the invitation,
   And sees the streaming eyes
Of the old man lost to the nation,
   And forgiven beyond the skies.

DOMINION OVER THE FISH.

" A GIFT-BOOK for Christmas. A poem preferred. Limited text, and profuse illustration." What should it be?

As if by invocation, the Ancient Mariner rose before me ! He stood in the doorway of my office, and held me with his glittering eye. He lifted his skinny hand to his long gray beard, and then gravely tipped his oiled hat. " The reader for Spry, Stromboli, and Smith ?"

I had that honor, and handed him a chair. He sat in it after the manner of a flounder, concentrated his eye upon me like a star-fish, and produced a roll of manuscript with the fluttering claws of a lobster. Then he stirred and squirmed, like an elderly eel, looking distrustfully into the vestibule. I closed the door and begged to be informed of his business.

" I have a great work for you," he said mysteriously, proffering his manuscript. As he leaned over to do this, I saw a shining something on the top of his head, but the thick white hair concealed it when he resumed his place. The manuscript smelled as if it had contained mackerel, and looked as if it had come from the bottom of the sea. I found, curiously enough, some fish-scales adhering to it, and its title very oddly confirmed these testimonies—" Five Years in the Great Deep."

I glanced at the author with some surprise. He was the quaintest of mariners, and if I had met him leagues under the sea, I should have thought him in his proper element. His locks were like dry sea-weed ;

his cheeks were so swollen that they might have contained gills, but this was probably tobacco. When he
wiped his nose with a handkerchief like a scoop-net,
some shells and pebbles fell from his pocket, and his
ears flapped like a pair of ventrals. I remarked as he
pursued the lost articles over the floor, that he wore
a microscope strapped in a leathern case, and a geo-
logical hammer belted to his side. He walked as if
habituated to swimming, and when he shrugged his
shoulders I expected to see a dorsal fin burst out of
the back of his jacket. He might have been sixty
years of age, but looked much older, and behaved like
a well-born person, though, superficially judged, he
might have lived in Billingsgate.

"A good title for a fiction," I said encouragingly.

"I never penned a line of fiction in my life," exclaimed my visitor sternly.

Referring to the copy again, I saw that it purported
to be the work of "Rudentia Jones, Fellow of the
Palæontologic Society, Entomologist to the Institute
for Harmonizing the Universes, and Ruler of Sub-
aqueous Creation, excepting the Finny Mammalia."

"Ah! I see," said I; "a capital title for a satire!"

"Life is too grave, and science too sacred," replied
my visitor, "for the indulgence of idle banterings.
The work is mine; I am its hero; and it is all true."
He wore so earnest a face, and looked so directly and
intelligently at me, that I forebore to smile. "I have
travelled in strange countries," he said; "Nature has
been bountiful in her revelations to me; indeed my
experiences have been so individual, that I sometimes
discredit them myself. I do not complain that others
ridicule them."

He spoke in the manner of one devoted to his species; and an easy dignity, which some trace to high
birth and the consciousness of dominion, became him
very naturally. The eldest of the admirals, or old
Neptune himself, could not have seemed more kingly;
but once or twice he started at a noise from the pub-

lishing-house, as if longing to get back to his legiti-
mate brine. I told him to leave the manuscript in my
hands for a fortnight, that I might form an opinion as
to its claims for publication.

"No!" he said quickly. "It is not a girl's romance, or a boy's poem, or the strollings of a man-
errant : it is of such rare value that gold cannot purchase it ; it is so priceless that I cannot own it myself ; it is like the air, or the water, or the light, or the
magnet—the property of all the peoples. It must not
leave my sight. I must read it to you now !"

He literally held me with his eye. He stood erect
dilating, until he seemed to reach the height of a main-
mast, as long and lank and brown as the subject of
the veritable *rime ;* and his ears, contracted, flapped like
the pectorals of a flying-fish. It was uncertain whether
he was going to fly or swim, or seize and shake me. I
believed him to be either a lunatic or an apparition ;
but when the frenzy of the moment was over, he became a very harmless, kindly, and grave old gentleman, who begged my pardon for transgressing decorum
in the enthusiasm for his "great work." He still
smelled abominably of fish, but I could not take it
into my heart to be harsh with this most pertinacious
of authors.

I had been but a short time in the service of Spry,
Stromboli & Smith, and my nerves had not yet been
exercised by sensitive and eccentric writers. I had
led a vagabond career myself, and had frequent reason, in my incipient literary days, to be grieved with
publishers' "readers ;" and when promoted to the
same exalted place, I resolved to be charitable, careful,
and obliging—to do as I would be done by—to crush
no delicate Keats, to enrage no Johnson, by slight,
prejudice, or deprecation. But to suffer the infliction
of a crack-brained old naturalist, repeating an inter-
minable manuscript in my own office, went beyond
my best resolve ! Still there was little to do. It
would be a paltry task to select a poem for illustration,

and had not this same Ancient Mariner suggested an admirable one ?

" I can grant your request in part, Mr. Jones," I said at length ; " you may read one hour ; and if at the end of that period I do not think favorably of your article, you must promise to read no further."

The old gentleman gave his parole at once, took a pair of great green spectacles from a sea-grass case, and blowing his nose again, rained pebbles and marine shells over the whole office. When he took the manuscript from my hand, I saw the shining something distinctly on the top of his head ; and when he sat back to read, he was a perfect copy of a dry old king-fish, looking through a pair of staring, glaring, green eyes. Without more ado, and in a rippling kind of voice, as of the rushing of deep water, the old naturalist read the following introduction to a most wonderful manuscript:

" At a very early period of my life I manifested an inclination for the study of the sciences. In my eighteenth year I submitted a theory of inter-stellar telegraphing to the Gymnotian Academy. It was my purpose to have placed the papers simultaneously before the scientific bodies of each of the seven planets in our constellation, but having no capital, the design failed, though I was complimented thereupon by the ' Institute for Harmonizing the Universes,' and elected a contributing member of that society. For several years I petitioned annually for outfit and transportation to Scilly Islands,* on the Ecliptic Circle, where I purposed to develop my scheme of transferring a portion of our globe to the system of Orion. In this I was opposed by the Palæontologic Society, on the ground that some valuable fossils were presumed to be there ; and Parliament, thinking that my protests were subversive of the law of gravity, rejected them. A number of projects, each of which, I firmly believe,

---

* This group of Scilly Islands is in the South Pacific : not on Land's End.

would have benefited my kind, and facilitated correspondence between all created beings, terminated un-
fortunately, and my relatives at length placed it out of
my power to continue these philanthropic exertions.
For some years I was denied the ear of man, and in
the interval my hair grew gray and my body a trifle
faint.   But the lofty impulses of youth survived.   My
mind could not be imprisoned, and I held communication with the stars through the grating of my chamber
in the still midnight.   At last the relief came.   I had
long prayed for it !   My deliverer was Sirius, the
brightest of the celestial intelligences.   He shone upon
my window bars with an intense, concentrated light,
and they reddened and melted before daybreak.   I
fled to Glasgow in the month of April, 184-, and obtained a captain's clerkship on the whaler Crimson
Dragon.

"We took in water at the Shetland Islands, and
sailing north-westward, skirted the coast of Greenland,
whence, cruising in a southerly direction, we lay off
Labrador, and waited for our prey.   Our crew was
fifty men, all told.   Our captain had been a whaler
thirty-eight years, and had killed five hundred and six
animals or eight more than the renowned Scoresby.
We carried seven light-boats for actual service, and
twenty-seven thousand feet, or more than five miles, of
rope.   Three men kept watch, day and night, in the
'crow's-nest,' at the maintop ; but though we beat
along the whole coast, through Davis' Strait, and
among the mighty icebergs of Baffin's Bay, we saw no
cetaceous creatures, save twice some floundering porpoises, and thrice a solitary grampus.   With these beings I endeavored to open communication, but they
made no intelligible responses.   The stars also of this
latitude failed to comprehend my signals, from which I
concluded that they were less intelligent than those of
more temperate skies.   But with the animalcules of
the sea I obtained most gratifying relations.   A series
of experiments with the *infusoria* satisfied me that they

were not loath to an exchange of information, and
finally they followed the ship by myriads, so that all
the waves were full of fire, which the sailors remarked ;
and fearful of being observed, I ceased my experiments
for a time.

" On the evening of the fifth Saturday of our cruise,
I waited till the changing of the watch ; then I stole
noiselessly upon deck, and secreted myself behind a
life-boat which hung at the side of the vessel. The
helmsman was nodding silently upon his tiller ; two
seamen sat motionless upon the bow, and the lookout
party in the crow's-nest talked mutteringly of our ill-
luck as they scanned the horizon. The Northern
Lights were pulsing like some great radiating heart,
and the sea was alternately flame and shadow. The
headlands of Labrador lay to the south—bare, bound-
less, precipitous ; and to the east a glittering iceberg
floated slowly towards us, like a palace of gold and
emerald. The ship rolled calmly upon the long swells,
the ripples plashing in low, lulling monotone, and her
hull and spars were reflected darkly beneath me. I
drew a long gray hair from my temple, and subjected
it to a gentle friction between my palm and finger ;
then I pricked my wrist, and leaning forward, placed it
against my heart : five blood-drops—symbols of the
five types of organized creation—fell simmering into
the depths, and the scintillant hair, floating after them,
described a true spiral. In an instant the Aurora grew
bright to blindness ; there was a rush of infinite stars,
and a host of beautiful beings fluttered to the surface
of the sea, within the shadow of the ship ! A gull
darted along the water, and in the far distance I heard
the bellow of the huge Greenland whale. All animate
nature had acknowledged my message ; I had touched
the nerve of the universes !

" ' Blow me if there warn't a whale, Ben ! ' said one
of the men in the maintop.

" ' My eyes ! but it wor like it,' replied the other.

" Fearful of being remarked, I slipped below, a second

time disappointed, but with such exultant feelings that
I tried in vain to sleep. The intimacy of species and
their common language, lost in the degeneracy of the
first human beings, were about to be restored by me.
Confusion had overcome the counsels of the count-
less things which had talked and dwelt together in
the past, but science was about to win back from sin
the great secret of communication. I should trans-
late the scream of eagles and the cooing of doves ;
I should hear the gossip of my household kittens,
and speak familiarly with the mighty hippopotami.
The serpent should teach me his traditions, and the
multitude of mollusks should develop the mysteries of
their sluggish vitality ; nay, the plurality of worlds
should be demonstrated, and with the combined intelligences of all the systems, we should wrest the
mysteries of life, matter, and eternity from their Divine
repository !

" I lay awake all night revelling in these anticipations,
and at dawn was quite weak of body. It was now
the Sabbath, and at nine o'clock all hands were summoned to the poop-deck for the customary worship.
I lay upon a coil of rope, when the mate commenced
to read the service, and a deep drowsiness came over
me. The lesson was a part of the first chapter of
Genesis—the weird history of creation. He had reached
the twenty-eighth verse when I dropped asleep. It
could have been only an instant's forgetfulness, for
when I awoke he had not finished the reading of the
same verse, but in that instant a vision had passed before me.

" A female of marvellous beauty rose from the water.
I had seen the long green locks, the eyes of azure, and
the glossy neck—it was Tethys, the queen of the sea-
nymphs. She was begotten of humidity in the remote
beginning, and seemed even now cloudy and incor-
poreal. Euripius, the divinity of whirlpools, lay in the
waves at her feet, projecting a spectrum of spray, in
an arch, above her head.

" ' Man,' she said, or rather rippled, for it was like
the even voice of waters, ' your love of nature, the
boundlessness of your kindness, the daring of your
speculation, the profoundness of your introspection,
have made you one of us. Awake, and hear our de-
cree ! '

" She melted into vapor, and disappeared. I
opened my eyes. The crew were grouped about the
deck, the mate was reading the lesson, the words which
I heard were : " Have Dominion over the Fish !"

" ' A fall ! a fall ! ' was shouted from the maintop.
The men on watch had discovered the long-expected
prey.

" ' Man the boats ! ' cried the captain ; ' all hands
be spry ! Where away, look out ? '

" ' Sou'-west ! ' answered the crow's-nest, ' about
two leagues. There must be hoceans of 'em ! They
'eave like water-spouts, and, lor ! how they lobtail ! '

" The seven boats were arranged in curved shape,
so as to form a semicircle around the animals ; and
the captain's, of which I took the helm, formed the left
tip of the crescent. We pulled steadily for a half-hour
over a smooth sea, and came at length so close to our
victims that we could count them. Truly it was ' a
fall '! A few cubs played recklessly around the surface ; but there was an enormous bull, whose bulk
was much greater than that of the ship's hull, which
came once in full view, dived vertically, and beat the
water with his terrible tail, making such billows that a
storm seemed to be raging. The other animals swam
in the froth and foam thus developed, now plunging
to the far depths, now shooting their huge bodies into
the air, and falling with a splash, as of the emptying of
the ocean. The scene was so exciting that even my
wonderful discoveries passed out of mind. Our oars
dipped noiselessly ; the crews were silent ; the harpoon-
ers stood, each in the bow of his launch, with naked
weapons extended, waiting to strike. The first opportunity occurred to the launch on our extreme right.

At the distance of twenty yards the executioner hurled his javelin full into the back of the great bull ; a roar ensued and a frightful leap. The other creatures repeated the agonized cry, and they swam southward with the velocity of a ship under full sail.

" ' Now, lads, bend your oars ! ' shouted the captain through his trumpet. The entire length of rope unwound directly from the reel or ' bollard ' of the first launch, and the line of a second boat was attached forthwith ; a third and a fourth were annexed, but the whale exhibited no sign of exhaustion, and dragged his pursuers like the wind. A fifth and a sixth line spun out. The captain's cheek grew pale, and he opened his clasp-knife with a curse upon his lips. There remained the line of our boat alone : unless the monster stopped within ten minutes, we should lose every foot of the ship's cordage, and this last rope would have to be severed. Tremulously a seaman attached it ; it was whirled out as if by a locomotive. The oars moved like light, but no human activity could approach that of our victim. He nearly swamped the launch, and the friction of the bollard threatened to set it ablaze.

" ' What devil of the deep is this ? ' said the captain, bending forward with his blade. The sailors ceased with hot faces, and stared aghast. I seemed to hear calling voices ; I grew faint and blind. The bollard snapped with a dead, dull sound ; I was entangled in the stout twine, and tossed into the sea. Some oars were thrown overboard, that I might be buoyed up. Three of the launches were turned toward me, and the seamen called aloud that I should keep up courage. But the line pulled me downward ; my heart ceased to beat ; I beheld with indescribable terror the pale surface receding, and the dark shapes of the vessels above me were finally lost to view. I knew that at the first inhalation the brine would fill my mouth and lungs ; I held my breath hard, and tried to pray. Down, down, down into the blue depths—a cycle of protracted years it seemed! My ears were stunned with strange noises; my lips parted, and at length the sea rushed into my throat; for an instant I seemed to strangle, but I did not perish.

"The fluid was mysteriously expelled from me. I breathed as freely of the water as a moment before I had breathed of the air! A weight was lifted from my brain, which had before been crushing it, and my temples grew suddenly cool. A spiracle had developed at the apex of my cranium, and I exuded water through a cavity or 'blow-hole' in the top of my head, like the cetacea around me!"

(The naturalist here paused and ran his hand through his hair. The shining something among his gray locks revealed itself as a plate of silver, circular in shape, covering what had evidently been an opening in the skull. He looked less like a man than ever, and when, consulting a glutinous old chronometer, like a jelly-fish, he found that his hour was passing, he begged so earnestly to be allowed to finish his "Introduction," that I gave him leave. A boy coming in with copy so frightened him, however, that I thought he was going to turn upon his stomach, and swim away through the window.)

"I became sensible directly of three organic changes: my heels clave together, my feet flattened, and my toes turned out, like a caudal fin; my integument grew thick and hard, and my blood thin and chill. But these conditions being novel to me, and my fears only equalled by my wonder as yet, I was paralyzed, and continued to sink. I had descended about one hundred fathoms, and was experiencing a strange oppression, as of the forcing together of my bones, when I heard a sonorous voice close below me say: 'If you go any deeper, you will sustain a pressure of twenty atmospheres, and may not get back at all.'

"I looked beneath, and to my horror a huge whale was coming upward with extended jaws. His half-human eyes were turned benignantly upon me; but he

was evidently in pain, and from a point in his back,
where a broken harpoon still remained, gouts of blood
curdled upward, coloring the water.   His vocal power
lay in his spiracle, and he said again :

" ' I should have been asphyxiated in five minutes.'

" ' Who is it that speaks ? ' I faltered.   ' Leviathan,
king of the sea, be merciful ! '

" ' I am called *New England Tom* by the creatures
of the upper element,' answered the whale, ' although
falsely thought to be of the family of the Spermaceti ;
but though my exploits have recommended me to my
species, I am not equal to the high title you have given
me.   *That* is possessed by You and our sovereign Jonah
only ! '

" The conviction rushed upon me that I had, indeed, ' Dominion over the Fish ' !

" ' I have suffered this wound for your majesty's
sake,' said the whale again ; ' for I had been deputed
to wait in this latitude for your arrival, and convey
you to our sovereign.   But though I am now in the
third century of my age, I can survive a dozen such
prickings, and if I chose could shiver the Crimson
Dragon with a blow of my tail, as in 1804 I stove the
Essex, and made driftwood of her spars.'

" In an instant I was seated within the mighty maw
of this famous monster.   His jaw-bones were forty feet
in length ; the roof of his mouth was fifteen feet high,
and formed of a spacious arch of " balleen," or whale-
bone.   His crescent-shaped tail, thirty-five feet from
tip to tip, swept the depths twice or thrice ; and when
we emerged into the air, the blood spouted from his
pores, and he threw cataracts of water through his
spiracle.   I saw the Crimson Dragon some miles away,
but there were no traces of her boats.   The crews of
the launches were fathoms deep in the ocean !

" I passed the cape of Greenland, rounded the base
of Mount Hecla, and was escorted to the abode of the
king of the cetacea by a multitude of his subjects.   A
submarine island, forty fathoms from the surface, had

been occupied three thousand years by this venerable
person. He came out to meet me upon the back of a
mighty ' rorqual,' and a body-guard of four hundred
picked narwhals swam before him. Fifty white whales
surrounded their monarch, and a host of dolphins,
grampuses, and porpoises brought up the rear. Ban-
ners of dyed seal-skin bore his arms—three gourds,
argent, upon a field *vert ;* and with these were carried
as trophies the wrecks of ships, including the identical
shallop whence he was expelled on the voyage to
Tarshish. But, marvellous beyond all, the ' great fish '
(falsely so translated, since no cetaceous creature can
be denominated a *fish*) into which he was received still
lived, and accompanied him. It was now the eldest
of the species, but very sprightly, and burdened with
dignities. The Seer-King saluted gravely, and gave
me a draught of spirits, distilled from the fronds of a
rare sea-tangle. His long tenure in the deep had obliter-
ated much of the similitude to man, but his memory of
terrestrial matters was extraordinary. The weeds were
wrapped about his head after the manner of a crown,
and he carried a sceptre of walrus tusk. He told me
that his original three days' experience under the sea
had so cooled his blood, that the suns of Nineveh
parched him, and he had cried for cooling water. I
informed him that Nineveh no longer existed, at which
he was gratified beyond measure ; for his only knowledge of events happening on the earth had been derived from the wrecks which had sunk into his domain.
I found that he was badly informed upon matters of
science, and he heard my theories of harmonizing the
universes with impatience. In his days, he said, no
such ideas were broached, and he was indifferent to
the intellectual development of his subjects.

" My visit was brief, for, though the palace of Jonah
had a sepulchral grandeur about it—a mighty cavern
beneath the waves—yet the glittering stalactites which
studded the roof, and the cold columns of ice support-

ing its halls, nearly froze me, and at length I made ready to depart.

"An escort of 'thrashers,' or grampuses, accompanied me. The Seër-King would have detached a cohort of white whales, but the animosity of my tribes might have provoked combat. I left the cetacea with some foreboding. They were allied in some degree to man ; they were capable of some human impressions ; their blood was warm like mine ; they breathed with lungs ; they had double hearts ; and nourished kindness for their offspring. But I was now about to be delivered over to the cold, cruel, gluttonous tribes of the fish. The family of sharks received me. They could not be counted for multitude. The terrible *requiem* of the storm—the cannibal white shark—welcomed me with open jaws ; the blue shark flung up his caudal for joy ; the fox-shark lashed the sea ; the northern shark glared through his purblind orbs ; the hammer-head dilated his yellow irides ; the purple dog-fish made a low purring huzza ; and the spotted eyes of the monk-fish glistened with satisfaction. The hound-shark, the basking-shark, and the port-beagle were not less loyal ; and these, the most perfectly organized of my cartilaginous tribes, handed me over to the deep-swimming Norwegian 'sea-rat.' Thus I kept steadily southward, the water growing warmer hour by hour, now riding on the serrated snouts of saw-fishes, now moving in the midst of battalions of sword-fish, now acknowledged by the great pike, now vaulting above the surface on the backs of flying-fish, now clinging to the spines of sturgeons, now passing through illimitable shoals of cod, now borne by the swift sea-salmon, now dazzled by the golden scales of the carp, now passing over miles of flat-fish, now hailed by monster conger-eels, now swimming down files of leering hippocampuses, now received by congregations of staid aldermanic lobsters. The torpedo telegraphed my coming to the tribes before, and at last I reached my abode, on the line of the equator, in mid-Atlantic.

" The magnitude and beauty of my court no mind can realize. A truncated cone of granitic rock, whose base extended to the profoundest depths of the sea—even to the region of perpetual fire—formed with its upper plane a circular lagoon at the surface of the ocean. Geysers or volcanoes of fresh water gurgled up through the centre of this palace, and vast submarine groves, intermixed with meadows, extended for leagues along its sides. My household consisted en·tirely of silver and golden carp, but my guards were of the loyal and gentle, yet courageous and powerful xiphias (sword-fish). These barred the unlicensed ingress of my subjects, and if the adventurous foot of man should profane my lagoon, I could close its inlet and cover it with floods. The dim aisles of the waters were full of wonderful lights : combinations of colors, unknown above, were here developed in gigantic *fuci*, around whose boles the scarlet tangle climbed, and parasites of purple and emerald played upon their rinds. Some of these forests pointed upward toward the sun ; some grew downward, deriving light and heat from the incandescent gulfs. My state apartments were built of coral, in wondrous architecture, and trumpet-weed clothed their battlements. Some cavernous recesses were lit with constellations of shining zoophytes, and there were floors of pearl, studded with diamonds. I could stroll through marvellous archways, gathering jewels at every step, or wander in my royal meadows, among the wrecks and spoils of hurricanes ; or rising through the mellow depths, sit among the palms of the lagoon, watching the white sails of ships or studying the awfulness of the storm.

" For a time I secluded myself, theorizing upon the policy of my government. My dominions were vast and venerable ; they comprehended two thirds of the surface of the globe ; no deluges had destroyed them, and they had been peopled ages before the coming of man. Life here inhabited forms, vegetable and animal, to which the greatest terrestrials were puny. But the darkness which of old rested on the face of the deep, now shadowed its depths. There was no *mind* here. These gigantic beings were shapes without souls. How should I reason with creatures who could not feel, whose heads could not know till to-morrow that their members had been severed to-day—some of whom, in a single moment, passed their whole existences, and fulfilled all the functions of eating, drinking, and generating—who were not only incapable of thoughts, affections, and emotions, but who could not see, smell, hear, taste, or touch ? But such subjects are among the afflictions of all wise rulers, and I resolved to conclude upon nothing till I had visited every part of my dominions.

"During three years of travel I classified the fishes anew, all previous enumeration being paltry, and made the notes and queries which form the staple of my manuscript. I found fresh-water creatures to which the sheat-fish would be a morsel, and hydras to which the fabled sea-serpent would be a worm. I ascended the rivers with the salmon, and fathomed the motives of the climbing-perch. I heard the narrative of a *siluris* tossed out of a volcano, and talked with a had-. dock which produced at a birth more young than there are men upon the globe. I have noted the harlequin-angler, which lived three weeks in Amsterdam, hopping about on his fins like a toad ; the sucking-fish which adhered to Marc Antony's galley and held it fast ; the horned-fish (*fil en dos*) which the savages discard from their nets in terror and prayer ; and the sprats which rise with vapors into the clouds, and are rained back into the sea. I have collected the traditions of many of these beings, and have translated some of their ballads. There is music under the ocean ; but most of the fishes sing with their fins, beating the water to rude measures. Among the traditions of all the tribes is that of a time when the waters were peaceful and the fishes happy, when none were rapacious, when death was unknown, when no storms lashed the ripples into billows, and when beings of the upper air bathed at the surface, and the fishes rendered them homage. But some foul deed of which the finny folk were guiltless brought confusion into the waters ; the ocean covered all the globe, corpses sank into the depths and were devoured, nets were let down from above, strange fires were kindled beneath, and whirl-pools, water-spouts, storms, and volcanoes began.

" I devoted a fourth year to perfecting my system of organic communication, and made some advance to-ward developing life in inorganic matter. From this latter attainment it would be but a step to *perpetuate* life, and I should thus restore immortality to man. But the shark family having threatened to revolt, I left off my investigations for some months, and organized a military force, with which I massacred the malcon-tents till my subjects swam in blood. Returning vic-toriously at the head of my legions, a sad incident occurred. A ship was crossing our line of march, and I had an unaccountable curiosity to hear something of terrestrial affairs. Five sawfish, at my bidding, staved in the ship's bottom, and she sank almost in-stantly. The corpses of the drowned drifted slowly down, and as I passed among them, turning up the faces, I recognized in one the features of my mother !

" After a season of remorse I continued my investi-gations, but a novel and unexpected discovery de-ranged my plans, and wrought a change in my destiny.

" The subtlest forms of matter, as commonly known, are the imponderables—light, heat, magnetism, and electricity. I had concluded that these were mani-festations of some still subtler form, and that this was *life*, beyond which lay the ethereal elements (called *principles*) of mind and soul—soul being ultimate and eternal. To demonstrate this I resolved to descend as far as possible into the depths of the sea, and ex-amine the beings which dwelt in the remotest darkness. The conical shape of my island allowed me to descend within its shelving interior, and yet sustain no great atmospheric pressure. I selected a sturgeon, whose body was so powerfully plated that he could not be crushed, and his long-pointed shape gave him great facility for penetrating dense waters.· I attached a phosphorescent light to his caudal, that I might not lose him in the gloom, and he preceded me along the sloping interior. We passed the foundations of my court, bade adieu to the deep-swimming hydras, left the profoundest polypi behind, and came at length to uninhabited regions, three thousand fathoms below the surface. My pioneer here suffered great inconvenience, and only by the most vigorous efforts was able to progress at all. The blackness was literally tangible, and our lantern, at most, only ' darkness visible.' By threat and persuasion I forced him forward, hardly able to make headway myself. He swept the almost solid element with his powerful tail, depressed his sharp snout, sucked a long breath, and we darted forward simultaneously. There was a cracking as of bones forced together, and my cranium seemed to split. We shot out of the density into lighter water, and the momentum carried us fifty fathoms beyond !

" We had passed out of the limit of solar attraction, and were being drawn toward the centre of the earth !

" Before, we had been descending ; now, we were rising. The fluid grew rarer and warmer as we proceeded, the darkness more luminous, and at last we became visible to each other, swimming in a ruby and transparent liquid, unlike any aspect or part of our native domain. The fluid became so rare finally, that the sturgeon was unable to go farther, kept down by his superior gravity. Some lights glimmering above us, and some mysterious sounds alarming him, he turned and fled. I was left alone.

" I reached the surface of this peaceful sea. A scene lay before me more beautiful than any wonder of the deep. I knew that I was among immortals, and that this was ' Happy Archipelago '!

" The surface was calm. Some purple islets were

sprinkled here and there, and creatures marvellously fair were basking in the roseate waters. They looked like angels half way out of heaven. Their faces were of a silvery hue ; their hairs shone on the stream like tremulous beams of light ; their eyes were of a tender azure, and their bosoms rose and fell as if they were all dreaming of blessedness. Some strains of ravishing harmony that were floating among the islands ceased when I appeared, and I thought I heard the snapping of a lute-string. All the spirits started at once. They were crescent-shaped, and stood upon their nether tips. A star upon their foreheads shone like a pure diamond. They saw me and vanished !

" All but one ! She was the fairest of the spirits, and looked, thus frightened, like the pale new moon. The violet veins faded from her lids, and her blue eyes were full of wonder. I felt as if, for the first time, a sinless being had looked upon me, and my heart grew so black and heavy that I sank a little way. I feared to breathe, for she might vanish. I wished to lie forever with her face shining upon me. What were science, and dominion, and the secret of man's immortality to one pure glance like hers ? In the agony of my soul I spoke : " Spirit ! Immortal ! Woman ! O stay ! Speak to me ! '

" ' Who are you ? Whence do you come ? You are not of us, nor of our element.'

" The voice was like a disembodied sound, coming from nothing, floating in space eternally.

" ' I am a creature of a cursed race—ruler of a blighted domain—a realm filled with violence : it lies beneath you.'

" The pale face grew tender ; the star on the forehead grew dim, like a tearful eye. She pitied me.

" ' There are beings above us,' she said, " winged beings, that talk with us sometimes ; but nothing below. Are *they* sorrowful as you are ? Are their brows all heavy with sadness like yours ? Why are they un· happy ? '

" I wept and moaned.

" ' They have not your pure eyes ; they cannot hear your voice. They have sinned.'

" She glided toward me. I felt my gray hairs dropping one by one ; my heavy heart grew light ; my groans softened to sighs.

" A shape came suddenly between us.

" I knew the long green locks, and the glossy neck. It was Tethys who spoke. ' Man,' she said, ' you were made one of us, not one of these. Go back to your domain, for you are mortal. Resume dominion over the fish, or, striving to win more, lose all !'

" I turned my face seaward bitterly. I looked back once ; the blue eyes were gleaming—oh, so tenderly ! —and I could not go. I muttered an execration at my bitter fate. Straightway the sky rocked, the sea rose, the pale star vanished. I had spoken a wicked word.

" I was consigned to Euripius, the divinity of whirlpools. In vain I struggled in his watery arms ; the swift current bore me circling away, and finally whirled me with frightful velocity. My feet were shaken asunder, my integument softened, my brain reeled. I was passed from eddy to eddy ; I became drunken with emotion ; I suffered all the tortures of the lost. A waterspout lifted me from the clutch of the sea, and deposited me upon the dry land, close to the home of my infancy.

" I have passed the weary hours of my penance in arranging the memoirs which follow. Science has again wooed me with her allurements ; the stars continue their correspondence. I have not despaired of the great secret of immortality ; and though these hairs are few and white, I shall be rejuvenated in the tranquil depths of the water, and reassert for ages my rightful dominion over the fish !"

" I was in doubt whether to laugh or wonder when the Ancient Mariner concluded ; but I was relieved from passing judgment upon his article by the unceremonious entrance of a tall, lithe, gray-eyed person, who

wore gold seals and carried a thick walking-stick.
The naturalist appeared to be bent on diving through
the floor, and swimming away through the cellar ; but
he caught the stern, keen eye of the stranger and
cowered. The tall man lifted his cane, and struck the
manuscript out of his Highness's hands ; he demol-
ished the microscope at a blow, and flung the geologi-
cal hammer out of the window.

" Come along," he said. " No ! drop that trash—
every article of it, or else you'll be experimenting
again. Come along !"

They went away together, leaving my office littered
with broken glass and sea-shells. With some astonishment I followed through the warehouse to the street ;
they had entered a carriage and were driving rapidly
away. The next morning's paper explained the whole
occurrence in the following paragraph :

"*Much Learning Hath Made Him Mad.*—Yesterday noon an elderly lunatic, named Robert Jones,
committed suicide by leaping over the parapet of
London Bridge. He was in the custody at the time
of Dr. Stretveskit, the celebrated keeper of the Asylum for Monomaniacs. He had been at large some
days, and was traced to several publishing-houses,
whither he had gone to contrive the publication of
some insane vagaries. He was finally overhauled at
the office of Spry, Stromboli & Co., and placed in a
carriage ; but seizing a favorable moment when travel
was impeded upon the bridge, he burst through the
glass door and cleared the parapet at a bound. Jones
was an adventurous and dangerous character. Some
years ago he set fire to the Shrimpshire Asylum, where
his family had confined him, and went abroad upon a
whale-ship ; but meeting with an accident, he under-
went the process of trepanning and came home more
crazy than before. At one time he attempted to drown
his mother, in furtherance of some strange experiment ;
but it was thought at the date of his death that he was
recovering his wits. Among his delusions was a

strange one—that he had been made viceroy over all the fishes.   His body has not been recovered."

I read the last sentence with a thrill.   My late visitor might even now be presiding at some finny council ; and as I should have occasion to cross the sea some day, an untimely shipwreck might place me in closer relations with him.   I determined, therefore, to print the manuscript which remained in my hands. May it appease his Mightiness, the King of the Fishes !

THE CIRCUIT PREACHER.

His thin wife's cheek grows pinched and pale with anx-
    iousness intense ;
He sees the brethren's prayerful eyes o'er all the confer-
    ence ;
He hears the Bishop slowly call the long " Appointment "
    rolls,
Where in His vineyard God would place these gatherers of
    souls.

Apart, austere, the knot of grim Presiding Elders sit ;
He wonders if some city " Charge" may not for him have
    writ ?
Certes ! could they his sermon hear on Paul and Luke
    awreck,
Then had his talent ne'er been hid on Annomessix Neck !

Poor rugged heart, be still a pause, and you, worn wife, be
    meek !
Two years of banishment they read far down the Chesa-
    peake !
Though Brother Bates, less eloquent, by Wilmington is
    wooed,
The Lord that counts the sparrows fall shall feed His little
    brood.

" Cheer up ! my girl, here Brother Riggs our circuit knows
    'twill please.
He raised three hundred dollars there, besides the marriage
    fees.
What ! tears from us who preached the word these thirty
    years or so ?
Two years on barren Chincoteague, and two in Tucka-
    hoe ?

" The schools are good, the brethren say, and our Church
  holds the wheel ;
The Presbyterians lost their house ; the Baptists lost their
  zeal,
The parsonage is clean and dry ; the town has friendly
  folk,—
Not half so dull as Murderkill, nor proud like Pocomoke.

" Oh ! Thy just will, our Lord, be done, though these
  eight seasons more,
We see our ague-crippled boys pine on the Eastern
  Shore,
While we, Thy stewards, journey out our dedicated years
Midst foresters of Nanticoke, or heathen of Tangiers !

" Yea ! some must serve on God's frontiers, and I shall fail,
  perforce,
To sow upon some better ground my most select dis-
  course ;
At Sassafras, or Smyrna preach my argument on ' Drink,'
My series on the Pentateuch, at Appoquinimink.

" Gray am I, brethren, in the work, though tough to bear
  my part ;
It is these drooping little ones that sometimes wring my
  heart,
And cheat me with the vain conceit the cleverness is
  mine
To fill the churches of the Elk, and pass the Brandywine.

" These hairs were brown, when, full of hope, ent'ring
  these holy lists,
Proud of my Order as a knight—the shouting Methodists—
I made the pine woods ring with hymns, with prayer the
  night-winds shook,
And preached from Assawaman Light far north as Bombay
  Hook.

" My nag was gray, my gig was new ; fast went the sandy
  miles ;
The eldest Trustees gave me praise, the fairest sisters
  smiles ;
Still I recall how Elder Smith of Worten Heights averred
My Apostolic Parallels the best he ever heard.

" All winter long I rode the snows, rejoicing on my way ;
At midnight our revival hymns rolled o'er the sobbing bay ;
Three Sabbath sermons, every week, should tire a man of
brass—
And still our fervent membership must have their extra
class !

" Aggressive with the zeal of youth, in many a warm re-
quite
I terrified Immersionists, and scourged the Millerite ;
But larger, tenderer charities such vain debates supplant,
When the dear wife, saved by my zeal, loved the Itinerant.

" No cooing dove of storms afeard, she shared my life's
distress,
A singing Miriam, alway, in God's poor wilderness ;
The wretched at her footstep smiled, the frivolous were
still ;
A bright path marked her pilgrimage, from Blackbird to
Snowhill.

" A new face in the parsonage, at church a double pride !—
Like the Madonna and her babe they filled the 'Amen-side '—
Crouched at my feet in the old gig, my boy, so fair and
frank,
Naswongo's darkest marshes cheered, and sluices of Chop-
tank.

" My cloth drew close ; too fruitful love my fruitless life
outran ;
The townfolk marvelled, when we moved, at such a caravan !
I wonder not my lads grew wild, when, bright, without the
door
Spread the ripe, luring, wanton world—and we, within, so
poor !

" For, down the silent cypress aisles came shapes even me
to scout,
Mocking the lean flanks of my mare, my boy's patched
roundabout,
And saying : ' Have these starveling boors, thy congregation, souls,
That on their dull heads Heaven and thou pour forth such
living coals ?

" Then prayer brought hopes, half secular, like seers by
       Endor's witch :
Beyond our barren Maryland God's folks were wise and
       rich ;
Where climbing spires and easy pews showed how the
       preacher thrived,
And all old brethren paid their rents, and many young ones
       wived !

" I saw the ships Henlopen pass with chaplains fat and
       sleek ;
From Bishopshead with fancy's sails I crossed the Chesa-
       peake ;
In velvet pulpits of the North said my best sermons o'er—
And that on Paul to Patmos driven, drew tears in Baltimore.

" Well ! well ! my brethren, it is true we should not preach
       for pelf—
(I would my sermon on Saint Paul the Bishop heard himself !)
But this crushed wife—these boys—these hairs ! they cut me
       to the core ;
Is it not hard, year after year, to ride the Eastern Shore ?

" Next year ? Yes, yes, I thank you much ! Then my re-
       ward may fall !
(That is a downright fair. discourse on Patmos and St.
       Paul !)
So Brother Riggs, once more my voice shall ring in the old
       lists,—
Cheer up. sick heart, who would not die among these Meth-
       odists ?"

THE BIG IDIOT.

"SISTER, thy boy is a big idiot—a very big idiot!" said Gerrit Van Swearingen, the Schout of New Amstel. Then the Schout struck his long official staff on the ground, and went off in a grand manner to frighten debtors.

The Widow Cloos made no reply, but dropped a couple of tears as she saw her son, Nanking, shrink away before his uncle's frown and roll his head in deprecation of such language.

"My mother," he whispered, "won't the big wild turkeys fly away with my uncle Gerrit if he calls me such dreadful names?"

"Nanking," said the widow, kissing the big idiot, "your uncle is a very great man. I don't know what is greater, unless it is an admiral, or a stadtholder, or maybe a king!"

"Yes," conceded Nanking, "he is a dreadfully great man. He puts drunken Indians in the stocks and ties mighty smugglers up to the whipping-pump. But Saint Nicholas will punish him if he calls me an idiot."

"Ah! Nanking," replied the widow, "nothing can curb your uncle—neither the valiant Captain Hinoyossa, nor the puissant director of every thing, great Beeckman, nor hardly Pietrus Stuyvesant himself."

"I know who can frighten him," exclaimed the big idiot. "Santa Claus! He's bigger than a schout. Mother, his whip-lash can reach clear over New Amstel —isn't it so? How many deers and ponies does he drive? Will he bring me any thing this year?"

"My poor son!" said the poor mother, "we are so far from Holland and so very humble here, that Saint Nicholas may forget us this year ; but God will watch over us !"

Nanking could hardly comprehend this astonishing statement : that Saint Nicholas could ever forget little boys anywhere.   So he went out by the river to think about it.   There were three or four Swedish boys out there rolling marbles and playing at jack-stones. They did not like to play with Dutch boys, but Nanking was only a big idiot, and they did not harbor malice against him.

"*He ! Zoo !*" they cried ; "wilt thou play ?"

"Yes, directly.   But tell me, Peter Stalcop, and you, Paul Mink, do the very poorest little boys in Sweden get nothing on Christmas ?"

"*Ah, Zon der tuijfel !* without doubt," cried the boys.   "Old Knecht Clobes, your Santa Claus, is a bad man.   That is why he gave the Dutch our country here.   And in Sweden, too, he turns people to wolves, and brothers and sisters tear each other to pieces."

"But not in Holland," exclaimed Nanking. "There he gives the strong boys skates and the weak boys Canary wine.   He brought, one time long ago, three murdered boys to life, so that they could eat goose for Christmas dinner.   And three poor maidens, whose lovers would not take them because they had no marriage portions, found gold on the window-sill to get them husbands."

"*Foei ! Fus !* You're lied to, Nanking !   There is no good Christmas in this land."

Nanking said they were very wicked to doubt true and good things.   He believed every thing, and particularly every thing pleasant.   His mother, whose house was on the river bank, looked out with a fond sadness as she heard him playing, his heart amongst the little boys, although he was so big.

"*Ach ! helas !*" she said to herself, "what will become of my dear man-lamb ?   He is simple and fatherless, poor and confiding. Thank God, at least he is not a woman !"

The Widow Cloos had come but recently from Holland, sent out by charity at the instance of her brother, Van Swearingen, the schout or bailiff of New Amstel colony. Her son, who was almost a man in years, had been kept in the Orphan House at Amsterdam until his growth made him a misplaced object there, and his feeble intellect forbade that he should become a soldier, and die, like his father, in the Dutch battles. So the Widow Cloos brought Nanking out in the ship Mill, to the city of Amsterdam's own colony on the banks of the South River, which the English called the Delaware. They came in a starving time, when the crops were drenched out by rains and all the people and the soldiery of the fort were down with bilious and scarlet fever. The widow was just getting over a long attack of this illness, and her brother, the schout, regarded the innocent Nanking as the cause of her poverty.

" Thou hadst better drown him," said the hard official ; " he'll eat all thy substance or give the remainder away, for he believes every thing and everybody."

" O brother !" pleaded the widow, " if he did not believe something, how sad would he be ! All the children love him, and he is company for them."

It was an odd sight to see Nanking down with the boys, as big as the father of any of them, playing as gently as the littlest. He rode them pig-a-back on his broad shoulders ; they liked to see him light his pipe and smoke without getting sick. He worked for his mother, carrying water and catching fish, and was the only person in New Amstel (or Newcastle) who could go out into the woods fearlessly among the Minquas Indians ; for the Indians all believed that feeble-minded people were the Great Spirit's especial friends, and saw beyond the boundaries of this world into that better heaven where shad ran all the year in the celestial rivers, and the oysters walked upon the land to be eaten. Nanking believed all this, too. It was his confiding nature which made him useless for worldly business. Hobgoblins and genii, charms and saints, and whatever he had heard in earnest, he held in earnest to be true.

"Dear me!" thought Nanking, when he was done playing marbles, "can't I be of use to somebody? Perhaps if I could do something useful my uncle would not think me a big idiot. Then, besides, little Elsje Alrichs might let me be her sweetheart and carry her doll!"

Elsje was the daughter of Peter Alrichs, the late great director's son, whose father slept in the grave-yard of the little log church on Sand Hook, beside Dominie Welius, the holy psalm-tune leader. Nanking believed that when the weathercock on the church tingled in the wind, it was Dominie Welius in the grave striking his tuning-fork to catch the key-note. Peter Alrichs inherited the well-cleared farm of his papa, and had the best estate in all New Amstel except Gerrit Van Swearingen, who was accused of getting rich by smuggling, peculating, and slave-catching. Little Elsje liked Nanking, but her father too, said he was a big idiot. So Nanking had a hard time.

"Elsje," cried Nanking one day, "don't tell anybody if I give you a secret."

"No, big sweetheart!"

"I'm going to catch a stork!"

"We don't have storks in New Netherlands, Nanking."

"That's just where I'm going to be smart," exclaimed Nanking. "Because there are no storks here I'm going to catch one. Then uncle Gerrit cannot call me a big idiot."

Elsje gave Nanking her doll to hold. He sat there as big as a soldier, and handled the doll tenderly; for he believed it to be alive as much as she did, and she was a little girl.

" In Holland," said Nanking, " there is a stork on every happy chimney. The farmers put a wagon wheel on the chimney-top, and along comes your stork and his family, and they build a nest on the wagon-wheel. There it is, Elsje, all twigs and grass, warm as pie, heated by the chimney-fire, and such a squawking you never heard. It keeps the devil away! The old stork sits up on one long straight leg, and with the other foot he hands the worms around to the family. I used to sit down and watch them by the hour in that other Amstel where ours gets its name."

" By the great city of Amsterdam ?" asked Elsje.

" That's it. In Amstel, the suburb of Amsterdam, where you can see such beautiful ships from all parts of the world. If I get a stork for our chimney may I hold your doll another day ?"

" Yes, Nanking, and I'll give you a kiss."

Nanking told his mother next day that he was going to the woods, and not to cry if he did not return at dark. The Widow Cloos kissed him, and saw him go happily up the street.

" *Om licht en donker!*" she moaned. " Between the hawk and the buzzard ! Poor, simple son ! The Indians may kill him, but here he will only get his uncle's curse !"

Nanking walked out through the little settlement of log and brick, and past the court-house, where the stocks and whipping-post were always standing. He saw his uncle Van Swearingen's smart dwelling, with its end to the street and notched gables, and many panes in its glazed windows, and two front doors, and large iron figures in front, telling the date his uncle built it. A little way off was the fine residence of Peter Alrichs, with a balcony on the roof where the family sat of evenings, smoking their pipes and seeing starlight come out on the river and the flag drop at sunset from Fort Casimir ; or hearing the roll of drums as they changed the guard or fired a gun to overhaul a vessel.

" If I get a stork and bring it back," thought Nan-king, " won't I astonish this town ? It'll be pro-claimed, I expect, in a public manner, that Nanking Cloos is no longer the big idiot."

The woods closed round New Amstel not very far from the houses, and only an Indian path led on through the strong timber or marshy copse. Nanking was unarmed and not afraid. He walked until long after sun-up, and waded the headwater swamps of Christine Kill, until he saw before him the hills of Chisopecke rise blue and wooded, and there he knew the Minquas kept their fort. But the Minquas had no storks. He turned the first and second of these hills and then crossed the range and descended to the rain-washed country on the other side, where, amid the low sparse pines on the lonely barrens, he could walk more readily, guided south-westward by the proceeding sun. The fierce Susquehannocks dwelt beyond the next high range, and Nanking had heard from other Indians that they, only, had some storks. Fierce Indians they were, but all Indians had been good to Nanking ; so he ad-vanced right merrily, and at the crossing of the second river snaked a fish out of the water with his line and made a fire with his flint and punk-wood to cook it. When he had finished his meal he looked up and was surrounded by Indians.

They were fierce, grave Indians, armed with spears and bows. Although they looked angry, Nanking wiped his mouth on his ragged sleeve and saluted them all kindly—shaking hands. He perceived that they formed around him closely, in front and rear, but he was not suspicious on this account. The Indians marched him over a long range of very high hills and stopped at a place where, through the timber, could be seen a noble bay.

" It is Chisopecke Bay," cried Nanking gladly, " and there, they say, are storks and plentiful geese. I suppose, when we come to a proper place, these Indians will ask me what I want."

The Indians turned down from the bay-view, backward, by another trail, and entered a very rocky glen, where rocks as big as the houses of New Amstel were strewn all over the country-side. Following downward, by a dangerous way like stair-steps, they entered at length a small shady amphitheatre, where a waterfall plunged down a gorge and foamed and thundered. Nanking fairly danced with delight.

"Oh !" he exclaimed, "I have seen paintings of cascades in Holland, but nothing like this. My mother and Elsje must come here."

The Indians, now present in great numbers, looked at Nanking dancing and laughing with the greatest wonder, but still they were far from affable. After a while they began to sit around in a large circle and sing a doleful sort of tune. Then two Indians produced a long piece of grapevine and tied one end of it to a tree and the other end around Nanking's wrists, which were fastened together behind his back. A fire had already been lighted at the foot of the tree, and the coals were now strewn over the ground.

"*Hond mold !* Keep courage !" thought Nanking. "It is only some kind of play or game. How can I get a stork from them unless I play with them ?"

But the Indians still sung their doleful tune and did not laugh a bit. The month was December, and the fire, at first grateful, grew unreasonably warm. At last Nanking trod on a hot coal, which burnt his old shoe through, and raised a blister on his heel.

"Such a game as this I never learned in Amsterdam or New Amstel," thought Nanking, laughing good-naturedly ; "I guess I will cut it short by riding one of their boys pig-a-back."

So he picked out a young Indian with his roving eye, one perhaps sixteen years old, and, darting upon him, lifted the Indian boy up in powerful arms and carried him around the fiery circle. The young brave struggled in vain. Nanking clinched his big fingers around the Indian and dandled him like a baby. The effect upon the Indians in the circle was exciting ; they seized their spears, stopped their singing, and rushed upon their guest with apparent or assumed fury.

" *Ha! herfe!* " cried Nanking, " I have changed the monotony of this game, anyhow ! "

At this moment an old Indian woman, the mother of the boy whom Nanking had desired to amuse, threw herself between the upraised spears and the laughing widow's son. She shouted something very earnestly, and then stretched herself at Nanking's feet. All the other Indians also flung themselves down in fear or revulsion of feeling, and some crawled in another minute to where the burning coals were strewn over the sward, and with their fingers or with tree-boughs returned these coals to the fire, while others quenched the fire itself with water from the torrent. Nanking had never lost his temper. He put the young Indian down and kissed him, and shook hands with one after another, who only rose as he approached them with a kind countenance. They unbound his hands and overwhelmed him with attentions and professions, and placed their fingers on their foreheads significantly, still looking at him.

" Well," exclaimed Nanking, " I hope they also don't take me for a big idiot ! No, they do not. It is only a part of the queer game."

It was now growing late in the day, and Nanking wanted some food. The Susquehannocks produced nuts, venison, fish, hominy, and succotash. Their formerly savage countenances beamed confidence and consideration. Nanking expressed his wishes by signs. He wanted a great, long-legged, long-winged bird, a stork, to carry back alive to New Amstel. The Indian chiefs conferred, and finally replied, by signs and assurances, that they had such a bird, but that it would take two whole days to procure one.

" Very well," thought Nanking, " I may as well stay here until I get it, and not return home like a fool. My mother will trust in God, if not in Saint Nicholas,

and I trust in both. Elsje will not forget me at any
time !"

All the next day Nanking played ball and bandy
with the Susquehannock boys, and taught them jack-
stones and how to make a shuttlecock. They put
eagle's feathers in his hair, and the old men adopted
him into their tribe. On the third day the absent Indians returned with a stork. It was a white stork with
a red bill and plenty of stork's neck, but short legs.
Nanking doubted if it could stand on one leg on the
top of a chimney and feed worms around to the young
stork family, but he felt very proud and happy. The
whole tribe seemed to have assembled to see Nanking
go away. He had become the friend of all the boys
and women and the *protégé* of the tall warriors. They
placed his stork in a canoe, and in a second canoe
following it were a couple of large deers freshly killed,
which he was to take to his mother as the gift of the
fierce Susquehannocks. Amid the cheers and adieus
of the nation the two canoes pushed off and entering
the broad bay, paddled up a river under the side of a
bar of blue mountains, until the river dwindled to a
mere creek, and finally its navigation ceased altogether.
By signs upon the head of the dead stag, indicating a
larger deer, Nanking knew they were at the " Head-
of-Elk " River. His fierce friends left him here with
many professions of apology and esteem, and soon
after they departed Swedes and Minquas appeared,
who had observed the hostile canoes from their lookout stations on the neighboring hills. These also welcomed Nanking, being already well acquainted with
him, and taking up his venison proceeded through the
woods toward New Amstel. He carried the live stork
himself—a rough bird, which would not yield to bland-
ishments or good treatment. After a very fatiguing
journey and four days' absence from home, Nanking
entered New Amstel in the dead of night.

" To-morrow," he thought, " I shall be repaid for
all this. They will say, ' Nanking Cloos is the smart-

est man in the colony of New Amstel.' Perhaps I shall be a burgomaster, and eat terrapin stewed in Canary wine !''

Nanking was up betimes, looking at the chimneys on his mother's dwelling, of which there were two, and both were the largest chimneys in New Amstel. The Widow Cloos lived in a huge log building with brick ends, long and rather low, which had been built by the commissary of the colony at the expense of the city of Amsterdam as a magazine of food and supply for her colonists ; but after several years of unprofitable experiment with the colony, it was resolved to give no more provisions away, and the director, great Captain Hinoyossa, when Van Swearingen became the schout, allowed the latter's sister to inhabit one end of the warehouse, and that the farthest end from the water. The rest was uninhabited, and Nanking, looking at the chimney which surmounted the river gable, said to himself :

'' That will never do for my stork, as there is no fire lighted there. I never saw smoke from that chimney in my life. The stork requires a nest where there is heat, and plenty of it.''

He therefore prepared to climb to the chimney on the land-side and establish a nest. There was a broken cart-wheel in the warehouse, which Nanking procured and drew to the roof, and when daylight broke upon the town the earliest loungers and fishermen saw the happy simpleton working like a chimney-sweep, as they thought, except that instead of brushing he was piling brush around the chimney on the cart-wheel. His mother came out and looked joy to see him back ; the soldiers strolled down from the fort and the boys and women from the town. Uncle Van Swearingen was there, smiting the ground with his shodden staff, and ejaculating, '' *Foei ! weg ! fychaam u !* Fie ! leave off ! fie on you ! What absurdity is this on the property of our *hoofstad,* our metropolis ?''

'' Never mind, uncle !'' answered the beaming Nan-

king. " I have been a great man in the last few days.
I have lived among the fierce Susquehannocks. Presently you shall see something that you shall see !"

Peter Alrichs also came down to the quay with his
pretty daughter, who could no longer keep her secret.
" Good Nanking," she whispered, " is building a nest
for a real stork. He has found one, just like the dear
creatures in Holland !"

The news was presently dispersed, and all felt an
interest, until finally Nanking produced his stork.

" It is like a stork, indeed !" uttered Peter Alrichs ;
" 'tis big as one, too, but its wings are all white !"

" 'Tis a stork, *yah, op myne eer !* Upon my honor,
it is !" muttered uncle Van Swearingen.

" Nanking is not an idiot, papa !" said Elsje, overjoyed.

The widow was delighted at the enterprise of her
son.

When Nanking had carried the great bird to the nest
he made a little speech :

" Worshipful masters and good people all, I have
been at great pains to get this stork, not for my own
gratification entirely, though there are some here I expect to please particularly. (He looked at Elsje and
his mother.) This stork will pick up the offal and eat
it, and we shall have no more bad fevers here for want
of a good scavenger. By and by he will bring more
storks, and they will multiply ; and every house, however humble, shall have its own stork family to ornament the chimney-top and remind us of our dear native land. I have done all this good with the hope of
being useful, and now I hope nobody will call me
wicked names any more."

Nanking cut the fastenings on the bird and set it on
the new-made nest. In a minute the stork stood up
on its short legs, poked its beautiful head and neck
into the air, and with its wings struck Nanking so heavy
a blow that it knocked him off the roof of the house,
but happily the fall did not hurt him. As he arose

the huge bird was spreading its wings for flight. Before Nanking could climb the ladder again, it was sailing through the air, magnificent as a ship, toward its
winter pastures on the bay of Chisopecke.

"*He ! Zoo !*" exclaimed the soldiers.

"*Foei ! weg !*" cried the fishermen.

Only three persons said "*Ach ! helas !*"—the Widow
Cloos, pretty Elsje, and Nanking.

"Thy stork is a savage bird !" cried Peter Alrichs.
"'The English on the Chisopecke name it a *swan !*"

Nanking burst into tears. His uncle struck the
ground with his schout's staff, swore dreadfully, and
shouted to the Widow Cloos :

"Sister, thy boy is nothing but a big idiot. Thou
hadst better drown him, as I told thee !"

Nothing could equal the mortification of Nanking.
He thought he would die of grief. He was now known
to be more of an idiot than ever, and the fickle Miss
Elsje would not let him hold her doll for a whole
week.

"My poor son," entreated the widow, "do not
pine and lose courage ! The venison will feed us half
the winter. You can help me smoke it and dry it.
Do not give up your sweet simple faith, my boy ! As
long as you keep that, we are rich !"

The next day Schout Van Swearingen, the great
dignitary, came in and said to Nanking : "As you are
a big idiot and good for nothing else, I will give you
an office. Even there you will be a failure, for you
are too simple to steal any thing."

Nanking's mother was happy to hear this, and to see
her son in a linsey-woolsey coat with large brass buttons, and six pairs of breeches—the gift of the city of
Amsterdam—stride up the streets of New Amstel, with
copper buckles in his shoes and his hair tied in an eel-
skin queue. The schout, his uncle, who was sheriff
and chief of police in one, marched him up to the jail
and presented him with a beautiful plaything—a handle
of wood with nine leather whip-lashes upon the end of

it. "Your duties will be light," said the schout. "Every man you flog will give your mother a fee. Come here with me and begin your labors!"

In the open space before the jail and *stadt huys* were a pair of stocks and a whipping-post. Nanking's uncle released a rough but light-built man, who had been sitting in the stocks, and taking off the man's jacket and shirt, fastened him to the post by his wrists.

"Give this culprit fifty lashes, well laid on!" ordered the schout.

Nanking turned pale. "Must I whip him? What has he been doing that he is wicked?"

"Smuggling!" exclaimed Schout Van Swearingen. "He has taken advantage of the free port of New Amstel to smuggle to the Swedes of Altona and New Gottenburg, and the English of Maryland. Mark his back well!"

The sailor, as he seemed to be, looked at Nanking without fear. "Come, earn your money," he said.

"Uncle," cried Nanking, throwing down the whip, "how can I whip this man who never injured me? Do not all the people smuggle in New Amstel? Was it not to stop that which brought the mighty Director Stuyvesant hither with the great schout of New Amsterdam, worshipful Peter Tonneman? Yes, uncle, I have heard the people say so, and that you have smuggled yourself ever since your superior, the glorious Captain Hinoyossa, sailed to Europe."

"Ha!" exclaimed the bold smuggler. "Van Swearingen, *dat is voor u!* That is for you!"

"*Vore God!*" exclaimed the schout; "am I exposed and mocked by this idiot?"

He took up the whip and beat Nanking so hard that the strong young man had to disarm his uncle of the instrument. Then, stripped of his fine clothes and restored to his rags, Nanking was returned with contempt to his mother's house.

"Mother!" he cried, throwing himself upon the

floor, " am I an idiot because I cannot hurt others ? No, I will be a fool, but not whip-master !"

The shrewd Peter Alrichs came to the widow's abode and asked to see Nanking. He brought with him the worshipful Beeckman, lord of all South River, except New Amstel's little territory, which reached from Christine kill to Bombay Hook. They both put long questions to Nanking, and he showed them his burnt heel, still scarred by the fagots of the Susquehannocks.

" *Ik houd dat voor waar !* I believe it is true," they said to each other. " They were burning him at the stake and he did not know it. Yes, his feeble mind saved him !"

" Not at all," protested Nanking. " It was because I thought no evil of anybody."

" Hearken, Nanking !" said Peter Alrichs, very soberly. " And you, Mother Cloos, come hither too. This boy can make our fortunes if we can make him fully comprehend us."

" Yah, mynheers !"

" He can return in safety to the land of the Susquehannocks, where no other Dutchman can go and live. Thence, down the great river of rocks and rapids, come all the valuable furs. Of these we Dutch on South River receive altogether only ten thousand a year. Nanking must take some rum and bright cloth to his friends, the chiefs, and make them promise to send no more furs to the English of Chisopecke, but bring them to Head-of-Elk. There we will make a treaty, and Nanking and thee, widow, shall have part of our profits."

" *Zeer wel !*" cried Nanking. " That is very well. But Elsje, may I marry her, too ?"

" Well," said Peter Alrichs, smiling, " you can come to see her sometimes and carry her doll."

" Good enough !" cried Nanking, overjoyed.

Before Nanking started on his trip, the sailor-man he had refused to whip walked into his mother's house.

"Widow Cloos, no doubt," he said, bowing.
"Madame, I owe your son a service. Here are three
petticoats and a pair of blue stockings with red clocks ;
for I see that your ankles still have a fine turn to
them."

The widow courtesied low ; for she had not received
a compliment in seven years.

Nanking now began to show his leg also, as modest-
ly as possible.

"Ah ! Nanking," cried the sailor, " I have a piece
of good Holland stuff for you to make you shirts and
underclothes. · 'Tis a pity so good a boy has not a rich
father ; ha ! widow ?"

The widow stooped very low again, but had the art
to show her ankle to the best advantage, though she
blushed. She said it was very lonely for her in the
New World.

"Now, Widow Cloos," continued the sailor, " I
am Ffob Oothout, at your service ! I am a mariner.
Some years ago, when Jacob Alrichs was our director,
I helped to build this great warehouse with my own
hands. They were good men, then, in charge of New
Amstel's government. Thieves and jealous rogues
have succeeded them. Would you think it, they sus-
pect even me, and ordered Nanking to whip me with
the cat ! But for Nanking I should have a bloody
back at this minute, and you would be wiping the
brine out of it for me, I do not doubt !"

Nanking had gone out meantime, seeing that he was
to get no clock-stockings.

"Widow, come hither," said the sailor. " Do you
know I like this big barn of a warehouse! It is my
handicraft, you know, and that attaches me to it.
Well, you say nothing to anybody, and let me sleep in
the river end. In a little while the noble veteran,
Alexander D'Hinoyosso, will be due from Holland on
the ship Blue Cock. Then we will all have good
protection. In that ship are lots of supplies of mine.
Of evenings we can court and drink liquor of my own

mulling. And when the Blue Cock comes to port
you shall have more petticoats and high-heeled shoes
than any beauty in New Amstel."

Ffob Oothout stole a couple of kisses from the
widow, like a bold sailor-man, and she promised that
he should lodge in the river end of the Amsterdam
warehouse.

For the rest of that afternoon Nanking carried
Elsje's beautiful doll, and his feelings were very much
comforted.

"Big sweetheart," she said, "what a smart man you
would be if you could only make me a bigger doll than
this, which would open and shut its eyes and cry '*fus ;*
hush !'"

Nanking left New Amstel at moonlight, at the head
of a little procession, carrying gay cloths and plenty of
rum for the Susquehannocks. The last words Peter
Alrichs said to him were : "You must talk wisely,
Nanking. It is a mighty responsibility you have on
this errand. Remember Elsje !"

Next morning Nanking pushed off in a boat, all
alone, from the Head-of-Elk, and rowed under the
blue bar of mountain into the Chisopecke, and turned
up the creek below the rocky mouth of the great river
toward the council-fire retreat of the fierce Susquehannocks. As he was about to step ashore a band of Englishmen confronted him, with swords and muskets.

"Whom art thou ?" cried their leader, a stalwart
man, with long mustaches.

"Only Nanking Cloos, mynheers, who used to be
the big idiot of New Amstel. But," he added, with
confidence, "I am now a great man on a very responsible mission to the Indians. I am to talk much and
wisely. They are to send to New Amstel thousands of
furs and peltries, and I am to give them this rum and
finery !"

"He talks beautifully," exclaimed the English ; and
the chief man added :

"Nanking, I know thee well. Thy mother is the

pretty widow in the house by the river. I am Colonel Utye, who swore so dreadfully when I summoned New Amstel to surrender. Come ashore, Nanking."

Nanking felt very proud to be recognized thus and receive such compliments for his mother. The English poured out a big flagon of French brandy and gravely drank his health, touching their foreheads with their thumbs. The brandy elated and exalted Nanking very much.

"Nanking," said Colonel Utye, "we desire to spare thee a long journey and much danger. Leave here thy rum and presents, and return to thy patrons, Alrichs and Beeckman, bearing our English gratitude, and thou shalt wear a beautiful hat, such as the King of England allows only his jester to put upon his head."

Nanking felt very much obliged to these kind gentlemen. They made the hat of the red cloth he had brought. It was like a tall steeple on a house, and was at least three feet long. As proud as possible he re-entered New Amstel on the evening of the day after he left it. It was now within a few days of Christmas, and the Dutch burghers and boors, and Swedes, English and Finns, were anticipating that holiday by assembling at the two breweries which the town afforded, and quaffing nightly of beer. Beeckman and Alrichs were interested in the largest brewery, and their beer was sent by Appoquinimy in great hogsheads to the English of Maryland in exchange for butts of tobacco.

As Nanking walked into the big room where fifty men were drinking, his prodigious red hat rose almost to the ceiling, and was greeted by roars of laughter.

"*Gœden avond! Hoe yaart gij!* How do you do, my bully?"

Nanking bowed politely, and singling out Beeckman and Alrichs, stood before them with child-like joy.

"Gentlemen," he said, "I gave all your presents to the noble Colonel Utye, who sends his deepest gratitude, and presented me with this exalted cap in acknowledgment of my capacity."

" Thou idiot !" exclaimed Beeckman ; " 'tis a dunce's cap !"

" Dunder and blitzen !" swore Peter Alrichs, " hast thou lost all our provision and made fools of us, too ?"

They struck the dunce's cap off Nanking's head with their staves, and threw their beer in his face.

" Two hundred guilders are we out of pocket," cried both these great men. " Was ever such a brainless dolt in our possessions ?"

The room rang with the cry, " Incurable idiot !" and Gerrit Van Swearingen cried louder than any, " Go drown thyself, and spare thy mother shame !"

" Then I shall not marry Elsje ?" exclaimed Nanking, bursting into tears.

" No !" stormed Peter Alrichs ; " thou shalt marry a calf. Away !"

When Nanking arrived home he found his mother sitting very close to Ffob Oothout. He told his tale with a broken heart.

" My man," exclaimed the rough sailor, in his kindest tone, but still very rough, " take this advice from me : Whatever thou believest, tell it not. Where thy head is weak, hold thy teeth tight. Then thou canst still have faith in many things, and make no grief."

The next day the Blue Cock sailed into the roadstead and the fort thundered a salute. Fort and vessel dipped the tricolor flag of the States-General and the municipal banner of Amsterdam. Beeckman surrendered all the country on South River to Hinoyossa, who came ashore very drunk and very haughty, and threatened to set up an empire for himself and fit out privateers against the world.

" Let him lose no time," muttered Ffob Oothout ; " the English have doomed these Western Netherlands !"

Amidst the festivity Nanking was in a condition of despair. He had seen Elsje on the street and she turned up her nose at him. Christmas was only one day off, and Santa Claus, the Swede boys insisted, never came to the sorrowing shores of New Amstel.

"My uncle Gerrit was right," thought Nanking. "I had better drown myself. Yes ; I will watch on Christmas eve for Santa Claus. I will give him plenty of time to come. He is the patron saint of children, and if he neglects poor, simple boys in this needful place, there is no truth in any thing. On Christmas morning I will fall into the river without any noise. My mother will cry, perhaps, but nobody else, and they will all say, ' It was better that the big idiot should be drowned ; he had not sense enough to keep out of the water.' "

Nanking spent half the day watching the chimneys of his mother's house. Both chimneys were precisely alike in form and capacity, and the largest in the place. But the chimney next the river did not retain the dark, smoky, red color of the chimney on the land side.

"No wonder," thought Nanking, "for no fire nor smoke has been made in that river chimney for years. It almost seems that the bricks therein are oozing out their color and growing pale and streaked."

Night fell while he was watching. Nanking hid himself upon the roof of the house, determined to see if Saint Nicholas ever came to bless children any more by descending into chimneys, or was only a myth.

It was a little cold, and under the moonlight the frost was forming on the marshes and fields. The broad, remorseless river flowed past with nothing on its tide except the two or three vessels tied to the river bank, of which the Blue Cock was directly under the widow's great dwelling. From the town came sounds of revelry and wassail, of singing and quarrel, and from the church on Sand Hook softer chanting, where the women were twining holly and laurel and mistletoe. Nanking lay flat on the roof, with his face turned toward the sky. The moon went down and it grew very dark.

" Lord of all things!" he murmured, " forgive my rash intention and comfort my poor mother !"

The noise of the town died on the night air, and every light went out. Nanking said to himself, " Is it Christmas at all, out in this lonely wilderness of the world ? Is it the same sky which covers Holland, and are these stars as gentle as yonder, where all are rich and happy ?"

He heard a noise. A voice whispered, just above the edge of the chimney on the river gable : " *Fus-s-s !*
Pas op ! "

" What is that ?" thought Nanking ; " somebody saying, ' Hist ! be careful ? ' Surely I see something moving on the chimney, like a living head."

The voice whispered again : " *Maak hast! Kom hier !*" Or, " Hasten ! Come here !"

Nanking raised up and made a noise.

" *Wie komt, daar ?*" demanded the voice, and in a minute repeated : " *Wie sprecht, daar ?*"

They ask, " Who comes and who speaks ?" said Nanking. " Blessed be the promises of heaven ! It is Santa Claus !"

Then he heard movements at the chimney, and people seemed to be ascending and descending a ladder. There seemed, also, to be noises on the deck of the Blue Cock, and sounds of falling burdens and spoken words : " Maak plaats !" or make room for more.

" I never heard of Santa Claus stopping so long at one humble house," thought Nanking.

After awhile all sounds ceased. Nanking crept to the chimney and touched it with his hand. It had no opening whatever in the top.

He felt around this mysterious chimney. " He ! Zoo !" he said aloud, " there is more wood here than brick. 'Tis a false chimney altogether!'

Then he saw that his close observation had not been at fault. The chimney over the river gable was a painted chimney, a mere invention. Yet, surely Santa Claus had been there.

After a time Nanking opened the top and side of this chimney as if they were two doors. He found it packed with goods of all kinds—a ton at least.

" I will run and awaken my mother," he thought. " But no. Did not Ffob Oothout tell me to blab no secrets and shut my teeth tight ? I will tell nobody. These costly things are all mine ; for there are no other boys in this whole dwelling but Nanking Cloos, the fatherless idiot !"

He slipped down and hastened to his boat, which lay in a cove not far below. Towing it along the bank to a sheltered place convenient, Nanking began to load up the goods from the chimney. Before daylight broke he had secured every thing, and hoisting sail was speedily carried to the island of the Pea Patch, far down the bay—that island which shone in the offing and seemed to close the river's mouth. Here, in the wreck of an old galiot, he hid every article dry and secure : kegs of liquors and wine, shawls and blankets, pieces of silk, gunpowder, beautiful pipes, bars of silver and copper, and a whole bag of gold. Nanking covered them with dry driftwood and boughs of trees, and sailed again to New Amstel, where he arrived before breakfast.

At breafast Nanking found upon his bench a beautiful new gun.

" It is thine, good child," said Ffob Oothout, " for sparing me those lashes. Thy churlish uncle felt so reproved by thy innocent words that he set me free. Widow, here is a *spiegel* for thee, a looking-glass to see, unseen, whoever passes up or down the street. That is a woman's high privilege everywhere. Thou shalt be, erelong, the best-dressed wife in all New Amstel. Nanking, wouldst thou like to have a father ?"

" I would like you, Ffob Oothout, for a father."

" Widow," said Ffob, " he has popped the question for me ; wilt thou take an old pirate for thy man ?"

" They are all pirates here," replied the blushing

widow, " and thou art the best pirate or man I have seen."

" Well, then, when the English conquer this region I have that will make thee rich. Till then let us wait on the good event, but not delay the marriage."

That Christmas Day they were married in form. As the three sat before the fresh venison and drank wine from the store of the Blue Cock, Nanking said :

" Father Ffob, you are wise. Give me yet another word of advice, that I may not continue to be a big idiot."

" Trust whom thou wilt, Nanking, yet ever hold thy tongue. If thou hast now a secret, hold it close. Begin this instant !"

" Even the secrets of Santa Claus ?"

" Yes, even them."

Nanking said no more. He found compensation for Elsje's contumely in his gun, and roved the forests through, and peeped from time to time at his mystic treasures.

One day the news came overland that the English had taken New Amsterdam. Then the great Hino-yossa and uncle Van Swearingen and Alrichs and Beeckman swore dreadfully, and said they would fight to the last man. Ffob Oothout went around amongst the Swedes and the citizen Dutch, and prepared them to take the matter reasonably.

One day in October of that same wonderful year, 1664, two mighty vessels of war, flying the English flag, came to anchor off New Amstel and the fort. They parleyed with the citizens for a surrender, and Ffob Oothout conducted the negotiations. The citizens were to receive protection and property. The fort replied by a cannon. Then the English soldiery landed and formed their veteran lines. They charged the ramparts and broke down the palisades, and killed three Dutchmen and wounded ten more. Proclamation was made that New Amstel should for all the future be named New-*castle*, and that Gerrit Van

Swearingen, the refractory schout, should yield up his noble property to Captain John Carr, of the invaders, and Peter Alrichs lose every thing for the benefit of the fortunate William Tom.

The English soldiery proceeded to make barracks of the Amsterdam warehouse. The first night they inhabited it they strove to light a fire under the wooden chimney in the river gable. The chimney caught fire and burnt out like an old hollow barrel.

"Wife," exclaimed Ffob Oothout, looking grimly on, "in that chimney was all my property and thine. Poor boy," he said to Nanking, "we must all be poor together now."

"No," cried Nanking, "I have yet the gifts of Santa Claus which I took from that chimney on the night before Christmas. Yours, father, may be burnt. Mine are all safe!"

He sailed his father and mother to the island since called the Pea Patch, and Ffob Oothout recognized his property.

"Wonderful Nanking!" he cried, "thy faith was all the wisdom we had. God protects the simple! Thou art our treasure."

The great Hinoyossa condignly fled to Maryland. Uncle Van Swearingen was exported to Holland, and in the dwelling of Peter Alrichs the family of Ffob Oothout made their abode.

"Nanking," asked the houseless Alrichs, "is not Elsje pretty yet?"

"Not as pretty," answered Nanking, "as my little baby sister. I will carry nobody's doll but hers."

"Humph!" said Peter Alrichs, "you are not the big idiot I took you for!"

A BAYSIDE IDYL.

BASKING on the Choptank pleasant Cambridge lies
In the humid atmosphere under fluttered skies,
And the oaks and willows their protection fling
Round the court-house cluster and the public spring.

There the streets are cleanly and they meet oblique,
Forced upon each other by the village creek
Winding round the ancient lawns, till the site appears
Like a moated fortress crumbling down with years.

Round the town the oysters grow within the coves,
And the fertile corn-fields bearing yellow loaves ;
And the wild duck flying o'er the parish spire
Fall into the graveyard when the fowlers fire ?

There the old armorial stones dwellers seldom read ;
There the ivy clambers like the rankest weed ;
There the Cambridge lawyers sometimes scale the wall
To the grave of Helen, loneliest of all.

Even here the fairest of the little band
Strangers call the fairest girls in Maryland,
Like the peach her color ere its dyes are fast,
And her form as slender as the virgin mast.

Like a vessel gliding with a net in tow,
Up the street of evenings Helen seemed to flow,
Leaving light behind her, and a nameless spell
Murmured in the young men, like an ocean shell.

Made too early conscious of her power to charm,
Still unconscious ever love of men could harm,
Voices whispered to her : " Beauty rare as thine
Princes in the city never drank in wine !

" Hide it not in Cambridge ! Cross the bay and see
How a world delighted hastes to honor thee.
Seek the fortune-teller and thy future hear ;
There is empire yonder ; there is thy career !"

Oh, the sad ambition and the speedy dart !
He, the fortune-reader, read poor Helen's heart ;
And a face created for the hearthstone's light—
Fishers tell its ruin as they scud by night.

Whisper, whisper, whisper ! leaf and wave and grass ;
Look not sidewise, maiden, as the place you pass !
If you hear a restless spirit when you pray,
'Tis the voice that tempted Helen o'er the bay.

SIR WILLIAM JOHNSON'S NIGHT.

AN extraordinary story, some say the recital of a dream, or scenes in somnambulism, is that of Andrew Waples, of Horntown, Va. He visited Saratoga twenty years ago, well-to-do, the owner of slaves, sloops, lands, and fisheries, and visits it now upon an income of $2000 a year, derived from boiling down fish into phosphates for the midland markets. He preserves, however, the habit and appearance of old days : that is to say, his chin is folded away under his lip like a reef in a mainsail ; his cheek-bones hide his ears, so tusky and prominent are the former, and tipped with a varnish of red, like corns on old folks' feet ; he has a nose which is so long and bony that it seems to have been constructed in sections, like a tubular bridge, and to communicate with itself by relays of sensation. A straight, mournful, twinkling, yet aristocratic man was Andrew Waples, "befo' de waw, sah ! befo' de waw !"

He had no sooner arrived at Saratoga than he met some ancient boon companions, who took him off to the lake, exploded champagne, filled his lungs with cigar-smoke, and sent him to bed, the first night, with a decided thirst and no occasion to say his prayers. For it was Andrew's intention, being a mournful man of the Eastern Shore, to pray on every unusual occurrence. Piety is relative as well as real, but Andrew Waples on this occasion jumped into bed, said hic and amen, and "times befo' de waw," and went to sleep in the somnorific air of the Springs.

He awoke with a dry throat, a disposition to faint and surrender his stomach, and an irresistible propensity to walk abroad and drink of the waters. He looked at his watch : it was two o'clock, and Saturday night. "Alas !" said Andrew Waples aloud, "the bars are closed. Even Morrissey has gone to bed, and the club-house is in darkness, but perhaps I can climb over the gate of some spring company, or find a fountain uninclosed. Yes, there is the High Rock Spring !"

He drew on his clothes partly, slipped his feet in slippers, and wrote on a piece of paper, which he conspicuously posted on the gas bracket :

"Andrew Waples, Gentleman (befo' de waw), departed from the United States Hotel, at two o'clock A.M., precisely. If any accident happens to him, seek at the High Rock Spring, or thereabouts."

It was a sad, green, ghostly moonlight streaming through the elms as Andrew Waples walked up Broadway. The moon appeared to be dredging for oysters amongst the clouds, circling around there by bars, islets, and shoals. Bits of spotted and mackerel-back sky swam like hosts of menhaden through the pearly sheen of the more open aërial main. The leaves of the tall domes and kissing branches of the elms, that peeped on either side into open windows of people asleep and told across the street to each other the secrets there, were now themselves heavy as if with surfeit of gossip and they drooped and hardly rustled. Not a tipsy waiter lurked in the shadows, not a skylarking couple of darkey lovers whispered on doorsteps. No birds, nor even crickets, serenaded the torpid night. The shuffling feet of Andrew Waples barely made watch-dogs growl in their dreams, and started his own heart with the concussions they produced on the arborescent and deeply-shadowed aisles of the after midnight. He saw the town-hall clock pallidly illuminated above its tower. The low frame villa of Chancellor Walworth, cowering amongst the pine-trees, expressed the burden of parricidal blood that had of late oppressed its memories. There were no murmurs from the court-room where Judge Barnard had been tried, but its deep silence seemed from the clock to tick : " Removed ! disqualified !" .and " Disqualified ! removed !"

Turning from Broadway to lesser streets of cheap hotels and plain boarding cottages, where weary women and girls had drudged all day long, and washerwomen moaned and fluting and ruffling were the amusements of the poor, Andrew Waples became haunted with the idea that Saratoga was poisoned, that every soul in the village was dead, and that he was to be the last man of the century to drink of the Springs. Nature and night were in the swoon of love or death. Parting their drowsy curtains went Waples through the muffled echoes, impelled by nothing greater than a human thirst.

He saw his shadow, at length, fall down the steep stairs of the valley of High Rock Spring, as he stood at the top of the steps uncovered to the moon. It was a shadow nearly a hundred feet long, a high-cheeked head without a chin and all nose, like the profile of a mountain. But what was extraordinary was the total absence of an abdominal part to Mr. Waples' exaggerated shadow, for he distinctly saw a young maple-tree, in perfect moonlight, grow through the cavity where his stomach ought to have been.

" I must be hollow," said Andrew, as he looked,— " the frame of a stomach removed ; for surely my whole figure is in blackness, except my bread-basket." But his fears were dissipated by the sound of voices, of glasses clinking and water running, and the evident semblance of life at the High Rock Spring in the ravine beneath, to which the steep stairs descended. At the same moment he descried another shadow propelled alongside his own, as if from some far distance in the rear a human object was slowly advancing to stand beside him.

There were very old wooden houses around this precipice or promontory of Saratoga, some of them a hundred years old, and decrepit and in ruins ; for here, at the High Rock, was the original fountain of the village. As if from the cover of one of these old and decaying tenements came a person of venerable aspect, with a tray of glasses fastened to the top of a staff, like a great caster of bottles on a broomstick. As this person stood by the side of Andrew Waples, and planted his staff on the top step of the stairs, his prolonged shadow, falling in the valley, gave him the appearance of a gigantic Neptune, with a trident in his hand.

" Hallo !" exclaimed Mr. Waples, " are you a town scavenger, to be up at this time of the clock ?"

The man replied, after a very curious and explosive sound of his lips, like the extraction of a cork from a bottle, " No, sir ; I'm only the Great Dipper."

" Very good," resumed Mr. Waples. " Then, perhaps, you'll explain to me a very great optical delusion, or tell me that I'm drunk. Do you see our two shadows as they fall yonder on the ground, and amongst the tree-tops ? Now, if I have any eyes in my head, there is a stomach in your shadow and no stomach whatever in mine."

" Quite right," answered the Great Dipper. " You are the mere rim of a former stomach. Abdominally, you are defunct."

Andrew Waples put his hand instinctively where his stomach was presumed to be, and he saw the hand of his shadow distinctly imitate the motion, and repeat it through his empty centre.

" This is Sir William Johnson's night," remarked the Great Dipper. " We have a large company of guests on this anniversary, and no gentleman is admitted with a stomach, nor any lady with a character. My whole force of dippers is on to-night, and I must be spry."

As the venerable man spoke, and ceased to speak, exploding before and after each utterance, it occurred to Mr. Waples that his voice had a sort of mineral-water gurgle, which was very refreshing to a thirsty man's ears. He followed, therefore, down the flight of rickety stairs and stood in the midst of a promenad-

ing party of many hundred people, variously dressed,
and in the costumes of several generations.

The canopy or pavilion of the spring, which, like a
fairy temple, seemed to have been exhaled from its
bubbles, was yet capped, as in the broad light of day,
by a gilded eagle, from whose beak was suspended a
bottle of the water, and no other light was shed upon
the scene than the silver and golden radiance emitted
together from this bottle, as if ten thousand infinitely
small goldfish floated there in liquid quicksilver. The
spring itself, flowing over its ancient mound of lime,
iron and clay, like the venerable beard over the Ara-
bian prophet's yellow breast, shed another light as if
through a veil fluttered the molten fire of some pulsat-
ing crater. The whole scene of the narrow valley, the
group of springs, the sandy walks, dark foliage, and inclosing ridges took a pale yellow hue from the effer-
vescing water and the irradiant bottle in the eagle's
beak. The people walking to and fro and drinking
and returning, all carried their hands upon their stomachs or sides, and sighed amidst their flirtations. Mr.
Waples saw, despite their garments, which represented
a hundred years and more of all kinds, from Conti-
nental uniforms and hunting shirts to brocades, plush
velvets, and court suits, that not a being of all the multitude contained an abdomen. He stopped one large
and portly man, who was carried on a litter, and said :

" Have you a window through you, too, old chap ?"

" 'Sh !" exclaimed one of the supporters of the litter, who wore the feathers and attire of an Indian,
" 'Tis Sir William Johnson—he who receives to-
night."

" Young man," exclaimed that great and first of
Indian agents, " this is the spot where all people come
to find their stomachs. Mine was lost one hundred
and ten years ago. The Mohawks, my wards, then
brought me through the forest to this spot. Faith ! I
was full of gout and humors, and took a drink from a
gourd. One night in the year I walk from purgatory

and quench my thirst at this font. The rest of the year I limp in the agonies of dyspepsia."

A large and short-set woman was walking in one of the paths, wearing almost royal robes, and her train was held up by a company of young gallants, some of whom whistled and trolled stanzas of foreign music. "Can you tell me her name!" asked Waples, speaking to a bystander.

"It is Madame Rush, 'the daughter of the banker who rivalled Girard. She was a patroness of arts and letters in her day, full of sentiment."

"But disguised in a stomacher!" interrupted our friend. The lady passed him as he spoke, and, looking regretfully in his face, murmured :

"Avoid hot joints for supper! Terrapin must crawl again. Drink nothing but claret. Adieu!"

"Really," thought Andrew Waples, "this is a sort of mass meeting of human picture-frames. But here is one I know by his portrait—the god-like head, the oxen eyes, the majestic stalk of Daniel Webster." He was about to address this massive figure, when it turned and looked upon him with rolling orbs like diamonds in dark caves.

"Brandy," said the great man, "'tis the drink of a gentleman, and the stimulus of oratory. But public life requires a thousand stomachs. Who could have saved the Constitution on only one?"

"Poor ghost!" thought Andrew Waples. "Yet here is a milder man, also of mighty girth, like the frame of a mastodon, transparent. Your name, my friend?"

"John Meredith Clayton, of Delaware! I filled my paunch of midnights with chicken soup. I arose from bed to riot in gravy. Ye who have livers and intestines, think of my fame and fate!"

The old man sobbed as he receded, and Waples had only time to get a glimpse of the next trio before they were upon him.

"I agree with Commodore Vanderbilt," said the

other, the wearer of a rubicund face, and great blue eyes. "My *forte* was oysters and economy. I grew wondrous fat and conservative, and one day awoke with a stomach that exclaimed, ' I have become round, so that you can trundle me for the exercise you deprived me of.' Henceforward, not even the unequalled advantages of the Baltimore and Ohio Railroad gave me pleasure. I live like a skeleton world, without an inner globe, without a paunch. Beware!"

" Well," cried Mr. Waples, " it is a singular thing that the conservative as well as the volatile lose their full habits. How is it with Colonel Tom Scott, I wonder ?"

" No rest," exclaimed a full-necked man, " I eat at figures, and think in my sleeping car. Go slow, go fast, young man, ' But it is even, heads I win, stomach you lose !' "

The shaggy iron-gray whiskers and hair of Charles Sumner were well known to Mr. Waples, as that great Senator strutted down the maple paths. " You here, also !" shouted Mr. Waples.

" Ay !" answered the champion. " Freedom is not worth enjoying without the gastric juice. The taste of Château Yquem pursues me through eternity. There are times when Plymouth Rock is a pennyweight in value compared to High Rock at Saratoga, and all the acts of Congress foolish beside a pint of Congress water !"

A tall and elegant man came by and said : " I was the reviver of the running turf. My stomach was tough as my four-in-hand. 'Twas Angostura nipped my bud. It was, by Saint Jerome !"

Another passer, with a dark skin and a merry twinkle, said : " Uncle John's under the weather tonight. But he can lay out another generation yet. While there's sleep there's hope. Cecil's the word ! Give me me an order !"

A tremendous fellow, with a foot a little gouty, gulped down a gallon of the water, and said : " Rufe

Andrews never gives up while on that high rock he builds his church !"

" The way to eat a sheep's head," exclaimed a florid man, " is with plain sauce. Clams are not kind after nightfall. Champagne destroyed the coats of W. Wickham, Mayor of the *bon vivants. Sic transit* over-took my rapid transit. Heigh-ho !"

" Hear me lisp a couplet," said the great poet Saxe. " Oh, how many a slip 'twixt the couplet and the cup ! Abdomen dominates. When Homer had no paunch, he went blind."

" Halt ! 'Sdeath ! is't I, that once could put the whole Brazilian court to bed, who prowls these grounds for midnight water now ? I am the Chevalier Webb. Who says it is dyspepsia ? I will spit him upon my walking-staff."

" Ees ! 'tis good drinkin' at the fount when one can naught sleep. Johnson, of Congress Spring, the resident cherub ; that's my name. I tipped the rosy, and it tripped on me. What measure I used to take around the bread-basket !"

" The top of the foine midnight to you !" said Richard O'Gorman. " I'm here, my lords and gentle folk, to find a portion of my appetite. It was not so when I could lead a revolution in a cabbage garden."

So went past Uncle Dan Sanford and Father Farrell, and arm-in-arm, on mutual errands of thirst, Judge Hilton and Joseph Seligman.

" Shudge," said Seligman, " when you refushed me a room, it was only becaush you had no stummicks ? Heigh, Shudge ?"

" Ay, Joseph, me broth of a darlint," answered Hilton, " when a spalpeen has no stummick, he speaks without circum—spection. Ye can impty yer stum-mick wherever ye loike over the furniture, if ye'll fill this aching void."

So went the procession. All walking with hands laid heavily on their paunches, or where they used to be. Lovers had lost the light of interest from their

eyes, wedded people the light of retrospection, states-
men the pride of intellect, princes and legates the pride
of power. Wealth flashed in a thousand diamonds to
contrast with the heavy eyes that had no vanity in
them, and religion wore the asceticism of everlasting
gloom instead of the hope of immortal life.

As Mr. Andrew Waples beheld these things, and felt
his thirst impel him toward the fountain of the High
Rock, he became sensible of a wonderful change in the
proportions of that object. It had always been a
mound or cone of sand, clay, magnesia, and lime, well
oxidized, and made rusty-red by the particles of iron in
the composition deposited with the other materials,
through ages of overflow. It had never been above
two feet in height, and of little more diameter than a
man's stature. The water, flowing through its middle,
sparkled and discharged diamond showers of bubbles,
and ran down the ochre-besmeared sides, to disappear
in the ground, the cavity through which it came not
more than ten inches wide. Such had been the dimen-
sions of the High Rock Spring.

But it was now a mountain, rising high in the air,
and flowing crystal and gold, like a volcano in an erup-
tion of jewels. The pyrites of sulphur and motes of
iron, that formerly gleamed in the rills that trickled
down its slopes, were now big as cascades, filled with
carbuncles and rocks of amethyst. A mist of soft
splendor, like the light of stars crushed to dust and
diffused around the mountain's head, revealed an immense multitudes of people scaling the slopes, and
drinking ; and some were raising their hands to Heaven
in praise, and some were drawing the water from the
mountain's base by flumes and troughs. This exten-
sive prospect fell to a foreground of people, such as
Mr. Waples had been mingling with, and these were
clamoring and supplicating for water faster than a
hundred dippers there could pass it up. The dippers
were of all garbs and periods, from Indians and rustics
to boys in cadet uniform. The vessels with which they

dipped were of all shapes and metals, from conch shells and calabashes to cups of transparent china, and goblets of gold and silver. Amongst the dippers, conspicuous by his benevolent face and clothing of a butternut color, was the Great Dipper himself, directing operations.

"Drink freely !" he exclaimed, "for the night is going by. Sir William Johnson has ordered his litter, and the company is breaking up. Drink while you may, for the sun is soon to arise, and ye who have no stomachs will be exposed and disgraced."

"Hark ye ! old friend," whispered Andrew Waples to the Great Dipper, "are there here people alive, as well as dead people, and why do they fear exposure ?"

The Great Dipper replied : "Nobody can be said to live who has lost his stomach. We make no other distinction here. There are thousands who have lost them, however, and who deceive mankind. Even these, you perceive, who drink at the High Rock Spring, flirt while they feel unutterable gloom, and so are dead women above the ground tied to living men, and men without a human hope of health mated to joyous beauty and animation."

It seemed at this point that Mr. Waples shrank away down to the ground, and the Great Dipper loomed up high as the mountain of High Rock. His drinking glasses were as large as Mr. Waples' body ; he was a mighty giant, clad in colors like those of the overflowing mountain.

"Old chap," cried Mr. Waples, "methinks your clothing up there is of much age and tarnish. Tell me its material ?"

A voice came down the long ravines of the mountain like rolling thunder. "It's calcareous tufa I'm a-wearing, wove on me by exudation and accretion in the past two thousand years."

At this point the head of the Great Dipper was quite invisible in the clouds, but the tray of glasses he carried, which were now big as barrels or full-sized

casks, was set down on Mr. Waples' toe. As he
sought to get out of the way a torrent of water
washed him up and away, and he was spilled into one
of the glasses ; and then, as it appeared, he was raised
an inconceivable distance in the air and plunged down
like a bursted balloon from the sky to the sea, and he
found himself immersed in mineral water and rapidly
descending, against the current, toward the centre of
the earth !

Before Mr. Waples could get his breath he was
landed in a bar or shoal of mineral salt, which came
nearly to the surface of the torrent in which he found
himself, and the current of this torrent was ascending
toward the surface, as full of mineral substances as a
freshet is full of saw-logs. Explosions of gas, loud
and rapid as the guns in a naval battle, took place on
every side. The walls of the inclosure made a large
and almost regular cave or tunnel of blue marl, and in
the contrary way from the course of the stream. Mr.
Waples sank along the sides of the cave in the swash
or backflow, until he arrived at a grand archway of
limestone, riven from a mass of slate. A voice from
the roof of the archway, whispering like a sigh of pain,
articulated shrilly :

" Who goes back ?"

Waples discerned, in the joint or junction of the
arch a huge deformed object, whose hands were
caught between the masses of stone, and he still desper-
ately pulled to divide them, so that the torrent could
escape through. The eyes of this object rolled in pain,
but he gave no sign of relinquishing his hold, and
again the painful whisper skipped through the abyss:
" Who goes back from the alluvial ?" Mr. Waples
got a breathful of air from an explosion of bubbles,
and boldly replied, " The Great Dipper's assistant."

" Tell him," whispered the hunchback in the roof,
" that Priam, the Fault Finder, is holding the strata
back, but wants the relief to come on three centuries
hence, that I may spit upon my hands."

Mr. Waples had no time to reply, for a large bubble of carbonic acid gas burst at that moment, and blew him through the gap or " fault " of the rock, into the coldest and clammiest cavern he had ever trodden. From every part of the walls, ceilings, and floor exuded moisture, which flowed off in rills and large canals, until they formed the torrent that disappeared at the Fault Finder's archway.

" Magnesia, faugh !" exclaimed Mr. Waples, unconscious that he was in the presence of somebody.

" You don't like Magnesia, then ?" rejoined a large, spongy object on the floor, whose forehead perspired while he looked up through the chalky-white sockets of sightless eyes. " Why, he's a sixth part of all that's drunk at the springs. Here, I'll call him up! Come Magnesia ! come Potash ! come Lime, Soda, Lithia, and Baryta ! Come ye all to the presence of Prince Saturation !"

There glided to the Sponge's feet a number of leather-looking beings, of broad, circular faces, and to every face a tail was appended on the other side.

" The gentleman don't like our laboratory," exclaimed the Sponge, purring the while like a cat. " Apply your suckers to him, ye percolating angels, and draw him to the forests of Fernandes !"

Mr. Waples felt a hundred little wafers of suction take hold of his body, and a sense of great compression, as if he was being pulled through a mortar bed. He opened his eyes on the summit of a stalagmite in a vast thicket or swamp of overthrown and decaying trees. Birds of buried ages, whose long, bittern-like cries flopped wofully through the silence, made ever and anon a call to each other, like the Nemesis of century calling to century. One of these birds, having authority and standing on one leg, observed to Mr. Waples, in a very philosophical manner :

" Stranger, are you of the Fungi family ?"

" No, Fernandes," answered our bold adventurer ;

" I live nearer the phosphates when at home, and it's a good article."

A mournful chorus of croons from the loons went round the solitude. " Phosphates ! phew ! Phosphates ! phew !"

" This apartment," exclaimed the one-legged bird, " is exclusively for fungi of the old families. Here we rot piecemeal and furnish gas to the nine-thousandth generation after us. By our decay the springs are fed with bubbles. Here is the world as it fell in the floral period, and our boughs are budding anew in the Eldorado of the waters above us."

" Phosphates ! phew !" shouted the great birds of this land of Lethe, as Mr. Waples' stalagmite broke off and dropped him and set him astride of an ancient pterodactyl bird that flew off with its burden to an immense height, and swinging him there by the seat of his breeches, as if he were to be the pendulum of a fundamental and firmamental clock, the griffin-bird finally let go. Mr. Waples was propelled at least six miles out of gravity, and tossed into a most deep and silent lake. Nothing affected its loneliness but an oppressive shadow that came from above, and seemed to sink every floating object in the scarcely buoyant waves. No shores were visible, but distant mountains on one side ; nothing lived in the waters but meteoric lights and objects that ran as if on errands for the spirit above. Broad, submissive, unevaporating, but sinking down, the great inland lonely pool was everywhere the creature of an invisible footprint. Mr. Waples knew the power it obeyed to be that prostrate, cloud-like, overbrooding presence far above, with outlines like a mountain range. The silent sea was the water-trough of Apalachia, the western dyke of the deluge of Noah. The oppressive spirit, stretching overhead, was Bellydown, or the thing that brooded over the waters of chaos, known to schoolmasters as Atmospheric Pressure.

Mr. Waples saw it all now. The spirit overhead,

with equal and eternal pressure, forced down this meteoric water through the slopes of stone, until it reas-
cended toward the clouds of its origin and was lost in
the forest of the fossils, where every decaying fibre
made bubbles to drive it forward, and hold in solution
the mineral substances it was to receive in the porous
magnesian barrier between it and freedom. Soaking
through this, the water escaped by the break in the
strata at the arch of the Fault Finder.

But who had ever passed back against the current of
the earth's barometry, from the spa to the reservoir,
like Andrew Waples of Horntown, Eastern Shore of
Virginia?

He felt a mighty vanity overwhelm him to get recognition of some kind from Bellydown, who disdained
even thunder for a language.

" Thou sprawling spirit, up yonder in the sky !"
shouted Mr. Waples, with much firmness, " if thou art
not mere nightmare, mere figment of the sciences, let
me feel thy strength unequally, for once !"

The vast cloud object moved and yawned. Something like a small world, wearing a boot, smote Andrew
Waples in the rear, as if the spirit above had kicked
him on the proper spot. He felt a pain and a flying sensation, that was like paralysis on wings, and he never
seemed to stop for years, until he fell and struck the
ground, and, after an interval, looked around him.

He was in his room, at the United States Hotel, and
had fallen out of bed. The clock in the Baptist church
cupola struck two. On the gas bracket was pinned a
written notice, not yet dry, that Andrew Waples had
just started for the High Rock Spring.

But he knew that his adventure continued to be true,
for when he went to breakfast at daylight, he found
he had no stomach.

THE PHANTOM ARCHITECT.

FOUR hundred miles of brawling through many a moun-
    tain pass,
From the shadow of the Catskills to the rocks of Havre de
    Grace,
The Susquehanna flashes by willowy isles of May
And deluges of April to the splendors of the bay.

It brings Otsego water and Juniata bright,
Chenango's sunny current and dark Swatara's night,
By booms of lumber winding and rafts of coal and ore,
And gliding barges crossing the dams from shore to shore.

It is an aisle of silver along the mountain nave,
Where towers the Alleghany reflected in its wave,
By many a mine of treasure and many a borough quaint,
And many a home of hero and tomb of simple saint.

The granite gates resign it to mingle with the bay,
And softened bars of mountain stand glowing o'er the way ;
The wild game flock the offing ; the great seine-barges
    go—
From battery to windlass, and singing as they row,

The negroes watch the lighthouse, the trains upon the
    bridge,
The little fisher's village strewn o'er the grassy ridge,
The cannoneers that, paddling in stealthy rafts of brush,
With their decoys around them, the juicy ducks do flush.

And oft by night, they whisper, a phantom architect
Lurks round the Cape of Havre, of ruined intellect,
Who had designed a city upon this eminence,
To cover all the headland and rule the land from hence.

And sometimes men belated the phantom builder find,
Lost on the darkened water and drifting with the wind ;
Then by his will a vision starts sudden on the night—
The city flashing splendor o'er all that barren height.

Its dome of polished marble and tholus full of fire ;
The dying look of sunset just fading from the spire ;
The towers of its prisons, the spars and masts of fleets,
And lines of lamps that clamber along the crowded streets ;

The ships of war at anchor in the indented ports,
The thunder of the broadsides, the answer of the forts—
These by his invocation arise and flame and thrill,
Raised on his faith tenacious and strengthened by his will.

My soul ! there is a city, set like a diadem,
Beyond a crystal river : the new Jerusalem.
The architect was lowly and walked with fishermen ;
But only He can open the blessed sight again.

THE LOBBY BROTHER.

I.

THE express train going south on the Northern Central Railroad, March 3d, 186-, carried perhaps a score of newly-elected Congressmen, prepared to take their seats on the first day of the term. For every Congressman there were at least five followers, adventurers or clients, some distinguished by their tighter-fitting faces, signifying that they were men of commerce; others, by their unflagging and somewhat overstrained amiability, not to say sycophancy, signifying that out of the aforesaid Congressmen they expected something "fat." Of the former class the hardest type was unquestionably Jabel Blake, and the business which he had in hand with the freshly Honorable Arthur MacNair, who sat at his side reading the Pittsburg newspaper, was the establishment of a national bank at the town of Ross Valley, Pennsylvania.

Jabel Blake had as little the look of a bank president as had his representative the bearing of a politician. MacNair was a thin, almost fragile young person, with light-red hair and a freckled face and clear blue eyes, which nearly made a parson of him—a suggestion carried out by his plain guard and silver watch and his very sober, settled expression. The Honorable Perkiomen Trappe, who had served three terms from the Apple-butter District, remarked of him, from the adjoining seat, "Made his canvass, I s'pose, by a-colporterin' Methodist books, and stans ready to go to his hivinly home by way of the Injin Ring!"

But, in reality, the Congressman belonged to the same faith with his constituent and client—both Presbyterians like their great-grandfathers, who were Scotch pioneers among the spurs of the Alleghenies ; and there still lived these twain, in fashion little changed—MacNair a lawyer at the court-house town, and Jabel Blake the creator, reviver, and capitalist of the hamlet of Ross Valley. Jabel was hard, large, bony, and dark, with pinched features and a whitish-gray eye, and a keen, thin, long voice high-pitched, every separate accent of which betrayed the love of money.

"It's an expensive trip," said Jabel Blake ; "it's a costly trip. More men are made poor, Arthur Mac-Nair, by travellin' than by sickness. Twice a year to Pittsburg and twice to Phildelfy is the whole of my gadding. I stop, in Phildelfy, at the Camel Tavern, on Second Street, and a very expensive house—two dollars a day. At Washington they rob everybody, I'm told, and I shall be glad to get away with my clothes."

"Tut ! Jabel," said MacNair, "brother Elk has taken rooms for me at Willards', and for the little time you stay at the capital you can lodge with us. A man who has elected a Congressman in spite of the Pennsylvania Railroad shouldn't grudge one visit in his lifetime to Washington."

"Oh !" said Jabel, "I don't know as I begrudge that, though your election, Arty, cost me four hundred and seven dollars and—I've got it here in a book."

"I know that," said MacNair quietly ; "don't read it again, Jabel. You behaved like a sturdy, indignant man, paid all my expenses, though you protested against an election in a moral land involving the expenditure of a dime, and though you pass for the closest man west of the mountains. And here we are, going upon errands of duty, as little worldly as we can be, yet not anxious to belittle ourselves or our district."

"I'd cheerfully given more, Arty, to beat that corporation. A twenty-dollar bill or so, you know ! But money is tight. I've scraped and scraped for years to start my bank at Ross Valley, and every dollar wasted retards the village. You boys have cost me a sight of money. There's Elk's sword and horse, and the schooling of both of you, and the burying of your father, Jim MacNair, eighteen years ago this May. Dear ! dear !''

The Honorable Perkiomen Trappe, catching a part of this remark, observed that Jabel Blake, judging by his appearance, shouldn't have buried MacNair's father, but devoured him. Jabel's unfeeling remark gave MacNair no apparent pain ; but he said :

'' Jabel, don't speak to Elk about father. He is not as patient as he should be, and perhaps in Washington they disguise some of the matters which we treat bluntly and openly. There's Kitty Dunlevy, you know, and she is a little proud.''

The glazed, whitish eye of Jabel bore the similitude of a beam of satisfaction.

'' It's nothing agin you boys,'' he said, '' that Jim MacNair, your father, didn't do well. He wronged nobody but himself, as I made the stonecutter say over his grave. *That* cost me upwards of eleven dollars, so I did *my* duty by him. You boys don't seem to have his appetite for liquor. You are a member of Congress, and Elk was one of the bravest ginerals in the war ; and I don't see, if he saves his money and his health, but he is good enough even for Judge Dunlevy's girl.''

Judge Dunlevy was the beau ideal of Jabel Blake, as the one eminent local statesman of the region round Ross Valley—the County Judge when Jabel was a child, the Supreme Justice of the State, and now a District Justice of the United States in a distant field. His reputation for purity, dignity, original social consideration, moral intrepidity, and direct Scotch sagacity, had made his name a tower of strength in his native State. To Jabel's clannish and religious nature Judge Dunlevy represented the loftiest possibilities of human character ; and that one of the two poor orphans—the sons of a wood-cutter and log-roller on the Alleghenies, and the victim of intemperance at last—whom Jabel had watched and partly reared, should now be betrothed to Catharine Dunlevy, the judge's only daughter, affected every remaining sentiment in Jabel's heart.

Absorbed in the contemplation of this honorable alliance, Jabel took out his account-book and absently cast up the additions, and so the long delay at Baltimore caused no remarks and the landscape slipped by until, like the sharp oval of a colossal egg, the dome of the Capitol arose above the vacant lots of the suburbs of Washington.

A tall, handsome, manly gentleman in citizen black, standing expectantly on the platform of the station, came up and greeted MacNair with the word:

" Arthur !"

" Elk !"

And the brothers, legislator and soldier, stood contrasted as they clasped hands with the fondness of orphans of the same blood. They had no superficial resemblances, Arthur being small, clerical, freckled, and red-haired, with a staid face and dress and a stunted, ill-fed look, like the growth of an ungracious soil ; Elk, straight and tall, with the breeding and clothing of a metropolitan man, with black eyes and black hair and a small " imperial " goatee upon his nether lip ; with an adventurous nature and experience giving intonation to his regular face, and the lights and contrasts of youth, command, valor, sentiment, and professional associations adding such distinction that every lady passenger going by looked at him, even in the din of a depot, with admiration.

To Jabel Blake, who came up lugging an ancient and large carpet-bag, and who repelled every urchin who wanted the job of carrying it, Elk MacNair spoke cordially but without enthusiasm.

" Jabel," he said, " if I hear you growl about money as long as you are here, I'll take you up to the Capitol and lose you among the coal-holes."

" It took many a grunt to make the money," said

Jabel Blake, " and it's natural to growl at the loss of it."

By this time they had come to the street, and there in a livery barouche were the superb broad shoulders, fringed from above with fleece-white hair, of Judge Dunlevy. Health, wisdom, and hale, honorable age were expressed attributes of his body and face, and by his side, the flower of noble womanhood, sat Catharine, his child, worthy of her parentage. Both of them welcomed Arthur MacNair with that respectful warmth which acknowledged the nearness of his relationship to the approaching nuptials, and the Judge said :

" Great credit to Jabel Blake as a representative citizen, in that his eyes have seen the glory of these fine boys, to whom he has been so fast a friend !"

Jabel's glassy eyes shone, and his mouth unclosed like a smile in a fossil pair of jaws.

" It's the nighest I ever come to being paid for my investment in Arty and Elk," he said, " to get sech a compliment from Judge Dunlevy ! They *are* good boys, though they've cost me a powerful lot, and I hope they'll save their money, stick to their church, and never forgit Ross Valley, which claims the honor of a buildin' 'em up."

" Get up here, Jabel, and ride !" cried Elk. " Remember that coal-hole, old man !"

" No ! no !" cried Jabel ; " I can walk. These fine carriages is expensive luxuries. They'll do for politicians, I 'spose, but not for business men with limited means."

The Judge made Jabel Blake sit facing him, however, and they rattled off to the hotel, where Elk MacNair had secured a parlor and suite for his brother in the retired end of the structure, commanding a view of Newspaper Row upon one side and of the Treasury façade on the other. The long, tarnished mirrors, the faded tapestry, and the heavy, soiled, damask curtains impressed Jabel Blake as parts of the wild extravagance of official society, and gave him many misgivings as to the amount of his bill. He retained enough of his Scotch temperament, however, to make no ceremony about a glass of punch, which the General ordered up for the old man, Arthur MacNair only abstaining, and the beauty and amiability of the Judge's daughter, who sat at his side and beguiled him to speak of his idolized village, his mills, his improvements, and his new bank, softened his hard countenance as by the reflection of her own, and touched him with tender and gratified conceptions of the social opportunities of his *protégés*. Miss Dunlevy's face, with the clear intellectual and moral nature of her father calmly looking out, expressed also a more emotional and more sympathetic bias. A pure and strong woman, whose life had ripened among the families and circles of the best in condition and influence, she had never crossed to the meaner side of necessity, nor appreciated the fact, scarcely palpable, even to her father, that he was poor. An entire life spent in the public service had allowed neither time nor propriety for improving his private fortune ; and as his salary continued over the war era at the same modest standard which had barely sufficed for cheaper years, he had been making annual inroads upon his little estate, which was now quite exhausted. His daughter might have ended his heartache and crowned his wishes by availing herself of any of several offers of marriage which had been made to her ; but the soldierly bearing, radiant face, and fine intellect of Elk MacNair had conquered competition when first he sought, through her father's influence, a lieutenancy in the army.

His career had been brilliant and fortunate, and when he was brought in from the field dangerously wounded, her womanly ministrations at the hospital had helped to set him upon his horse again, with life made better worth preserving for the promise of her hand, surrendered with her father's free consent. It was a love-match, without reservations or inquiries, the *rapport* and wish of two equal beings, kindred in youth, sympathy, and career, earnest to dwell together and absorbed in the worship of each other. Folded in full union of soul as perfectly as the leaves of a book, which are in contact at every point equally, they felt at this period the wistful tenderness of a marriage near at hand, and their eyes anticipated it, seeking each other out. She was cast in the large stature of her father, and her dark brown hair and eyes betokened the stability of her character, while her graces of movement and speech no less revealed her adaptability to the social responsibilities which she had solely conducted since her mother's death. Together, Catharine and her affianced made a couple equal to the fullest destiny, and they won praise without envy from all.

" It is a happy fortuity," said Judge Dunlevy, putting aside his glass ; " Catharine's marriage to a worthy man, native to my own part of the country ; Arthur's induction into national life ; and hard-working Jabel Blake's final triumph with his bank ! There is no misgiving in the mind of any of us. The way is all smooth. Perfect content, perfect love, no stain upon our honors or our characters . with such simple family democracies all over the land we vindicate the truthfulness of our institutions, and grow old without desponding of our country !"

" I feel almost religiously happy," said Arthur, the Congressman ; " not for myself, particularly ; not for my mere election to Congress, for in our district there are many abler men to make representatives of—I hope none with more steadfast good intentions !—but Elk . here always had so much health, blood, wayward will, and brilliancy that I sometimes feared he might abandon the safe highways of labor and self-denial and try some dangerous short-cut to fortune. To see him survive the battle-field and begin the longer campaigns of peace with a profession, a reputation, no entanglements, and such a wife, makes me a religious man. God bless you, brother Elk !"

General MacNair said, in a jesting way, that Arthur

was the truest, most old-fashioned, and most ridicu-
lously scrupulous brother that ever grew up among
the daisies ; but he was affected, as were they all.

" Elk MacNair," asked Jabel Blake, in ·his hard,
incisive, positive, business voice, " what do you mean
to do after you are married ?"

The General looked at Jabel as if he were a little
officious and with large capacities for being disagree-
able.

" I have arranged to buy a partnership in a legal
firm having the largest practice in the North west.
This is better than beginning alone and waiting to
make a business."

" How much will that cost ?" persisted Jabel Blake,
not remarking the growing repulsion with which the
General answered, after some little embarrassment :

" One hundred and sixty thousand dollars."

" Why !" cried Jabel Blake, " that is nearly as
much as it takes to start the Ross Valley bank. Take
care ! Take care ! Beware, Elk MacNair, of getting
into debt at your time of life. It makes gray hairs
come. It breaks up domestic pleasure. It mortgages
tranquil years. Neither a borrower nor a lender be !
That's Bible talk, and the Bible is not only the best
book for the family, but the best business book besides."

" I don't mean to run in debt," said the General,
with a look, perhaps surly ; " I mean to buy into the
firm with cash."

" Bosh !" said Jabel Blake, rising up, " where did
you get one hundred and sixty thousand dollars, Elk
MacNair ?"

" If you were not claiming to its fullest extent the
privilege of my father's friend, Jabel, I should tell
you that it was none of your business ! I will have
made the money by the practice of law in the City of
Washington."

" Dear me, Elk!" said his brother, quietly ; " I don't
presume to be worth five thousand dollars, all told.
But I suppose you have genius and opportunity, and

the times are wondrous for men of acquaintance and
enterprise.''

Jabel Blake stared at Elk MacNair a long while without speaking.

II.

The sudden revelation that Elk MacNair was very
rich had, on the whole, a depressing effect. Kate
Dunlevy, who had expected to marry purely for love,
found with a little chagrin that she was also marrying
for money. The Judge was led to remark upon the
curiosities of a speculative age and a fluctuating currency, and said he longed for the solid times of hard
coin, cheap prices, easy stages, and a Jeffersonian re-
public. As for Jabel Blake, he was too late for that
day to deposit his bonds at the Treasury and obtain the
currency for the Ross Valley bank, so he went saunter-
ing around the city, grim as a defeated office-seeker.

The brothers also made some calls, and Arthur
MacNair was puzzled and at the same time pleased, to
find that his dashing junior knew everybody, had
something to chat about with innumerable strangers or
members, and was freely admitted to any public office
he desired. They came home at twilight, quite
fatigued, and found Jabel Blake lying on a bed in the
inner chamber, fast asleep.

"Dreaming of his bank!" said Elk MacNair;
"what a metallic soul must Jabel's be! His very
voice rattles like money. His features are cut hard as
a face on a coin.''

"Jabel has good points, Elk," said the Congressman; "if you can understand the passion of the town
builder you can apprehend him. He has devoted his
life to Ross Valley, and the only text of Scripture he
finds it hard to understand is, that he who ruleth his
soul is greater than he who buildeth a city.''

The two brothers sat together in the main room;
the day, at the windows, was growing grayer, and they
were silent for a while.

The face of Elk MacNair had been growing long during the whole afternoon, but with an assumed gayety he had sought to make the hours pass pleasantly, and when his thoughtful and modest brother endeavored to argue with him that his legal labors were wearing him out, Elk MacNair turned the conversation off in a cheerful way by saying :

"Arthur, I have arranged that you shall have the chairmanship of a first-rate committee."

"How arranged it ?"

"Oh, these things can be managed, you know. Every good position in Washington has to be begged for, or brought about by strategic approaches. I know the Speaker and the Speaker's friends below him, and the old chairman of the committee where I wish you to be ; and, among us all, you have obtained the rare distinction, for a new member, of going to the head of one of the best of the second-class committees."

"I do not like this, Elk," said Arthur. "I hope I am without ambition, particularly of that sort which would annihilate processes and labors, and seek to obtain distinction by an easy path. I do not know that I shall make a speech during the whole of this Congress, although I shall try to be in my seat every day, and to vote when I am well informed. What committee is it, that you have been at such pains to put me at the head of it ?"

"The Committee on Ancient Contracts."

Arthur MacNair, who had not much color at the best of times, turned a little pale.

"Elk," said he, "there is a bad sound in that word 'contracts.' Of course, I do not take much stock in the widespread scandal about our Government giving away contract work to do from base or personal considerations ; but I have a little belief that one ought to avoid even the appearance of evil. I think I must refuse to go on that committee."

Elk MacNair seemed to grow darker and older, and

his face assumed an intensity of expression which his brother did not perceive.

" Pshaw ! Arty," he said, with agitation, " every-thing here goes by friends.   You brought with you no renown, no superstition, nothing which would entitle you to the Speaker's consideration.   He might have put you, but for me, away down on the Committee on Revolutionary Pensions."

" I think I would like that committee," said Arthur MacNair quietly.   " In it I might be the means of do-ing gratitude to some old and needy hero.   I like those tasks which involve no notoriety.   At home, in our church and among our townsfolks, I always tried to get on the societies which are unknown to public fame ; and there, any little thing which I can diligently do brings its own reward.   I must decline to go on the Committee on Ancient Contracts, Elk !"

The younger brother, with his dark burning eyes, met at this point the cool, unsuspecting glance of the coun-try lawyer, and something in it seemed to embarrass even his worldliness, for he rose from his seat and threw up his hands impatiently.

" Oh ! very well," he said.   " I thought I was do-ing you a service, and now I see that it has been love's labor lost.   In fact, I want you on that committee to serve a little turn for me !"

The country brother looked up with truthful sur·prise.

" For you, Elk ?"

" Yes," cried the younger, striding up and down the floor with the step of one made decisive by being put at bay ; " I want you upon that committee, not only to do me a turn but to do me a benefit ; to come to my rescue ; to fulfil the expectations of many hard-working months ; to make me happy.   Yes, Arthur, to make my fortune !"

Arthur MacNair followed the rapid walk and excited voice of his brother with astonishment.   His small, thin, commonplace face seemed to develop lights and intelligences which were painful to him, the clearer his apprehensions became. He said, in a quiet, still voice, as if he also were interested now :

" I am afraid I am on the eve of hearing something bad, my brother. If it must come, let it all come."

" Arthur MacNair," said Elk, his voice raised above the ordinary pitch, and the recklessness of an officer in the ardor of battle showing in his working face, quick talk, and rapid gestures, " you *are* on the eve of hearing something. In your answer lies my destiny. I told you I was a lawyer, and had made one hundred and sixty thousand dollars with which I was to buy my way into an attorney's firm and establish myself in business. It was true. I have made that engagement. My talent and energy are recognized, and the place of which I spoke is waiting for me immediately after my marriage. The lady who is to be my bride is divided from me by no other consideration than this—that I have not obtained the one hundred and sixty thousand dollars."

The Congressman grew paler, and he made an effort to say " go on," but his voice was scarcely audible, and Elk MacNair saw that he seemed to be suddenly sick. With self-reproach the younger brother observed all this, but it was too late for him to falter ; the time was too precious.

" Arty," he said ; " oh, my brother, the whole story must be told and the full crisis met. I am dependent upon you for the price of my happiness ; for the hand of my wife ; for the key to my fortune ; for all that makes the future auspicious and the past clear. I am not a lawyer, as I have said, in the common sense in which, with modest effort and goodness, you have followed out your career. I am a lobbyist !

"I returned from the war flushed with my success, and told on every hand that an immediate and profound prosperity were close before me. These politicians and speculators around the capital took me by the hand, flattered me, and showed me where my fortune was within my own grasp. Little by little they led me on, using my reputation and influence to accomplish their ends ; and my mode of living, my acquaintances, my expectations, increased with my facilities, until, chafing under the consciousness that I was working out the private interests of others, I resolved to stake all upon one large hazard, conclude this wayward, self-accusing life, and depart from the purlieus of legislation. Up to the present time no stigma has been attached to my irregularities, none have suspected that I was less than I claimed to be—a soldier and a gentleman, betrothed to the noblest woman in the world. But this manner of living in the end works the destruction of habits and reputation to any who continue in it. To be brief, I have found political life nothing but a commerce. All have their price, and the highest sometimes sell out the cheapest. Men are estimated here by their boldness and breadth only, and a single successful venture of the kind I have in hand will dismiss me from this city rich and without exposure, and I swear never again to be seen in the lobbies of the Federal legislature. All my dependence in this, however, is upon you. I watched your campaign in our native region—how gallantly and how exceptionably you fought it, none knows so well !—and I took to heart the belief that, wishing to see me distinguished, wedded, and settled, your old scruples might give way, and you would afford me this last, best chance. Shall I go on ?''

The small, thin face of the elder brother seemed to have lost all of its vitality ; his fragile form was even more diminished ; it might almost have been paralysis which had seized him.

" Water !'' he muttered. " I cannot talk.''

The younger brother ran for a glass, and with a look of mingled guilt and affection sought to support him with his arm. Arthur MacNair feebly repelled his assistance.

" You may finish, sir,'' he said.

"God forgive me," cried Elk MacNair, sinking into a chair ; "my brother, I beseech you, do not think so evil of me as to suppose that in this enterprise I would compromise your character for one minute, and if it shall be necessary, all the fault shall be mine by open confession. There is an old claim for postal services rendered many years ago, which has reposed in the catacombs of one of the departments. The claimant has long been dead, and it was purchased for a small sum from his heirs. There are some equities about the claim ; the attestations in its favor are purely documentary, and I have so entirely manipulated every instrumentality on the way to its passage, judicial, legislative, and executive, that if the Committee on Ancient Contracts should report favorably upon it at the beginning of the session, my confederates in the House will see that it goes along, and the department will pay it immediately. Congress will then at once adjourn, within a day or two, for such is the usage here. With my share of the money, which will be large, I will be a man of wealth and able to turn my back once and for all upon this Capitol. You are to be the chairman of the committee ; the other members, as is habitual here, will intrust the whole matter to you ; a few words explanatory of this claim will send it on its way, and the crisis of my life will have passed."

When the younger brother had finished, he also seemed to have expended his strength in the effort he had made, and he sat limp and despondent. The elder brother, on the contrary, appeared to recover his strength by a vigorous effort of the will. He stood up. He walked straight before his brother and looked down upon him with his penetrating blue eyes.

"Elk MacNair," he said, "tell me—by our common origin, solemnly, truthfully, and on your honor, tell me—will this claim stand the test of full investigation ? Is it right ?"

"Arthur," said the younger, feebly, "under that appeal I must speak truthfully. The claim is irreg-

ular ; perhaps it has been paid already. There is no
time for investigation. I have stocked the cards, and
the trick must be taken at once or never. You have
this alternative: I can take you off that committee,
and I have a man in reversion who will get the post
and pass the claim.''

The stature of Arthur MacNair seemed to expand,
and he became the positive spirit of the room.

" Not so," he said ; " it shall not pass, Elk Mac-
Nair, neither by my help nor by any other man's !
You have acknowledged to me that there is no justice
in this thing. You have made me a party to a fraud.
You shall know that the only oath I came here to take
is that of allegiance to the interests of the country.
No brotherhood, no sympathy, no ambition, no pity,
nothing shall be able to swerve me from my full duty.''

" What would you do, fanatic ?" cried Elk Mac-
Nair.

" I will denounce that claim upon the floor of Congress, and couple with the denunciation the story of
this infamous proposal you have made to a member of
Congress.''

The younger brother gave a laugh.

" What nonsense, Arthur," he said. " If you expect to find any large class of Americans who will appreciate such heroism, exhibited at the sacrifice of your
own blood and family, you do not know your countrymen in these days. The only men who deal in sentiment in our time are demagogues, who never feel it.
A sneer will go up from all the circles of the capital,
from all the presses of the land, at a man who seeks,
in a political age, to play the part of the elder Brutus.''

" Miserable, lost, dishonored man !" said Arthur
MacNair. " In the valleys of my State, in the quiet
farming districts all through the Union, among the
hard-working, the penurious, and the plain—such as
you and your class despise—there are armies of men
who would rise and march upon this capital if they appreciated the whole of the scene in which you have

figured to-day! You would steal the money of the people that you may buy a character and a position among your countrymen. Shame upon the man who would defend the acquisition of such booty to wed the woman he loves."

Every word which Arthur MacNair had uttered, and most of all the last, cut like a knife into the pride of Elk MacNair.

" I thought I was pleading with my brother," he said hoarsely, " not to a stone. I shall say no more. I have placed myself in your power. Remember this : if my point is not carried within three days, or if it be balked by your interference, I will blow out my brains. I have walked to the door of hell on the battle-field, and I can go further."

He seized his hat and hurried away like a fury. Arthur MacNair stood motionless an instant in the middle of the floor, and then, worn out with the intensity of the scene, his limbs gave way beneath him, and he fell unconscious.

In a moment the hard, strong face and giant form of Jabel Blake appeared over the threshold of the bedroom ; he lifted his Congressman and counsel in his arms and carried him grimly to a sofa.

III.

The Honorable Perkiomen Trappe was much delighted, on the morning subsequent to the occurrences related in our last chapter, to see Jabel Blake walk down Pennsylvania Avenue with the pensive air of a man whose heart had been broken. The Honorable Perkiomen supposed that Jabel had failed to receive some drawback or other upon his income-tax, and he rejoiced in the reverses of the close and thrifty.

But Jabel Blake was now concerned solely with the sudden and violent rupture between the MacNair brothers. He had little acquaintance with Elk Mac-Nair, and no great fondness for him ; but, being well

informed as to the positive, combative traits of character in Arthur MacNair, Jabel knew very well that what
his counsel had threatened to do he would do, though
his own heart-strings might be sundered.

The deepest wish in Jabel's heart, next to establish-
ing a national bank in Ross Valley, was to see the
marriage between Kate Dunlevy and the MacNair
family brought to pass ; yet such was his reverence for
the Dunlevys and so great his antagonism to the
Washington Lobby that he was half inclined to be
himself the means of breaking off the match between
the daughter of his great neighbor and exemplar and
the son of his old chum and companion.

Jabel took his way to the house of the old Circuit
Judge, which was one of a row of tall brown-stone
structures not far from the city hall, and when he rang
the bell a servant showed him to a library in the second
story, where the Judge was dictating certain judicial
opinions to his daughter.   The two elderly men retired
to an adjacent apartment, which seemed, from its ap-
pointments and the character of needlework and liter-
ature strewn about, to be the *boudoir* of Miss Dunlevy ;
and the Judge, who was somewhat past the prime of
life, plunged into a long story about Ross Valley and
its early settlement, speaking much of the time with his
eyes closed in a sort of half reverie, while Jabel, who
occupied a seat nearer to the library, was meantime
overhearing a conversation between Kate Dunlevy and
young Elk MacNair, who had followed hard upon
Jabel's heels.   The old Judge meantime, used to their
voices, paused only to remark that he thought Elk
MacNair one of the strongest, most brilliant, and most
promising men in the nation, and then went on with
his dissertation upon pioneer days among the spurs
of the Alleghenies.   Jabel, however, who was an attentive, inquisitive busybody, and who lived in a part
of the country where folks of quality and large pursuits
were few, observed that the two voices in the next room

were lowered, and that their key, while not so high, was yet even more startling than before.

" Kate," said Elk MacNair, " I had counted upon my brother as an assured ally in something of the most momentous importance to me at this juncture, before our marriage. My brother is a man of power, but of narrow views, and I have unconsciously aroused his animosity. He is not to be appeased. Nothing can divert him from his purpose.

" It can be nothing ,if Arthur is the arbiter and your happiness the subject," said Miss Dunlevy.

" It is a point of honor differently taken by two men," said Elk MacNair ; " and the issue is a matter of character. It is a matter of fortune besides, and if neither relents both will suffer."

These words were attended with some emotion which smote the rough feelings of Jabel Blake, and he was a witness of some subsidiary endearments, besides,. which softened his indignation against the young officer. So he followed Elk MacNair from the house and accosted him upon the street.

" General," he said, " I claim the privilege of a guardian over you boys—over your brother in particular, who is a true man and an obstinate one. I know the matter of your difference. If you do not yield, Arthur MacNair will keep his word ! You will be exposed on the floor of Congress, exactly as he promised, and your engagement with Kitty Dunlevy broken forever."

" Jabel Blake," answered the soldier, " I know just what I am about. I told my brother that I would blow my own head off if he sacrificed me for a sentiment. And just that I mean to do."

" I know the devil in the MacNair blood," said Jabel Blake ; " but you are playing a false part and Arthur a true one. He fought his campaign against the corruptions and chicanery of power, and he will trample you out like a snake."

" He thinks he's correcting a boy," said Elk Mac-
Nair ; " he shall find me a soldier."

" And you will find him a Christian soldier, truer to
his allegiance than to rob his country !"

" Pshaw !" laughed Elk MacNair ; " a skinflint
who has raked up fortune with his fingers, ground
down his laborers, pinched his soul, and stooped his
stature for money, has no right to be my chaplain,
Jabel Blake ! You have grown rich like a scavenger.
What matter if I bring down fortune with my rifle,
though the American eagle be the bird. I would spare
my body some of the dirty crawling you have done to
get your bank !"

" Base boy !" cried Jabel Blake, with more contempt than anger ; " I will live to teach you that a life
of thrift and honest toil is above your power to insult
it. You can neither repel me nor break your brother's heart. The time will come when you will weep to
deserve the respect you have lost from these gray
hairs."

He passed away with his old, heavy, deliberate gait,
and left the young man almost repentant.

IV.

The galleries and floors of the House of Representatives were crowded, as was usual upon early working
days of the session. Among the members in a retired seat, his red shock of hair, clerical dress, and
thin, worn, commonplace, freckled face denoted the
new member from the Scotch district of Pennsylvania.
The gay daughter of the Honorable Perkiomen Trappe,
picking him out from the diplomatic gallery by the aid
of her opera-glass, remarked that she mourned for her
country when Europe could behold such a specimen
of homespun among American Congressmen.

" And what's more, pet," said the Honorable Perkiomen, " he's a bin put on a fat committee. He
has the cheer in the room on Ancient Contracts, and

your unfortnit father is only a member under him. I
think that staving cavalry brother of his'n, Elk Mac-
Nair, fixed his feed for him !"

They turned to look at Elk MacNair, sitting in the
gallery near by with the venerable Judge and the
Judge's daughter. His dark goatee, eyes, and hair, were
set in a face unusually pale and intense, and his manly
and refined worldly bearing suited his associations.
Kate Dunlevy, with her charms of bloom, repose, and
stateliness, looked like the wife of such a public man.

" Elk," said she, " you do not seem to be at ease
to-day. You are pale and nervous, and you have
stared down there at your brother's seat till people are
taking notice of you."

" I am suffering a little, Kitty ; that is all. My
case comes up within five minutes, and I might as well
blow my head off if it shall stick anywhere."

His eyes seemed to flame out with a reckless light as
he said this.

" Arthur has a sick look as well," said Kate.
" This public life is too exciting for him. See how
nervously he sips that glass of water."

" Sick !" exclaimed Elk MacNair, with a voice of
bitterness, yet with a melancholy glance of admiration
in the direction of the Congressman ; " he is more dangerous than sick. His will is sublime, Kate ; nothing
can soften it, not even pity."

The committees were now being called by the
Speaker, and chairman after chairman rose to make his
report. As the list diminished more and more, and
the Committee upon Ancient Contracts approached
its turn, there were no two such livid, deathly faces in
all the crowded house as these two brothers wore.
Elk MacNair's had a settled ferocity. The youthful-
ness and comely moods were gone from it, and the
burnt-out countenance of a man of the world looked
dead and ashen above the exhausted reservoirs of a
diseased mind. Nothing was left but the last chance
before despair, and apprehensive of the failure of this

hope also, his gloved hand, resting upon a pocket hidden at his hip, sought support from the hilt of a pistol secreted there. Was *this* the meaning of the sullen and ghastly determination glaring from his eyes? Yes, love and death were almost mated; and so in every busy Congress do the spectres of temptation and ill-omen lurk in wait.

The country brother on the floor showed also his tenacious purpose in his compressed lips, straight, expanded breast and shoulders, and clear and direct but grave look. No extremity of occasion could make a heroic figure of him, but in his plain face was the beauty of moral courage. He rose to his feet when the Speaker cried:

"Committee on Ancient Contracts is next in order. The gentleman from Pennsylvania!"

The people in the galleries were not disappointed that such a homely man should have no voice nor grace, and that he spoke only with the gravest effort.

"The gentleman's voice is inaudible to the chair," said the Speaker.

But Elk MacNair had heard it from where he sat. He had distinguished the fitful words:

"The committee reports against the —— claim for postal services, desires that it do not pass, and the chairman wishes to make a personal explanation relative to the claim."

"Kitty," said Elk MacNair, in a coarse whisper, "my brother has broken my heart!"

"Stay!" said Miss Dunlevy; "he staggers in his seat as if he were about to fall. A page has run to him with a letter. He reads it. Elk, for Heaven's sake, go to his help! He is dying!"

There was a rush of members about the new chairman of committee. Confusion reigned upon the floor of Congress. The lobby brother had apprehended it all. He cleared the gallery at a run, passed a familiar doorkeeper like a dart, and raised his senior to his breast.

" Arty," he whispered, " may Heaven forgive me !
I repent of my folly and wickedness, and entreat you
to speak to me !"

" Heaven has forgiven you, Elk MacNair !" muttered
the spent Congressman. " Your father's friend has
spared your fame and my feelings at the expense of his
fortune. It has taken the bank of Jabel Blake—the
dream of his life—to save you from a dishonored name,
and to give you a wife too worthy for you !"

He put a piece of paper in the lobbyist's hands. It
said :

" Arthur, I have given you the last gift in my power
—a costly and a dear one—to keep your brother from
disgrace, and to save you both remorse. I have bought
the ——— claim, and destroyed it, but Ross Valley has
lost the bank.   JABEL BLAKE."

V.

On the terrace of the Capitol, while all this was oc-
curring, a gaunt, gigantic, aged figure might have been
seen, looking away into the city basking in the plain
at his feet, with almost the bitterness of prophecy. He
carried an old worn carpet-bag, and a railroad ticket
appeared in his hat-band. It was Jabel Blake, shaking
the dust of the capital city from his feet !

To him the soft and purple panorama brought no
emotions, as pride of country or æsthetic associations :
and even the bracing savor of the gale upon the eminence seemed laden, to his hard regard, with the corruptions and excesses of a debauched government and
a rank society. The river, to him, was but the fair
sewer to this sculptured sepulchre. The lambent amphitheatre of the inclosing ridges was like the wall of a
jail which he longed to cross and return no more. He
saw the dark granite form of the Treasury Department,
and groaned like one whose heart was broken there.
The bank of Ross Valley was never to be !

Jabel thought in one instant of the inquiries which

should be addressed to him on his return, the prying
curiosity of the hamlet, the strictures of his neighbors
and laborers, the exultation of his enemies, the lost
chance of his cherished village to become the mart of
its locality and dispense from its exchequer enterprise
and aid to farms and mines and mills.

"The good God may make it up to my children
some day," he said; "but the bank is never to be in
the life of old Jabel Blake!"

So Jabel went home and met with all obtuseness the
flying rumors of the country. His worst enemies said
that he had fallen from grace while in Washington, and
"bucked" with all his bonds against a faro bank.
His best friends obtained no explanation of his losses.
He kept his counsel, grew even sterner and thriftier than
he had ever been, and only at the Presbyterian church,
where he prayed in public frequently at the evening
meetings, were glimpses afforded of his recollections of
Washington by the resonant appeals he made that the
money-changers might be lashed out of the temples
there, and desolation wrought upon them that sold
doves.

There was no bank at Ross Valley, but people began
to say that old Jabel Blake had particles of gold in the
flinty composition of his life, and that his trip to Washington had made him gentler and wider in his charities.
He was attentive to young children. He encouraged
young lovers. He lifted many errant people to their
feet, and started them on their way to a braver life of
sacrifice. And fortune smiled upon him as never before. His mills went day and night, stopping never
except on Sabbaths. The ground seemed to give forth
iron and lime wherever he dug for it. The town became the thriftiest settlement in the Allegheny valleys,
and Jabel Blake was the earliest riser and the hardest
delver in the State.

It happened at the end of two years that rheumatism
and an overstrained old age brought Jabel Blake to
bed, and a flood, passing down the valley, aroused him,

despite advice, to his old indomitable leadership against its ravages. He returned to his rest never to arise ; for now a fever laid hold upon the old captain, and he talked in his delirium of Judge Dunlevy and his bank, and he was attended all the while by Arthur MacNair.

One night, in a little spell of relief, Jabel Blake opened his eyes and said :

" Arty, I dreamed old Jabel Blake was in heaven, and that he had founded a bank there !"

" Jabel," said the young Congressman, " you must have some treasure laid up there, old friend. And not only in heaven, but in this world also. Look on this happy family redeemed by your sacrifice !"

Jabel Blake opened his eyes wider, and they fell upon Judge Dunlevy.

" This is a great honor," he said ; " Ross Valley brings her great citizen back."

" No !" cried the Judge, " it is you, Jabel, who have brought us all to your bedside to do ourselves honor. Here are Elk MacNair and my daughter, who owe all their fortune to your fatherly kindness, and who have come to repay you the uttermost farthing. Providence has appreciated your sacrifice. They bring for your blessing, my grandson, and the name they have given him is Jabel Blake."

" Jabel," said General MacNair, " take with our full hearts this money. It has been honestly earned with the capital of your bank. We return it that you may fulfil the dream of your life !"

Jabel Blake took the money, and a smile overspread his face. His hard lineaments were soft and fatherly now, and their tears attested how well he was esteemed. He drew Elk MacNair's ear to his lips, and said feebly, and with his latest articulate breath ·

" General, you owe me two years' interest !"

They laid Jabel Blake away by his fathers, and on the day of the funeral Ross Valley was crowded like a shrine.

POTOMAC RIVER.

BRAVE river in the mountains bred,
　And broadening on thy way,
So stately that thy stretches seem
　The bosom of the bay !
Thy growth is like the nation's life,
　Through which thy current flows—
Already past the cataracts
　And widening to repose.

Thy springs are at the Fairfax stone,
　Thy great arms northward course,
They join and break the mountain bars
　With ever rallying force ;
But in thy nature is such peace,
　The beaten mountains yield,
And lie their riven battlements
　Within thy silver shield.

Through battle-fields thy runnels wind,
　In fame thy ferries shine ;
Thy ripples lave the ancient stones
　On Freedom's boundary line ;
Where every slave the border crossed,
　A living host repass'd,
And of the sentries of thy fords,
　John Brown shall be the last !

Yet, O Potomac ! of thy peace
　Somewhat let faction feel,
And Northern pilgrims patient hear
　Of Mosby and MacNeill.
The long trees bloom where Stuart cross'd,
　And weep where Ashby bled,
And every echo in thy hills
　Seems Stonewall Jackson's tread.

The love we bore in other days
   No difference can bar,
And truce was kept at Vernon's grave
   However rolled the war.
Like thee, oh river! human states
   By many a rapid rage,
Before they reach the deeper tides
   And glass the perfect age.

Brief is the span since Calvert's huts
   Were still the Indian's sport,
And Braddock's columns stumbled on
   The borderer Cresap's fort,
Till now the tinted hills grow fond
   Around yon marble height,
Where Freedom calmly rules a realm
   That tires her eagle's flight.

And still the wild deer sip thy springs,
   The wild duck haunt thy coves,
And all the year the fisher fleets
   Bask o'er thine oyster groves ;
The strange new bass thy trout pursue,
   And where the herring spawn,
The blue sky opens to let through
   Thine own majestic swan.

Haste, Nature ! Raze yon shiftless halls,
   Where pride penurious hides,
The while the richness of the hills
   Runs off to choke the tides ;
Where every negro cabin stood
   A freeman's hearthside warm,
And broad estates of bramble wood
   Expunge in many a farm '

Fill and revive these fair arcades,
   O race to Freedom born !
The tinkling herds that roam the glades,
   The barge's mellow horn,
The lonesome sails that come and go
   Repeat the wish again :
The ardent river yearns to know
   Not memories, but MEN !

TELL-TALE FEET.

THE din of the day is quiet now, and the street is deserted. The last bacchanal reeled homeward an hour ago. The most belated cabman has passed out of hearing. The one poor wretch who comes nightly to the water-side has closed her complaint ; I saw her shawl float over the parapet as she flung her lean arms against the sky and went down with a scream. Here, in the busiest spot of the mightiest city, there is no human creature abroad ; but footsteps are yet ringing on the desolateness. They are heard only by me. There are two of them ; the first light, timorous, musical ; the other harsh and heavy, as if shod with steel. I recognize them with a thrill : for they have haunted me many years, and they are speaking to me now. The one is soothing and pleading, and it implores me to write ; but the second is like the striking of a revengeful knell. "Confession and Pardon," says the one ; "Horror and Remorse," echoes the other. They tinkle and toll thus every midnight, when my hour of penance arrives and I have tried to register my story. It is almost finished now. Let me read the pages softly to myself :

"My life has been a long career of suffering. The elements, whose changes and combinations contribute to the pleasure of my species, have arrayed themselves against me. I am fashioned so delicately that the every-day bustle of the world provokes exquisite and incessant pain. Embodied like my fellows, my nerves are yet sensitive beyond girlishness, and my organs of sight, smell, and hearing are marvellously acute. The inodorous elements are painfully odorous to me. I can hear the subtlest processes in nature, and the densest darkness is radiant with mysterious lights. My childhood was a protracted horror, and the noises of a great city in which I lived shattered and well-nigh crazed me. In the dead calms I shuddered at the howling of winds. I fancied that I could detect the gliding revolution of the earth, and hear the march of the moon in her attendant orbit.

"My parents loved me tenderly, and failing to soothe or conciliate me, they removed from the busy city to a secluded villa in the suburbs. Those labors which necessitated abrupt or prolonged sound were performed outside our grounds. The domestics were enjoined to conduct their operations with the utmost quietude. Carriages never came to the threshold, but stopped at the lodge ; the drives were strewn with bark to drown the rattle of wheels ; familiar fowls and beasts were excluded ; the pines were cut down, though they had moaned for half a century ; the angles of the house were rounded, that the wind might not scream and sigh of midnight, and the flapping of a shutter would have warranted the dismissal of the servants. Thick carpets covered the floors. My apartments lay in a remote wing, and were surrounded with double walls, filled with wool, to deaden communication. Goodly books were provided, but none which could arouse fears or passions. Fiery romances were prohibited, and histories of turmoil and war, with theology and its mournful revelations, and medicine, which revived the bitter story of my organism. My library was stocked with dreamy and diverting compositions—old Walton, the pensive angler ; the vagaries of ancient Burton, and the placid essayists of the Addisonian day. Of poets I had Cowper and Wordsworth, who loved quiet life and were the chroniclers of domestic men and manners. Pictures of shadowy studios and calm lakes, unfrequented coverts and sleepy wayside inns, covered my wall. The tints of tapestry, panel, and furniture were subdued, and the sunshine which mellowed a stained window was softened by an ingenious arrangement of shades and refractors. Art opposed her quaintest contrivances against the intense and violent moods of Nature, and my retirement was secure from the inroads of all except my careful guardians.

" But I was still unhappy, and the prey of vivid fancies. This privacy suggested the great world without, where men were wrestling with dangers. I imagined ships upon stormy seas, and whirlwinds around mountain-homes ; the chaos of cities, the rout of armies, dim arctic solitudes, where the icebergs tumbled apart and the frozen seas split asunder. They had banished painful occurrences, but the sensitive organism could not be destroyed, and I bore up until almost insane, struggling to be cheerful when stunned and dazzled. At last, when my mother stole into my room one day—it was October, I think, for I could hear the tiniest leaves dropping to the grass far below —I laid my head wearily in her lap and covered my ears with my hands. My eyes were filled with tears.

" ' My dear mother, I cannot bear this life. I suffer as of old, though there be not a mote across the sun nor a breath in the air. If my mind could be led from these consciousnesses, I might be calm.'

" ' Luke,' said my mother, ' you need a companion.'

" 'The thought was a new one, and so thrilled me.

" ' No, mother,' I replied ; ' strong, healthy beings could not exist thus cloistered.'

" ' For less than money,' she responded, ' they have done more.'

" ' We should not agree,' I said ; ' I would be peevish and he would despise me.'

" ' Your companion must be a woman, my son.'

" A succession of short chills passed through every nerve, and a moment's faintness possessed me.

" ' It must not be,' I pleaded ; ' a restless, chatting, plotting woman would be worse than all.'

" My mother marked my rising agitation and glided away.

" ' Whatever can relieve you, dear Luke,' she said, ' your father shall obtain.'

" I now fancied that they believed me mad, and that a keeper was to be introduced to me, under the guise of a companion. I formed many mental portraits of this fierce person, and they kept me awake through the long watches. I even meditated escape, and unclosed my casement with that design, but the sunlight, the bird songs, and the zephyrs rushed into my window and staggered me like so many sentinels. One day I slept fitfully, and dreamed that I was poor and orphaned, with the alternatives of death or work before me. I had wandered to a village and thrown myself beneath some elms, with a horrible despair sealing my eyelids. Suddenly the grass was stirred by some human footfalls, and two soft voices were speaking close beside me.

" ' It is strange,' said the first voice ; ' he is pale and delicate, but with no evidences of heavier afflictions.'

" ' You do not know him,' murmured the other ; ' wait and see !'

" A face bent down to mine, and the lips of a woman touched my cheek. I started in my sleep, caught my breath gaspingly, and quivered like an aspen.

" ' This is indeed terrible,' said the soft voice compassionately ; ' but do not despair! It cannot be nature. It must be habit, or bashfulness, or the effect of some childish and forgotten fright. Cheer up, and hope !''

" ' Be kind to him, Heraine,' resumed the other ; ' you are my last resort, and becoming his companion you become my child. Do not vex, do not excite him. Be yourself—always calm, gentle, and affectionate—and the kindness which you show my boy may God return to you in mercy and blessing !'

" I unclosed my eyes ; the scene was resolved to my quiet library. Something glided through the door, but a form from the other side flung a shadow across my face. A premonition of the keeper thrilled me a moment, but I turned slowly at length and looked into the intruder's face.

" A woman, or rather a girl with a woman's face, serene and placid, as if never ruffled by care or passion, sat between me and the window, and the gloomy light softened her calm countenance. As I looked up her lashes fell, and her blue eyes were bent fixedly upon the floor. She seemed like one of my sedate portraits, which had come down from its case. She waited, apparently for some sign of recognition, or until my surprise should have passed away, and did not move while I ran her over with keen curiosity. She was, probably, of my own age, though her self-possession might have stamped her as much older ; but the bloom of her cheek and her bosom just ripening were indices of a girl's year's. She raised her eyes at length and bade me good afternoon in a voice which reminded me of the faintest lullaby. The quiet tone was seconded by an assuring glance, and directly we were conversing without restraint, as if friends of years rather than acquaintances of an hour.

" Heraine was the impersonation of composure. The neutral tint of dress corresponded with the smooth tresses of her brown hair. Her touch was magnetic, and petulancy vanished at her smile as at a charm. Her intelligence was, doubtless, the secret of her power. She divined my moods without inquiry, and cheered them without effort. She led me out of the unhealthy atmosphere engendered by my sensitiveness, and I sometimes forgot my disability for hours. She was as good as she was capable, and as amiable as she was resolute. We fraternized immediately, and I felt all the newness of a regenerated life. My temperament was fitful as of yore, but the gloomy spectres vanished ; and my attention being weaned from the slighter occurrences of nature, I was no longer racked by their tremors and jars. The soft face of Heraine seemed to hush all chaos, and when she smiled I thought that the very earth had ceased to roll. When her large liquid eyes were fully opened upon me, I seemed to be looking into the hungry blue of the sky, and carried aloft by the look beyond the influence of matter. For the moment my nerves grew numb, the compass of my senses narrowed to her wondrous face, and the fetters which bound me to it were forged of gold.

" The months went by like the stars, which wheel eternally, but seem motionless as we watch them. Sometimes we read aloud, but our voices were low and lulling, as if quieter than silence. Then we talked of my calm paintings, shadowing deeper lonelinesses in them. But it was my highest rapture to sit in stillness for hours while Heraine, cushioned at my feet, made cunning embroideries, like some facile poet whose fingers were dropping rhymes.

" l remarked that our conversations were progressive. My companion led me gradually into forbidden themes, as if to strengthen and embolden me. We went forth, in fancy, from our shadowy chamber, through deep groves, into twilights, beneath soft skies, even into the glare of the sun, and, at last, among the storms and the seas. l may have quivered, but I was not shocked ; for the wrack and roar of the universe were drowned in the quietness of her voice. Then we walked abroad a little way, and, though pained, I endured ; for she did not abuse these successes. She had travelled in far countries, and often read me friendly letters which attested how well the world esteemed her. Sometimes her acquaintances came to the house, but never to my room ; and once or twice she was absent a whole day, when my nervousness returned. There was one correspondent whose missives were never read to me—a fine, bold hand, which at length became familiar. Their receipt pleased her, I thought, and once I ventured to say :

" ' Heraine, you have a pleasant letter there.'

" She only blushed very much, and all her quietness was gone for a moment.

" As the months expanded into years, a new feeling engendered from our intimacy. I did not comprehend it at first. It crept upon me like the unfolding of a new sense, or the gradual realizing of the earliest profound thought. An unexpected event gave it recognition.

" The boldly-indorsed letters came twice a month at first, afterward four times, and finally twice, thrice, and even five times a week. Heraine was quick and flushed. She passed but two or three hours daily in my apartment, and substituted for the embroidery a dress of such bright hues that it dazzled my eyes. One day she took her accustomed seat, with a face subdued to sadness and an irresolute manner.

" ' Luke,' she said, after a long pause, ' we have passed many days pleasantly together?'

" She did not wait for me to speak, though I thrilled and turned deadly white.

" ' And because so pleasantly, I contemplate my farewell with regret.'

" ' Your farewell, Heraine?'

" ' Yes,' she said firmly ; ' to-day—this afternoon —this hour—I bid adieu to Glengoyle !'

" I fell forward in my seat, forcing down my heart, which sobbed and swelled, and the whole world rang, flared, and burst into violence. If the seas had opened their fountains and the crust of the globe crushed up, there would have been no greater chaos. But in my faintness and agony I caught the blue eye which had soothed and melted me so often, and, clasping my hands, I fell at her knees and said,

" ' Heraine, I love you !'

" It was her time to tremble now, and I interpreted the pallor of her cheek as a signal of hope.

" ' I know that I love you.' I said ; ' if the earth and the stars were to be blotted out, and you remain, I should not miss them. You are my universe. Without you there is no creation, and the elements are at war. If you leave me, you have left only a bright space in a wretched eternity. No voice but yours can say " peace" to me. Be merciful and remain !'

" She was moved with my appeal, and tears came to her eyes.

" ' I did not know that it had come to this,' she said. Then her composure returned, and she raised me with a smile.

" ' If you would win any woman,' she said meaningly, ' you must first be a man. You are not a man, Luke. You are a child ! You have shut the sunlight from you, and the trill of a thrush pierces you like an arrow. Would you cage your wife in the gloominess of this sepulchre ? Would you hush her songs, and tremble beneath her caresses, and die in the delights of her love ? Go ! Open the window of this vault ! Mingle with the crowds of cities ! Ascend into the mountains ! Cross the seas ! Become worthy of my affection, and then entreat me again !'

" She had shown me the abject thing I was. Her conditions were harder than death ; but the hope she had spoken was like a glimpse of Heaven, and I answered,

" ' Heraine, I will do it !'

" In a month I set out for my travels. An easy coach conveyed me to London, and the third day I lay sick in Paris. Sore of body and brain, strained in nerve and stunned in sense, I persisted in my resolve, and was whirled, more dead than alive, across the Continent to Berlin. In the period of three months I had traversed all the leading kingdoms and pushed my purpose to the sandy banks of the Nile. Every moment in this journey was an infinity of torture ; but in the bitterest pangs I remembered the divine consummation, and kept on. My infirmities were increased rather than diminished. In the deepest thunder I could hear the delving of the beetle ; and though the whole

vault blazed with electric light, I could see the twinkle
of the glow-worm. But among the multitude of noises
which haunted me, the most persistent were the footfalls of men. There were pauses in the lives of all
other beings. The weasel and the hyena rested sometimes, and I could avoid their haunts, but men were
forever alert and ubiquitous. I heard them in abysses,
upon peaks, and in wildernesses. They trod upon my
nerves ; they crushed sleep from my soul. I closed my
ears in vain ; I fled without refuge ; I prayed without
avail. The patter of little children, the footfall of the
maiden, the elastic pace of the youth, the racking limp
of the cripple, the veteran hobbling upon his wooden
stump, the confused tread of crowds, the steady tramp
of soldiers—these tortured me by daylight, and I kept
penance at midnight with the going of outcasts and
vagrants.

"I learned to classify these footfalls. My sensations of them were so keen that my memory retained
them. I recognized individuals, not by their faces but
by their feet. A solitary tourist met me among the
ruins of Luxor ; I knew his tread, though months had
elapsed, among the thousands on London Bridge.
A gypsy family, whom I passed on the Spanish sierras,
went under my window in Paris, and I missed the feet
of the lad who had been hanged. Ten thieves were
marched to the pillory in Kiev ; I counted the paces
of the four who escaped, from a closed diligence on the
Simplon. I lost not one among the millions of footfalls. But there were two which I distinguished every
where. When I pursued, they retreated ; when I fled,
they followed me. They were like two echoes in
different keys ; and one of them I loved, the other I
hated. The first was soft, tinkling, harmonious, like
a memory rather than a sound ; the other was firm,
vigorous, and vehement, and it kept time with the soft
footstep, as if to drown it to my ears. When I was
fagged and wretched, the light footfall approached me ;

but when, inspirited, I rose to behold its owner, it died away in the thunder of its companion tread.

"At last I embarked for America, and when the land disappeared I said to myself, ' At sea, at least, no footfalls can follow.' But one night, when the clangor of the screw drove me upon deck, I heard, far astern, through the deep fog, the sound of two haunting feet. Next morning a swifter steamer overtook us. The waves revelled between, and the winds were high, but above the bellow of our engines and the elements, those thrilling footfalls rang out. I caught a glimpse of a familiar something, as the rival craft went by, and reeled and fell upon the deck.

" I found New York the noisiest city in the world, and felt that a week's tenure there would drive me mad. A fire occurred in Broadway the night of my arrival, and the din of the mobs which ran to its relief was greater than all the combined clamors of Europe. So I resorted to a beautiful village called Wyoming, in the heart of the Susquehanna mountains, and passed the month of September in comparative quiet. If any place in the world is shut in from brawls and storms, it is this historic valley. Its reminiscences were sad and painful to me, but its scenes were like soft dreams.

" During a part of my tenure in the village I missed my shadowy attendants ; but when, one day, I ascended to Prospect Rock, I heard amid the hum of farms and mines and mills, those same audible repetitions floating up the sides of the mountain. The valley grew dim upon my sight, and I hastened nervously to my cottage. Thenceforward I seldom lost them. When I penetrated the wild glen of the Lackawanna, or climbed the Umbrella Tree, or ventured into the Wolf's Den, or sat upon Queen Esther's Rock, or sailed upon Harvey's Lake, they followed me, the one lulling, the other maddening—invisible but omnipresent types of the good and the evil which forever hover in the air.

" One day I ventured to Falling Waters, a reservoir which is precipitated from a cliff, called Campbell's Ridge, into a gorge of the Shawnee Mountains. The deafening roar of the cataract would be almost deathly to me ; but, strengthened by the promise of Heraine, I determined to add this achievement to the long list of inflictions endured for her sake.

" I made the ascent on foot, and could see, from the base of the ridge, the skein of foam shining through the pines in its everlasting flight down the rocks. I became accustomed to the sound as I gradually approached, and mused, with gladness, of an early return to England. Heraine would acknowledge my vindication. Suffering more anguish from a sunbeam or a song than others from the knout or the rack, I had yet run the gauntlet of the intensest horrors, cheered by the certainty of her regard. She would confess her error. We should shut out the world again from our shadowy home at Glengoyle, and go down together, hand in hand, to a deeper stillness. As I mused thus I heard the haunting footfalls again, going up the mountain before me. To my delight, their attendant demon was inaudible, and I pursued them rapturously. The rush of waters grew louder. They had moaned before ; they shrieked and screamed now, as if in the agony of their suicidal leap. But, clear and musical above the hell of sound rang the tinkling feet which had led me around the globe.

" I called aloud. I quickened my pace. I could see only in glimpses through my tears ; but along the steep sinuosities of the path something fluttered and vanished, and fluttered again—I recognized Heraine.

" I knew now the fidelity of her affection. She had followed my invalid wanderings, to be near me in want and prostration. I could have knelt in the aisle of the dim woods, with God's choir of waters pealing before me, to weep my gratitude. But as the figure of Heraine disappeared above, those other abhorred footfalls rang keenly below. Deep, rapid, and elastic, they were sonorously defined above the clash of the cataract. I fled, with my hands upon my ears.

" On and on ! winding among boles, creeping beneath branches, climbing ledges, vaulting over fissures
and chasms, I reached the open plain at last, and
halted unnerved upon the brink of the abyss.

" The glory of the prospect filled me with exquisite
pain. A mist, arched by a delicate rainbow, rose from
the tumbling flood, and the sunny valley was visible,
at intervals, beyond it, inclosed by blue mountains and
intersected by the pale, ribbon-like Susquehanna. It
was my fate to endure, not to enjoy ; but at this
moment the cataract was forgotten in a deeper torment ; the boughs opened, the sky split with the shock
of feet, and a man bounded from the wood.

" He was tall, handsome, and athletic, and his ruddy
cheeks were flushed with exercise. He made a trumpet of his hands, and hallooed, long and clear,

" ' Hera—a—a—ine !'

" Then he whistled through his fist till the rocks
and water rang.

" ' Where the deuce is the dear girl ?' he said, and
his eyes fell upon me.

" A terrible hatred rose in my heart against this
man. It was the first great passion I had nurtured,
and had received no other provocation than the empty
sounds of his footfalls. But antipathies are not acci-
dental merely ; they are organic ; and my quick sense
took alarm even from his tread. One's character may
be defined in his gait, but I knew from the tramp of
this person that his nature was averse to mine. Why
had he followed my affianced across the seas ? Why
had his crashing drowned the music of her steps ?
Why had he uttered her name with an endearment ?
Why had he been retained at her side, and I sent alone
and wretched before ? My wrists knotted nervously as
these accusations took shape, and my blood became gall.

" ' I beg pardon,' he said curtly ; ' but are you the
young man we are looking for ?'

" I asked through my teeth whom he designated in
the term ' *we*.'

" ' Heraine, of course,' he replied ; ' give me your hand ! We have followed our little invalid—that's what we call you—over many a league, and may make his acquaintance at last. Ralph Clendenning, at your service !'

" I shrank menacingly from him, and counted the dull throbs of my heart.

" ' What ! timid !' he said ; ' and with so old a friend ? I never met you, indeed, but then I have talked of you so often that you have grown to be quite a brother.'

" I saw that he was frank and winning, and hated him the more.

" ' Upon my word,' he added, ' there was none whom I had resolved in my mind to love so well, for the sake of Heraine.'

" A cry escaped me, so bitter that it seemed a howl, and I clenched my hands.

" He still followed me along the very edge of the cliff, extending his hand. A horrible impulse rushed upon me, and a thought darker than jealousy caught it up. I hurled myself against him. He staggered on the brink of the abyss, and went down with a sharp, half-stifled scream !

" My eyes followed the dead weight, as it rolled from ledge to ledge, accelerated each instant by the force of the cataract. A world, tossed out of gravity and crashing among the planets, could not have been more awfully distinct. Down—down—down—a formless mass of fibre and bone, the mist seemed to buoy it up when it reached the deepmost cascade, and as it disap·peared through the tops of the pines, I heard the coming of footfalls.

" Mine was a soul in torment, listening to music in heaven. I stood, stiff and numb in horror, staring into the gulf. The roar of the cataract was smothered to a babble. The rainbow vibrated tremulously to the dropping harmonies. I saw the familiar shadow as it gided to my feet. A soft hand thrilled me with its touch, and the old voice said:

"'Dear Luke, I am Heraine, come back.'

"I could not stir. My eyes were forged to the abyss.

"'Why do you glare so wildly?' she said. 'Come! you have been brave, and must not fail now. Have you no kind greeting for Heraine?'

"Down in the abyss, swaying and rocking upon the pine bough, with the frank smile as when I murdered him, I saw my victim in fancy.

"'Speak, Luke,' she repeated. 'I have a dear friend here ; he has made the long pilgrimage with me, fondly anticipating this meeting. You will know him to-day, and I am sure you will love him.'

"Still surging upon mist and spray and bough, with the halo of the rainbow shimmering above it, the noble face turned upward forgivingly.

"We have planned for your happiness, dear friend. Compared to the retreat we have fashioned for you, Glengoyle is a Babel. But you are ill, Luke! What terrible allurement lies in the waterfall? Come away from the brink! Ralph! Ralph!'

"She called in clear tones. The woods and waters answered back.

"'He is there,' I stammered ; 'down—deep—dead —do you see him?—how he smiles and surges on the tufts of the pines ! I—thrust him over—in rage—even as he gave me his hand—I slew him !'

"'Merciful God !' she whispered in horror ; 'he was my husband !'

"The rainbow dissolved ; the waterfall deluged the valley ; the mountains were covered with waves ; the skies grew pitchy dark ; I saw nothing more.

.   .   .   .

"My sensations upon waking were those of a diver who has risen from the tranquil depths to the surface. Hubbub recommenced ; horror returned. My hair was shaven close to my skull ; my head ached dismally ;

I moved my hand with an effort, and my eyelids were
so weak that I could not unseal them for a time.

"I was lying in my old chamber at Glengoyle, and
Heraine was sitting at my bedside. Her garments
were sable, her brown hair thin, her face placid, as of
yore, but marked by deep-seated grief, and the magnetism of will and courage was gone from it. To the
eye she was the same ; to the mind, a weak and broken
thing. Crime had changed both our natures ; she had
been tutor and governess before, and I the passive,
submissive creature ; but sin had made me bold, and
sorrow worn her to a woman.

"'Luke,' she said, in the same lullaby tone, 'do
you know me ? do you recognize the place ? are you
still weak ?'

"'Heraine,' said I, sternly, 'do not the wrongs we
have done each other forbid this intimacy ?'

"'Oh, Luke !' she replied, 'let us not uncover the
past. I have buried your sin with its victim, and
watched you through weary months, and prayed God
to pardon you.'

"'Can God pardon your sin to me, Heraine ?'

"'I trust so, Luke,' she said feebly, 'if ever in my
life I treasured you a hard thought or did you any injury.'

"'Is it no injury,' I said, 'to have lured me by a
false promise from my quiet home ? I have endured
the torture of cities, seas, suns, and storms. Your
pledge was my spur and talisman through all. But you
had cheated me with a lie. You were another's
already. For you I have stained my hands with blood
and shut heaven against my soul !'

"'As I have an account to settle, Luke,' she
pleaded, 'I meant your happiness only. To have told
you that I was wedded would have pained you. I
thought to familiarize you with scenes and sounds, by
making my regard an incentive to adventure. It was
your mother's plan. I yielded to the deception, and
believed it good.''

" ' It was a wicked falsehood," I said ; ' you knew the weakness of my nature—that my sensitiveness was a disease—that to cross me was to kill. You have made both of us wretched forever.'

" My cruelty was murdering her ; her face grew deathly in its pallor, and she pressed her hands upon her heart.

" ' Let the dead man lie between us,' I proceeded ; ' it is not seemly for you to be my friend ; and to me you are an ever-present accusation. We must not see each other !'

" ' Oh, Luke !' she cried, falling upon her knees imploringly : ' I am a bruised thing, a-weary of the world. This silence and darkness are endeared to me. Do not send me away !'

" ' You agitate me,' I said ; ' let us do our penance, each in loneliness. There was a time when our sorrows were mutual ; it is past ; we have only to say farewell.'

" I covered my face with my hands ; she touched my brow with her lips, and when the door had closed upon her sobbing I heard her footfalls making mournful music on the stairs. They rang upon the lawn, then pattered down the drive ; they passed desolately out of the gate, they were lost on the highway, and then the world became blank again.

. . . .

" ' Luke,' said my mother timidly, ' Mrs. Clendenning—Heraine—is—dead.'

" ' I know it,' said I quietly.

" She seemed surprised, and interrogated me with her eyes.

" ' She died at twilight yesterday,' I stated ; ' as the first candles were lit in the lodge and the earliest star appeared—I heard her footsteps.'

" ' At that time she passed away,' sobbed my mother. ' Oh, Luke ! you were cruel to the poor girl.

Her parting prayer was made for you.   To the last you
stood between Heraine and heaven.'

   " ' At that time, mother, I was sitting at my window.   Tears and thrills haunted me during the afternoon, and I was frightened in the silence and darkness.
And I heard Heraine's footsteps come up the road,
pass the lodge, ascend the stairs, and cross my threshold.   They were like echoes rather than sounds—hollow and ghostly ; and mingled with them were the
deeper footfalls of my other spectre, her husband.'

   " I could not inhabit my chamber now.   These
awful sounds drove me into the open world, where I
hoped to lose them in the tread of multitudes.   I wandered to the old church on the day of the funeral, and
looked upon the bier with dry and burning eyes.   The
pastor read of the holy Jerusalem, and said that her
pure feet were walking the golden streets.   But in the
hushes of the sobbing I heard them close beside me,
and while children were strewing her grave with flowers they followed me over the stile and through the
village till I gained the fields and took to my heels in
fright.
   " I sought the resort of crowds, and lived amid tur-
bulences.   In busy hours I baffled my pursuers ; but in
the dark midnights, when only the miserable walked, I
suffered the agonies of remorse and penance.   The
ever-flowing stream of life on London Bridge became
my solace.   My apartments are here, and I sit con-
tinually at an open window, leaning far forward, to
catch the thunder of the tramp.   I know the footfalls
as of old.   I see the suicide pace to and fro, to nerve
herself for the deed.   I hear her sleek betrayer, and
detect their wretched offspring as he first essays to
filch a handkerchief or a purse.
   " Oh, the footfalls ! the footfalls !   Each tread
marks a good or a wicked thought.   A fiend or an
angel starts beneath every heel.   They write an eternal

record as they go. Their voices float forever to witness against or for us. We people space as we cleave
it. The ground that is dumb as we spurn it has a
memory and a revenge. I am more sensitive than my
kind ; and my penance to these moniters of my sin is
but a realization of the terror which all must feel at the
accusation of their footfalls.''

UPPER MARLB'RO'.

Through a narrow, ravelled valley, wearing down the farmer's soil,
The Patuxent flows inconstant, with a hue of clay and oil,
From the terraces of mill-dams and the temperate slopes of wheat,
To the bottoms of tobacco, watched by many a planter's seat.

There the blackened drying-houses show the hanging shocks of green,
Smoking through the lifted shutters, sunning in the nicotine ;
And around old steamboat-landings loiter mules and overseers,
With the hogsheads of tobacco rolled together on the piers.

Inland from the river stranded in a cove between the hills,
Lies old Marlb'ro' Court and village, acclimated to her chills ;
And the white mists nightly rising from the swamps that trench her round,
Seem the sheeted ghosts of memories buried in that ancient ground.

Here in days when still Prince George's of the province was the queen,
Great old judges ruled the gentry, gathering to the court-house green ;
When the Ogles and the Tayloes matched their Arab steeds to race,
Judge Duval adjourned the sessions, Luther Martin quit his case.

Here young Roger Taney lingered, while the horn and hounds were loud,
To behold the pompous Pinkney scattering learning to the crowd ;
And old men great Wirt remembered, while their minds he strove to win,
As a little German urchin drumming at his father's inn.

When the ocean barks could moor them in the shadow of
    the town
Ere the channels filled and mouldered with the rich soil
    wafted down—
Here the Irish trader, Carroll, brought the bride of Darnell
    Hall,
And their Jesuit son was Bishop of the New World over all.

Here the troopers of Prince George's, with their horse-tail
    helmets, won
Praise from valiant Eager Howard and from General Wil-
    kinson ;
And (the village doctor seeking from the British to restore)
Key, the poet, wrote his anthem in the light of Baltimore.

One by one the homes colonial disappear in Time's decrees,
Though the apple orchards linger and the lanes of cherry-
    trees ;
E'en the Woodyard * mansion kindles when the chimney-
    beam consumes,
And the tolerant Northern farmer ploughs around old Rom-
    ish tombs.

By the high white gravelled turnpike trails the sunken, copse-
    grown route,
Where the troops of Ross and Cockburn marched to victory,
    and about,
Halting twice at Upper Marlb'ro', where 'tis still tradition's
    brag.
That 'twas Barney got the victory though the British got the
    swag.

But the Capital, rebuilded, counts 'mid towns rebellious
    this—
Standing in the old slave region 'twixt it and Annapolis ;
And the cannon their embrasures on the Anacostia forts
Open tow'rd old ruined Marlb'ro' and the dead Patuxent
    ports.

---

* "The Woodyard," the finest brick mansion on the western peninsula of Maryland, the seat of the Wests, twelve miles from Washington, burned down a few years ago by the unaccountable ignition
of the great beam of wood over the big chimney-place, which had
stood there for nearly 200 years. E'ther seasoned by the fire or
fired by spooks, it caught in the night and a heap of imported bricks
stood next morning in place of The Woodyard.

Still from Washington some traveller, tempted by the easy
    grades,
Through the Long Old Fields continues cantering in the
    evening shades,
Till he hears the frogs and crickets serenading something
    lost,
In the aguey mists of Marlb'ro' banked before him like a
    frost.

Then the lights begin to twinkle, and he hears the negroes'
    feet
Dancing in the old storehouses on the sandy business street,
And abandoned lawyers' lodges underneath the long trees
    lurk,
Like the vaults around a graveyard where the court-house is
    the kirk.

He will see the sallow old men drinking juleps, grave and
    bleared—
But no more their household servants at the court-house
    auctioneered ;
And the county clerk will prove it by the records on his
    shelves,
That the fathers of the province were no better than our-
    selves.

PREACHERS' SONS IN 1849.

WHEN I admit that these reminiscences are real, it will at once be inferred that I am a preacher's son. The general reputation of my class has been bad since the day of Eli ; but I affirm and maintain that reason does not bear out this verdict, however obstinate experience may be. For why should the best parents have the worst children ? and that our itinerant sires were godly and self-sacrificing men the most prodigal of their boys must confess. No flippant or errant example rises before me when I take my father's portrait in my hand and recall the humility and heroism of his life. A stern and angular face, out of whose saliences look two ruddy windows, lit by a steadfast cheerfulness, is thinly thatched by hairs of iron-gray, and around the long loose throat a bunch of frosted beard sparkles as if the painter's pencil had fastened there in reverence. I do not need to study the bent, broad shoulders and thin sinewy limbs to measure the hardness and steepness of his path ; he climbed it like a bridegroom, humming quaint snatches of hymns to lull his human waywardnesses, and all the fever and errantry of our own vain career shrink abashed before his high devotion.

That I have turned out a rover is not odd ; for the travelling preacher's son is cradled upon the highway. Three months after my birth we " moved" a hundred miles ; by my sixteenth year we had made eleven migrations.

We children little sympathize with our weak and sickly mother on these occasions, but look forward to a change of abode as something very novel and de-

sirable.   We count the days between Christmas and
April, after which the annual "Conference" assembles
in the distant city, and we see our father, in his best
black suit, quit the parsonage door with an anxious
face, cut to the heart by his wife's farewell, " May
they give you a good place, Thomas !"

Then come letters—one, two, three : " The bishops
are friendly ;" " The Presiding Elder has promised to
do the best for us that he can ;" " The influential
Doctor Bim has praised our missionary sermon, and
Brother Click, the Secretary, has applauded our
Charge's large subscription to the *Advocate ;*" " Our
character has passed even the severe approval of the
great theologian, Steep ;" " Take courage, my dear,
and hope for the best !"

The membership, meanwhile, are dropping in by
couples to say kindly words to our mother, whom they
pity, and it is rumored that they are collecting a purse
to help us on our way.   At last our father returns,
striving to hide his solicitude in a smile, for no fate
to which they could consign himself would scathe that
grisly servant of his Master ; but for his family, who
do not altogether share the spirit of his mission, he
has a little fear.   He kisses us all in order, from the
least to the biggest, commencing and ending with our
mother, and playfully prevaricates as to our " appointment," the name of which we noisily demand,
until his wife says timidly,

" Where do they send us, Thomas ?"

He tries to smile and trifle, but the possibility of her
discontent gives him so great pain that we children perceive it.

" How would you like to go to Greensburg ?"

" Not *Greensburg !*" she says, with a sudden paleness.

" Isn't it a good circuit ?" he says smilingly ;
" they paid the last preacher three hundred dollars,
and his marriage fees were a hundred more.   They say
he saved fifty dollars a year !"

"Oh, Thomas, I thought I had fortitude, but this—"

"Is only to test your faith," he cries. "A poor preacher's wife should be willing to go anywhere—even to Greensburg ; but that is not our appointment, dear ; we move to Swan Neck."

Then the fun begins in earnest. The church people come to look at our contribution bedquilts, and help us pack up the blue earthenware. The legs of the prodigious box, yclept a milk chest, are summarily amputated and laid away in it, with the parental library, which, we are sorry to say, is equally doubtful in point of both ornament and use. The good gossips slyly peep into the covers of Matthew Henry, and regard their retiring pastor as a more learned man than they had suspected, while the black letter-press of Lorenzo Dow, and John Bunyan, and Fox's "Book of Martyrs" touches them like so much necromancy. The faithful old clock, whose disorders are crises in our humdrum pastoral year, is stopped and disjointed, much to our marvel, and all the spare straw in the barn is brought to protect the large gilt-edged cups and saucers, which say upon their edges, "To our pastor," and "To our pastor's wife." The thin rag carpets are folded away ; the potatoes in the bin are sold to Brother Bibb, the grocer, and to a very few of the select sisters we present a can of our preserved quinces, with directions how to prepare them. Poor Em., the black domestic, drops so many tears upon the parlor stove as she carries it out to the wagon that the fresh blackening she has so industriously given it goes for nothing ; for Em. is to be discharged, and the fact troubles her, though a preacher's servant has little to eat and plenty to do.

At last the old parsonage is quite bare and deserted, though our successors, box and baggage, have moved in upon us, much to the annoyance of the females, who see with jealousy that the new arrival gets the lion's share of attention, and that Brother Tipp, whose class-book we took from him, and who has backbitten us ever since, is courteous as a dancing-master with our rival. We shall talk for six years to come—that is, our mother—of Bangs's, the new-comer's, impudence in feeding his horse on our oats, and shall never speak of him as Brother Bangs, but simply call him *Bangs*, emphasized. We are not even sure that he will not turn his poultry loose before ours has been secured, and we boys, with great zeal, run down the roosters and ducks, giving them, if the truth must be told, longer chase than is necessary. The aged muscovy, we are sorry to say, lames himself in the retreat, and the only goose on the premises hides among Powell's, the neighbor's, so that we cannot tell which from which. However, the property is tied up at last in the several wagons; Sister Phœnix's lunch has been eaten, and our father, the itinerant, in his shirt-sleeves, stands up, with pain and perspiration on his brow, to bid his flock good-by.

" Now, brethren," he says, with a quiver at his throat, " my time is passing ; I have finished the work appointed for me to do. Renew the kindnesses you have done me and my little ones upon the good steward who is to replace me. My heart weeps to cut the bonds which have held us so long together ; but in this world I am a pilgrim and a stranger. Let us all pray !"

As his shrill, broken voice goes up in a mingled wail and hosanna, we children peep by stealth into the working faces of the bystanders, and our own grow tearful, till our little sister cries aloud, and our mother falls into some fond matron's arms.

Immediately our wagons are on the way. The clustering village roofs and the church spire sink down behind. We are too full of excitement to share the silence of our elders, and the passing objects while us to laughter and debate.

Swan Neck is a representative circuit. It lies, as everybody knows, somewhere upon the Eastern shore—

that landmark and stronghold of Methodism. The
parsonage is in Crochettown, the county-seat, and the
circuit comprises half a dozen churches down the
neck, among the pine forests and on the bay side.
Our father tells our mother on the way of the advantages of the place, till we take it to be quite a metropolis. He says that Wiggins, whom we succeed, gives a
first-rate account of it. One of the members (Judd)
is a judge, and our church, in short, rules the roast
thereabout, and makes the Episcopalians stand around,
not to speak of the Baptists, who try as usual to edge
us out.

The boys ask with glowing cheeks if there is a river
at Crochettown, and are thrown into ecstasy by the
reply that a large steamboat touches there twice a
week, and that there is a drawbridge. We are less interested in the statement that the schools are good,
but hear with delight the history of one Dumple, an
innkeeper, who persecutes our church and sells quan-
tities of " rum" to our young men. William, the son
of Wiggins, our predecessor, was once seen in the bar-
room and reported to his father, who fetched him home
by *posse comitatus*, and found that he smelled strongly
of soda water.

As we go along the road in this way, our furniture
mean time having been shipped by water, a very com-
pact and knotty young man rides up behind us upon
a nag which we at once identify as church property.
The sleekness of the flanks betokens his conversance
with other people's corn-cribs, and he has a habit of
shying at all the farm-house gates as if habituated to
stopping whenever he liked and staying to dinner. His
Perseus has a semi-gallant, semi-verdant way of lifting
his hat, and his voice is hard as his knuckles.

" Woa, Sal !" he says (all preachers drive mares, it
may be interpolated), " have I the pleasure of addressing Brother Ryder?"

" The same, sir."

" My name is Chough, sir ; the annual Conference

has done me the favor of associating my name with yours at Swan Neck."

" Oh, ho !   You are my colleague ; my wife, Brother Chough !''

The wife runs Brother Chough over immediately, who looks very red and awkward, and she gives her estimate of him in an undertone.   It will be bad for Chough if he is at all airish or scholastic, or individual in his opinions, for between a senior pastor's wife and his young assistant there is an hereditary distrust ; conceit has no show at all in a young itinerant.

But Chough wisely confines his remarks to asking questions about the bishops, and agrees with us that Doctor Bim's address on the church extension cause was sound as the Fathers, and finally gives us his own extraction, which we trace to the respectable Choughs of Caroline County, and at once fraternize with him.

Those were happy days for us children !   Cornfield and barn and negro quarter rolled by us like things of fable.   We watched the squirrels in the scrubwood as never again we shall take interest in human companionship, and stopped at farm-house troughs to water our nag with keener joy than that with which we have since gazed upon far blue seas or soft cis-alpine lakes and rivers.

At last we reach the place ; the complement of free negro cabins lies on its outskirts ; we ask the way to the Methodist preacher's residence, and learning with feigned surprise that " he has just gone an' lef town for good," cross a sandy creek and bridge, climb a hill, and stop at our future threshold.

It is an ancient edifice of brick ; a pigmy stable stands beside it, with a gate intervening, and in the rear we have a lot big enough to graze one frugal horse, and a garden sufficiently large to employ us boys.   Our father starts off immediately to find the keys ; but in the face of a gathering of small lads in pinafores and jack-knives, who come to gaze at us, we

scale the gate, enter a back shutter, and cry a welcome
to our mother from the second-story front.

We hastily scan the several chambers to claim all
that we find in the drawers and closets ; are gratified
to observe the bow-gun and shinney-sticks of the young
Wigginses departed, and quite fall out among ourselves
over the wooden effigy of an Indian which has
tumbled down from the barn-top.

Soon the nearest neighbor of our persuasion arrives
with our father, and takes our mother and the baby
away to his dwelling. A fat old trustee and local
preacher carries off ourself and sister, and we go bash-
fully and wonderingly into the heart of the town, past
the church, past the market-house, past the tavern and
court and public hall, until the door of our host closes
upon us, and our short sandy hairs appear at the windows to scan the street and the people.

Yeasty, our host, is the only local preacher in
Crochettown, where he also keeps a store, but is said
to be as rich as Crœsus, and miserly as get out ; and
he has a pretty daughter, Margot, who sweeps into the
room like a little queen, and, being older than ourselves,
patronizes us till we blush. She rattles off all the town
talk, the parties in the winter season, the terrible master of the academy, and the handsomest boys, including Barret, who is dissipated and writes poetry ; the
beauty of Marian Lee, who seems to be the terror of
young gentlemen, though Margot don't see any thing
in her, the proud piece !

And so we pick up the history of the village with
the diligence of Froissart or Jean de Troyes, and eat
last winter's apples by the ruddy grate, listening to
Margot, with our very round tow head upon our sister's, filled with vague dreams of greatness and wealth,
and old Yeasty's silver half dollars piled up around us,
and Margot to chat at our side forever.

Oh ! innocent days of itinerant urchinhood, your
freshness comes no more ; we "move on" as of old—
waifs in the wide circuit of this nomad life—but with

the hymns which lulled us in the neglected meeting-house, the prophecies they told us of toil, duty, reverence, and content, have floated into heaven whither our father has gone !

The bulk of our furniture being delayed, and our mother impatient of accepting hospitality, we move into the great, bare parsonage house on Saturday, and sit in the only furnished room. It grieves even ourselves to see how this merry moving has thinned her anxious white face, and therefore we forbear to fret her when we read the three long Bible chapters she exacts. Josh, our brother, does not purposely pronounce physician " physiken," as he is in the habit of doing, and our sister remembers for once that ewe lamb is to be called " yo," and not " e-we" in two syllables. The dinner is quite cold, but Josh, who complains, is reminded of the poor Shepherd of Salisbury Plain, who could not afford salt with his potatoes. Josh says that for his part he don't like potatoes anyhow, and will not be comforted.

In the afternoon we present ourselves at Sunday-school, and as the preacher's sons are supposed to be first-class ecclesiastical scholars, are put in the Bible-class. Here we surprise everybody by the quantity of verses we know by heart, and get many red and blue tickets for our reward. It must be confessed that we had been twice before paid for the same lesson, it being our perquisite to carry all that we know from school to school. We see Margot among the girls, swinging her feet under the seat as she hummingly commits her lesson to memory, and as her feet are very pretty, they do not perhaps move unconsciously. But Josh and we have quite a battle as to Margot, Josh saying, " She's my girl," and we averring that " we know better—she's mine," until finally our sister disposes of the matter by betraying us to the little coquette, whereat we are both ashamed, and go home hastily.

We feed and curry the horse by turns, and hunt

eggs in the stable with boisterous rivalry, and have quite a contest as to who shall go down upon " the circuit " first, which is at last settled in favor of the first person.

On the appointed Sunday we rise betimes, " gear up" the nag to the sulky, and depositing a carpet-stool in the foot, sit upon it between our father's legs, and trot out of town at a respectably slow gait to clear the preacher of any suspicion of keeping a fast horse. Fairly out of town, however, we switch up somewhat, ourself watching over the dasher the clods and dust thrown from the mare's shoes, and our father humming snatches of hymns, with his grave eyes twinkling.

We say " How de do," of course, to every passer-by, as it is the pride of the profession to lead the etiquette of the country ; and, passing remarks upon the badness of the fences, the staunchness of the barns, and the coziness of the dwellings, soon leave the cultivated high-road for one of the by-ways which lead down the sparsely-settled " Neck." The sombre pine forests gather about us : a squirrel or two runs across the route, and a solitary crow caws in the tree-top ; we hear the loud " tap-tap-tap" of a woodpecker, and see through the sinuous aisles of firs some groups of negroes pattering to church. The men take off their hats obsequiously, and the women duck their heads, and our father says benignantly, " Going to church, boys ? that's right ! I like to see you honor the Great Master !" At which the younger Africans show their teeth, and the more forward patriarchs reply, " Yes, massar, bress de Lord !"

So the teams increase in number like the wayfarers, all with the same object in view, until we see the church at last, standing behind a line of whitewashed palings, flanked by less pretentious worm fences, and in the rear a long shed for horses, open in front, shadows the few tomb memorials of stone and stake.

Several lads and worldlings at the gate, slashing their boots with riding-whips, make obeisance, while two or three plain old gentlemen walk down to meet us, saying :

"Brother Ryder, we *pre*-sume ! Welcome to Dodson's Corner, Brother Ryder !"

We tie up the nag, loosen her bridle bit, and follow into the meeting-house—a lofty building unplastered at the roof, whose open eaves and shingles give place in summer to nests of wasps, and in the winter to audacious birds, some of which swoop screaming to the pulpit, and beat the window panes in futile flight. Two uncarpeted aisles lead respectively to the men's side and the women's side—for, far be it from us, primitive Methodists, to improve upon the discipline of Wesley—and midway of each aisle, in square areas, stand two high stoves, with branching pipes which radiate from their red-hot cylinders of clay. The pulpit is a square unpainted barricade, with pedestals on each side for a pair of oil-lamps ; the cushions which sustain the Bible are the gift of young unconverted ladies, and are sacredly brought to the place of worship each Sunday morning and taken away in the afternoon.

By the side of the stove the old stewards and the new minister stand awhile talking over the moral *status* of the country, the advances made by the Baptists, and the amount of money contributed by Dodson's Corner to the various funds of the church. The folk, meanwhile, drop in by squads, the colored element filling the unsteady gallery in the rear, until our father looks at his open-faced watch, and says :

"Bless my soul, brethren, it is time to begin the services !"

He ascends into the pulpit. We sit on what is known as the "Amen side," with our thumb in our buttonhole, and watch the process of the chief steward, who is unlimbering his tuning-fork. He obtains the pitch of the tune by rapping the pew with this, or, if his teeth be sound, which is rare, touches the prongs with his incisors. Then his head—whose baldness, we imagine, arises from the people in the rear looking all the hair off—is thrown back resolutely, his jaws fly wide open, he projects a tangible stream of music to the roof, to the alarm of the birds, and comes to a dead halt at the end of the second line—for here we have congregational singing, and even those without hymn books may assist to swell the music. But very often the leader breaks down ; the vanguard of old ladies cannot keep up the tune ; volunteers make desperate efforts to rally the chorus, but retire discomfited, and the pastor, in addition to praying, reading, and preaching, must finally, in his worn, subdued voice, lead the forlorn hope.

The sermon on this inaugural occasion may justly be termed a work of art. It must be conclusive of the piety, learning, eloquence, and sound doctrine of the preacher, and be by turns argumentative, combative, stirring, pathetic, practical, and pictorial. The text has about the same connection at first with the discourse that a campanile has with a cathedral. A solid eulogium upon the book from which it is taken gives occasion for some side-slashes at Voltaire, Hume, and Gibbon ; the deaths of these are contrasted with the obsequies of the righteous, and the old-fashioned, material place of punishment · is reasserted and minutely described. The text is then said to naturally resolve itself into three parts—the injunction, the direction, and some practical illustrations. The injunction, it is further allowed, re-subdivides itself, and these parts are each proclaimed in the form of speech of "Once more." We are quite too old a hand at listening to imagine that "once more" means *only* once more, and start to enumerate the beams in the roof, the panes in the windows, and the gray hairs in the old gentleman's head before us. About the time that we feel sleepy an anecdote arouses us : then the iteration of expletives from the membership succeeds ; we see that the owner of the tuning-fork has fallen to sleep in so ingenious an attitude that he would never have been detected but for his snore, and are amused by the fashion one good lady has of slowly wagging her head as she drinks in the discourse. A slight commotion in the gallery arises, which gives a steward excuse to steal down the aisle and hasten to the scene of disturbance ; the final appeal, brimming with the poetry of mercy, grace, patience, and salvation is said ; we all kneel down upon the hard cold floor while the last prayer is being made, and receive the benediction, as if some invisible shadow of bright wings had fallen upon the dust and fever of our lives.

To say that the first person is weary but vindicates the sagacity of our father, who steals down to our side and whispers, " You may go out, Fred, if you are tired." But curiosity compels us to remain after the congregation is dismissed, that we may hear the class-meeting experiences.

Those solemn corollaries to the service thrill me with their recollection even now. The almost empty church echoing the sobs of the weary, and heart-bruised, and spirit-broken ; the pinched, hard faces of the older people telling their bitter trials in bereavement, misappreciation, and poverty. But bursting through all, that unconquerable enthusiasm which lends to the face more than the glow of intelligence, and to the heart more than the recompense of riches ; the timid utterance of the younger converts, outlining the rebellious instincts of their tempted bodies, and their need of more faith, grace, and help divine. While these speak in order, the bald-headed chorister interpolates appropriate snatches of psalms, and the preacher cries, " Patience, my brother ! All will be well ! Hope on, hope ever !"

At last the impatient negroes in the gallery have their opportunity, and roll down thunders of exuberant piety, which, by their natural, almost inspired eloquence, pathos, and vehemence, stir even their masters to ejaculations of praise.

How must such spiritually social reunions cheer the

long, hard lives of these poor, remote believers ! He was a profound statesman who, projecting a gospel for the lowly, devised the class-meeting as an outlet for their suppressed emotions, sympathies, and sorrows.

However, it is all over, and there is quite a dispute after the "class" as to who shall have the pastor's company to dinner. It is a piece of fine diplomacy to determine this. Policy dictates the most influential ; feeling, the most reverend and poor. But the interest of the church is paramount ; a compliment or a promise appeases the vanity of the humbler, and we follow the double team of the great landholder, Tibbet, and are soon sitting before his roaring fire.

Itinerants are notoriously big eaters. Our father keeps a weather eye on the provender as it is brought in smoking, and it being soon apparent that the dinner is to be orthodox, if not apostolic, his social attributes improve wonderfully. He breaks out in little spurts of anecdote, not entirely secular, nor yet too didactic to be jovial. They run upon young Brother Bolt, who once, after an unusual happy "revival" night, to show his great faith, tried to leap over a creek and doused himself to the ears ; upon the great controversialist, Whanger, who, being invited to preach in a "High Church" pulpit, improved the occasion to trace apostolic succession as far back as Pope Joan ; upon the first intelligent contraband of his kind, whose mistress affirmed that if one's ill deeds were numerically greater than his good ones he would be—jammed, and if the contrary, saved, and who responded, "Spose'n dey boff de same, missus ?"

These are told with inimitable spirit and mimicry, as want of clerical wit is a direct impeachment of the validity of one's "call" to preach ; and when the table is filled, and with outstretched hands the blessing said, our father gets a universal compliment for his carving. There is roast turkey, with rich stuffing, bright cranberry sauce, and savory pies of pumpkin, mince, and persimmon, cider to wash down the mealy ripeness of the sweet potato, and at the end transparent quinces drowned in velvet cream.   How glibly goes the time ! We play with a young miss, who shows us her library, in which, we are sorry to say, a book about pirates deeply absorbs us.   But at last the sulky comes to the door ; we say good-by with touched full hearts, and pass hummingly to appointment No. 2.

This is " Sand Hill," perhaps, or " Mumpson Town," or " Ebenezer," or " Dry Pond ;" and when we have mustered again in the afternoon, and in the evening for the third time, turn Sal's head toward the parsonage, and sail along in the night, cold and worn, past fields of stubble, over which the wind sweeps, past negro cabins, watching like human things upon us, through dreary woods where the tall pines rock against the stars and the clouds sail whitely by like witches going to a rendezvous, past cheerful homes, gleaming light and rest and worldly competence, the owners whereof have heard no deep command to carry the gospel into wildernesses, or hearing disobeyed. And all the while our father sings softly to himself, looking now and then at us who are his cross, and again into the shining constellations which hide his crown.

But we " preacher's sons," by which name we are universally distinguished, have our own crosses as well. It is generally agreed that much ought to be expected of us and little obtained.   Let one of us play truant from school, or use a naughty word in play, or make marbles a source of revenue, or fight on the common when provoked, or steal a cherry, and the fact travels our town over like a telegram.   We once suffer greatly in repute by selling our neighbor's old iron and brass to an itinerant pedler, and are alleged to have run up a debit account of one dime with an old negro who sells spruce beer and " horse cakes"—whereafter we fail.

The church people, much to our dissatisfaction, present us with castaway coats and boots, which we are made to wear, and once or twice, when we encounter

Margot in this shape, we burst into tears and run home
to hide our wounded vanity in the stable loft. There,
in the " mow," while we devise bitter and futile con-
spiracies against society, the mare, munching her
fodder, looks up at us with patient eyes, as if to say :
" Am I not also mortified for the faith ?" But we are
cut to the heart to think that Margot may contrast us
with better-dressed boys, and therefore think us of
little spirit, learning, and courage. It is for you,
pretty coquette, that we carry many scandals and
scars ! We do not quite love you, Margot ; but we
are foolishly vain and sensitive, and your eyes are very
beautiful !

Still we are acknowledged at school to be " smart."
All preacher's sons are so by common concession, and
though we may not visit the circus, like others, we get
abundance of free tickets for concerts. panoramas, and
glass-blowers. Once, indeed, the great Chippewa chief,
Haw-waw-many-squaw, having thrown the town into
consternation by placards of himself scalping his enemies and smoking their tobacco, makes a triumphal
entry into the main street at full gallop, and pitching
his tent before the court-house, walks into the parsonage—war plumes, moccasins, and all—gives us complimentary seats, and eats the better half of our dinner. This incident is a source of pride to ourself
beyond any thing experienced by any urchin besides.
We boast of it frequently, and, being disliked therefor,
commit several impromptu scalpings on our own account.

Vagabonds unnumbered beg our hospitality, and
get it. Some of these it would be difficult to determine, either as to profession or destination. Many of
them are systematic pensioners upon the preacher, and
plead devotion to our denomination as a means of
gaining our hearts. They have the gossip of the " Conference" at their tongues' ends, and lead our family
devotion with the grace and hypocrisy of Belial.

The weddings that we hold are frequent and various.   Runaway couples come to us, blushing and short-winded, satisfy us of their lawful age, are united, and pass into the moon, leaving a five-dollar bill behind them.   We cannot quite find it in our hearts, even at this late day, to forgive those numerous candidates for felicity who hold the par value of a wedding ceremony to be no more than two dollars.   Yet, though we grieve to admit it, two dollars is the average fee.   At one time the negro population, anxious to be wived by a white preacher, makes inroads upon us *en masse* to the detriment of decorum and our carpets. We summarily shut down upon this business when we find that their fees come to but half a dollar a pair.

However, the year drifts by, and we are greatly concerned to know if it is the sentiment of Swan Neck that we shall continue its pastor another year.   Old Yeasty, Margot's father, as we are aware, feels himself slighted because we do not call upon him of Sundays to make the closing prayers ; for Yeasty's prayer is a sermon under another name, and runs the morning into twilight ; but a sly compliment that we pay him in a diplomatic sermon at the end of the conference year brings him round all right, and back we go to Swan Neck.

So with burying the dead and writing their obituaries ; making the babes pure with that holy sprinkling which gives them, dying early, to a Christian immortality ; launching our thunders upon the bold, softening the hearts of the errant, mingling with our unbending creed the more pliable ethics of worldly graces, and, in a word, walking like Saint John on the savage border of civilization, to thrill the brutal and unlettered with the tidings of one just day to come—our itinerant lives drift on till the marble slab in the meeting-house wall writes the itinerant's only human memorial.

We have dreamed our last.   Burst from the narrow chrysalis which we would gladly rebuild again, the seething, churning sea is before us and around us ; we only catch, like the strains of bells through the fog, the hum of hymns, the drowsy murmur of the buzzing Sabbath-school, and the nasal ring of the itinerant's summer sermon. Margot is married to Chough, our whilom colleague, and makes her migration in his Bedouin train, and does not know how once she thrilled us. The tuning-fork is rusty, and the chorister in his coffin may hear, if he can, his successor stirring the birds in the roof with his sonorous melody. All are at rest, and we live on—moving, moving, moving—so deeply fastened into our natures are our early instincts ; but every night we say the same parsonage prayer, and every morning look upon the wall where hangs the grave, grim features we revere—the Itinerant Preacher.

CHESTER RIVER.

WISE is the wild duck winging straight to thee,
River of summer! from the cold Arctic sea,
Coming, like his fathers for centuries, to seek
The sweet, salt pastures of the far Chesapeake.

Soft 'twixt thy capes like sunset's purple coves,
Shallow the channel glides through silent oyster groves,
Round Kent's ancient isle, and by beaches brown,
Cleaving the fruity farms to slumb'rous Chestertown.

Long ere the great bay bore the Baltimores,
Yielded thy virgin tide to Virginian oars ;
Elsewhere the word went, '' Multiply ! increase !''
Long ago thy destinies were perfect as thy peace.

Still, like thy water-fowl, dearly do I yearn,
In memory's migration once more to return,
Where the dull old college from the gentle ridge,
O'erlooks the sunny village, the river, and the bridge.

On the pier decrepit I do loiter yet,
With my crafty crab-lines and my homespun net,
Till the silver fishes in pools of twilight swam,
And stars played round my bait in the coves of calm.

Sweet were the chinquapins growing by thy brink,
Sweet the cool spring-water in the gourd to drink,
Beautiful the lilies when the tide declined,
As if night receding had left some stars behind.

But when the peach tints vanished from the plain,
Or struggled no longer the shad against the seine,
Every reed in thy march into music stirred,
And to gold it blossomed in a singing bird.

Eden of water-fowl ! clinging to thy dells
Ages of mollusks have yielded their shells,
While, like the exquisite spirits they shed,
Ride the white swans in the surface o'erhead.

Silent the otter, stealing by thy moon,
Through the fluttered heron, hears the cry of the loon ;
Motionless the setter in thy dawnlight gray
Shows the happy hidden cove where the wild duck play.

Homely are thy boatmen, venturing no more
In their dusky pungies than to Baltimore,
Happy when the freshet from northern mountains sweeps,
And strews the bay with lumber like wrecks upon the deeps.

Not for thy homesteads of a former space,
Not for thy folk of supposititious race ;
Something I love thee, river, for thy rest,
More for my childhood buried in thy breast.

From the mightier empire of the solid land,
A pilgrim infrequent I seek thy fertile strand,
And with a calm affection would wish my grave to be
Where falls the Chester to the bay, the bay unto the sea.

OLD WASHINGTON ALMSHOUSE.

A STRANGER in Washington, looking down the wide outer avenue named "Massachusetts," which goes bowling from knoll to knoll and disappears in the unknown hills of the east, has no notion that it leads anywhere, and gives up the conundrum. On the contrary, it points straight to the Washington Asylum, better known as the District Poor-House, an institution to become hereafter conspicuous to every tourist who shall prefer the Baltimore and Potomac to the Baltimore and Ohio Railroad; for the new line crosses the Eastern Branch by a pile-bridge nearly in the rear of the poor-house, and let us hope that when the whistle, like

> "the pibroch's music, thrills
> To the heart of those lone hills,"

the dreary banks and bluffs of the Eastern Branch will show more frequent signs of habitation and visitation.

To visit the poor-house one must have a "permit" from the mayor, physician, or a poor commissioner. Provided with this, he will follow out Pennsylvania Avenue over Capitol Hill, until nearly at the brink of the Anacostia or Eastern Branch, when by the oblique avenue called "Georgia" he will pass to his right the Congressional burying-ground, and arriving at the powder magazine in front, draw up at the almshouse gate, a mile and a quarter from the palace of Congress.

It is a smart brick building, four stories high, with green trimmings, standing on the last promontory of some grassy commons beloved of geese and billygoats.

The short, black cedars, which appear to be a species
of vegetable crape, give a stubby look of grief to the
region round the poor-house, and, thickest at the Congressional Cemetery, screen from the paupers the
view of the city. Across the plains, once made popu-
lous by army hospitals, few objects move except
funeral processions, creeping toward the grave-yard or
receding at a merry gait, and occasional pensioners,
out on leave, coming home dutifully to their bed of
charity. The report of some sportsman's gun, where
he is rowing in the marshes of the gray river, sometimes raises echoes in the high hills and ravines of the
other shore, where, many years ago, the rifles of Graves
and Cilley were heard by every partisan in the land.
Now the tall forts, raised in the war, are silent and
deserted ; the few villas and farm-houses look from
their background of pine upon the smart edifice on
the city shore, and its circle of hospitals nearer the
water, and its small-pox hospital a little removed, and
upon the dead-house and the Potter's Field at the river
brink. We all know the melancholy landscape of a
poor-house.

The Potter's Field preceded the poor-house on this
site by many years. The almshouse was formerly
erected on M Street, between Sixth and Seventh, and,
being removed here, it burned to the ground in the
month of March, fourteen years ago, when the present
brick structure was raised. The entire premises, of
which the main part is the almshouse garden, occupy
less than fifty acres, and the number of inmates is less
than two hundred, the females preponderating in the
proportion of three to one. Under the same roof are
the almshouse and the work-house, the inmates of the
former being styled " Infirmants," and of the latter
" Penitents." The government of the institution is
vested in three commissioners, to whom is responsible
the intendent, Mr. Joseph F. Hodgson, a very cheerful and practical-looking " Bumble."

Every Wednesday the three commissioners meet at

this almshouse and receive the weekly reports of the intendent, physician, and gardener. Once every year these officers, and the matron, wagoner, and baker are elected. Sixteen ounces of bread and eight ounces of beef are the ration of the district pauper. The turnkey, gate-keeper, chief watchmen, and chief nurses, are selected from the inmates. The gates are closed at sunset, and the lights go out at eight P.M. all winter. The inmates wear a uniform, labelled in large letters " Work-house," or " Washington Asylum."

The poor-house is an institution coeval with the capital. We are told that while crabbed old Davy Burns, the owner of the most valuable part of the site of Washington City, was haggling with General Washington over his proportion of lots, his neglected and intemperate brother, Tommy, was an inmate of the poor-house.

Thus, while the Romulus of the place married his daughter to a Congressman, and was buried in a " mausoleum" on H Street, Remus died without the walls and mingled his ashes, perhaps, with paupers.

The vaunted metropolis of the republican hopes of mankind—for such was Washington, the fabulous city, advertised and praised in every capital of Western Europe—drew to its site artists, adventurers, and speculators from all lands. From Thomas Law, a secretary of Warren Hastings, who wasted the earnings of India on enterprises here, to a Frenchman who died on the guillotine for practising with an infernal machine upon the life of Napoleon Bonaparte, the long train of pilgrims came and saw and despaired, and many of them, perhaps, lie in the Potter's Field. Old books and newspapers, chary on such personal questions, contain occasional references as to some sculptor's suicide, or to the straits of this or that French officer, a claimant about Congress ; and we know that Major L'Enfant, who conceived the plan of the place, sought refuge with a pitying friend and died here penniless. The long war of twenty years in Europe brought to America thousands in search of safety and rest, and to these the magnetism of the word "capital" was often the song of the siren wiling them to the poor-house. By the time Europe had wearied of the sword, the fatality attending high living, large slave-tilled estates, the love of official society, and the defective education of the young men of tide-water Virginia and Maryland, produced a new class of native-born errants and broken profligates at Washington, and many a life whose memories began with a coach-and-four and a park of deer ended them between the coverlets of a poor-house bed. The old times were, after all, very hollow times ! We are fond of reading about the hospitality of the Madisonian age, but could so many have accepted it if all were prosperous ?

In our time, work being the fate and the redemption of us all, the District Almshouse contains few government employés. Now and then, as Mr. Hodgson told us, some clerk, spent with sickness or exhausted by evil indulgences, takes the inevitable road across the vacant plains and eats his pauper ration in silence or in resignation ; but the age is better, not, perhaps, because the heart of man is changed, but in that society is organized upon truer principles of honor, of manfulness, and of labor. The class of well-bred young men who are ashamed to admit that they must earn their living, and who affect the company of gamesters and chicken-fighters, has some remnants left among us, but they find no aliment in the public sentiment, and hear no response in the public tone. Duelling is over ; visiting one's relatives as a profession is done ; thrift is no more a reproach, and even the reputation of being a miser is rather complimentary to a man. The worst chapters of humanity in America are those narrating the indigence of the old agricultural families on the streams of the Chesapeake ; the quarterly sale of a slave to supply the demands of a false understanding of generosity ; the inhuman revelling of one's friends upon the last possessions of his family, holding it to be a jest to precipitate his ruin ; the wild orgies held on the glebe of some old parish church, horses hitched to the grave-stones, and punch mixed in the baptismal font ; and at the last, delirium, impotence, decay ! Let those who would understand it read Bishop Meade, or descend the Potomac and Rappahannock, even at this day, and cross certain thresholds.

The Washington poor-house seems to be well-arranged, except in one respect : under the same roof, divided only by a partition and a corridor, the vicious are lodged for punishment and the unfortunate for refuge.

We passed through a part of the building where, among old, toothless women, semi-imbecile girls—the relicts of error, the heirs of affliction—three babies of one mother were in charge of a strong, rosy Irish nurse. Two of them, twins, were in her lap, and a third upon the floor halloaing for joy. Such noble specimens of childhood we had never seen ; heads like Cæsar's, eyes bright as the depths of wells into which one laughs and receives his laughter back, and the complexions and carriage of high birth. The woman was suckling them all, and all crowed alternately, so that they made the bare floors and walls light up as with pictures. A few yards off, though out of hearing, were the thick forms of criminals, drunkards, wantons, and vagrants, seen through the iron bars of their wicket, raising the croon and song of an idle din, drumming on the floor, or moving to and fro restlessly. Beneath this part of the almshouse were cells where bad cases were locked up. The association of the poor and the wicked affected us painfully.

Strolling into the syphilitic wards, where, in the awful contemplation of their daily, piecemeal decay, the silent victims were stretched all day upon their cots ; among the idiotic and the crazed ; into the apartments of the aged poor, seeing, let us hope, blessed visions of life beyond these shambles ; and drinking in, as we walked, the solemn but needful lesson of our own possibilities and the mutations of our nature, we stood at last among the graves of the almshouse dead—those who have escaped the dissecting-knife. Scattered about, with little stones and mounds here and there, under the occasional sullen green of cedars, a dead-cart and a spade sticking up as symbols, and the neglected river, deserted as the Styx, plashing against the low banks, we felt the sobering melancholy of the spot and made the prayer of " Give me neither poverty nor riches !''

1871.

OLD ST. MARY'S.

THIS is the river.   Like Southampton water
It enters broadly in the woody lands,
As if to break a continent asunder,
And sudden ceasing, lo ! the city stands :
St. Mary's—stretching forth its yellow hands
Of beach, beneath the bluff where it commands
In vision only ; for the fields are green
Above the pilgrims.   Pleasant is the place ;
No ruin mars its immemorial face.
As young as in virginity renewed,
Its widow's sorrows gone without a trace,
And tempting man to woo its solitude.

The river loves it, and embraces still
Its comely form with two small arms of bay,
Whereon, of old, the Calvert's pinnace lay,
The Dove—dear bird !—the olive in its bill,
That to the Ark returned from every gale
And found a haven by this sheltering hill.*

Lo ! all composed, the soft horizons lie
Afloat upon the blueness of the coves,
And sometimes in the mirage does the sky
Seem to continue the dependent groves,
And draw in the canoe that careless roves
Among the stars repeated round the bow.
Far off the larger sails go down the world,
For nothing worldly sees St. Mary's now ;
The ancient windmills all their sails have furled,
The standards of the Lords of Baltimore,

---

* The Catholic settlers of Maryland had a ship called The Ark,
and a pinnace called The Dove.

And they, the Lords, have passed to their repose ;
And nothing sounds upon the pebbly shore
Except thy hidden bell, Saint Inigo's.

There in a wood the Jesuits' chapel stands
Amongst the gravestones, in secluded calm.
But, Sabbath days, the censer's healing balm,
The Crucified with His extended hands,
And music of the masses, draw the fold
Back to His worship, as in days of old.

Upon a cape the priest's house northward blinks,
To see St. Mary's Seminary guard
The dead that sleep within the parish yard,
In English faith—the parish church that links
The present with the perished, for its walls
Are of the clay that was the capital's,
When halberdiers and musketeers kept ward,
And armor sounded in the oaken halls.

A fruity smell is in the school-house lane ;
The clover bees are sick with evening heats ;
A few old houses from the window pane
Fling back the flame of sunset, and there beats
The throb of oars from basking oyster fleets,
And clangorous music of the oyster tongs,
Plunged down in deep bivalvulous retreats,
And sound of seine drawn home with negro songs.

Night falls as heavily in such a clime
As tired childhood after all day's play,
Waiting for mother who has passed away,
And some old nurse, with iterated rhyme
Of hymns or topics of the olden time,
Lulls wonder with her tenderness to rest :
So, old St. Mary's ! at the close of day,
Sing thou to me, a truant, on thy breast.

THE END.

www.ingramcontent.com/pod-product-compliance
Lightning Source LLC
Chambersburg PA
CBHW021049030726
47496CB00006B/1760